CW01011188

Last Chance

Last Chance

A Novel by:

R.D. NATHANIEL

AuthorHouse™
1663 Liberty Drive
Bloomington, IN 47403
www.authorhouse.com
Phone: 1-800-839-8640

Published by AuthorHouse 09/05/2012

ISBN: 978-1-4772-1955-3 (sc)
ISBN: 978-1-4772-1954-6 (hc)
ISBN: 978-1-4772-1956-0 (e)

This book is printed on acid-free paper.

"People come into your life for a reason, a season or a lifetime. When you figure out which it is, you know exactly what to do."

Michelle Ventor

This book is a reality because of the encouragement of many. Firstly I thank God for the gifts He has entrusted me with and for loving me exactly as I am. I give thanks to my mother for her unfaltering love. To my friends in no particular order-my heart felt thanks for their support, encouragement and belief in me; Bayo, Santi, Jide, Zubes, Nnamdi, Peter, Adam, Janko and especially Vince. Special thanks to my friend Abdul, an extraordinary man. Thanks to the warm and helpful staff at Authorhouse. Thanks also to those not mentioned here but who remain close to my heart. To you my readers, for accompanying me on this journey and inspiring me to keep doing what I enjoy and love doing.

Dedicated to the memory of Noel

Contents

1. Once upon a time

I looked in the mirror and the man looking back at me was tall, dark, handsome, intelligent and solvent. I'd come a long way baby. Along that way I had kissed a lot of frogs; sure not all of them had turned into princes, but I was still in the game, still standing. My life was definitely coming together, everything, that is, except my love life.

They say the quickest way to a man's heart is through his chest with a sharp knife and I had the scars to prove it. My heart had been broken more times than I cared to remember. However, I was optimistic that I would one day get the fairy tale ending. I had the ability to see the glass half full, though at times it seemed more like a curse, than a blessing.

I would describe myself as a romantic man, eternally hopeful that I would one day meet my prince. He'd be the love of my life and, when our eyes meet across that crowded room, my dream would finally come true. Although it had eluded me for the better part of my adult life, I held firm to my belief that I'd love again-and next time it would be forever.

Gay relationships were fraught with difficulties, but my dreams were worth holding on to. I had arrived at a place in my life where I knew exactly what I wanted in a man, without being afraid to go after it.

After much introspection I'd come to realise that articulating that became much easier once I acknowledged it. I still dreamed of the handsome stranger who would sweep me off my feet, but I was more realistic in the choices I made. I approached finding a partner in the same manner as I would approach shopping for an expensive item; for example, a car.

When purchasing my last car, I used three columns to represent the areas I wished to cover. In the first column, I wrote down the qualities that were essential; like the car's safety record, its engine size and how much I was willing to spend to obtain it.

In the second column I wrote the qualities I desired. These were things I wanted, but which were not essential. Things like my favourite colour, leather interior, or gadgets.

In the final column, I documented the qualities I didn't want; such as a high mileage, or a history of extensive repairs. It was very easy to decide the things that went into this column, because I knew exactly what I didn't want.

Utilising this method in my search for a partner made a lot of sense to me, but, in matters of the heart, logic was rarely effective. The qualities I felt were essential in the man I hoped to find were: honesty, integrity and trustworthiness. Ambition was not at the top of that list but, since I was ambitious myself, it made sense that we would be more compatible if we had some similar interests in common. He didn't have to be wealthy, but he needed to have goals to strive for in his life. These were not qualities I would be willing to compromise on.

One of the qualities I reserved for the second column in my search for Mr Right was pride in one's appearance. He didn't have to be tall, dark and handsome with supermodel looks, although one or two of these qualities would go a long way with me! Personal hygiene care would have to be at least average, and it would be nice if my man looked after his physical appearance.

Identifying the qualities I didn't want in a partner was easy. I could recite them by heart due to my past experiences. In a nutshell, I didn't want a cheating, lying, down and dirty, good-for-nothing dog. I had no time for a brother who was incapable of loving, or being loved by me.

Nor did I want someone looking for fun with no strings attached. I needed strings. While he was on that bus leaving town he could make room for those confused men with extra baggage who wanted to keep me on the *down low* while taking care of their wives and kids. If he could so easily cheat on his family, then it would only be a matter of time before he cheated on me.

I believed that I had a lot of good qualities to offer a prospective partner. A little over six feet tall, I was noticed when I walked into a room. I had my hair cut every two weeks and I had regular manicures. Keeping in shape was also important to me, so I visited the gym twice weekly; sometimes more often if I felt particularly vain.

My values had been drilled into me as a child living in the Caribbean. Back then, I hadn't a clue about my sexuality. It was only when I arrived in London that I blossomed like a flower in spring.

Life on the Caribbean Island of Grenada was ideal until I completed my Advanced Level studies and realised my parents were unable to afford the university fees. I was faced with the harsh reality of finding a mundane job and putting my dreams of becoming an architect on hold.

My father's youngest sister had lived most of her adult life in England, after migrating in the early 1960s to study nursing. I'd met her on the few occasions she had visited the land of her birth. She had never married and didn't have any children of her own. My father persuaded her to sponsor me to join her in London so I could continue with my studies, thus making a better life for my family and myself.

I'd just turned twenty when Aunt Maggie sent for me to join her. I was very excited and felt it was the best thing that could've happened to me. I had an opportunity to break the cycle of poverty. The world was my oyster. My parents naturally expected me to provide some financial support to them once I'd established myself. I was the family's investment, their pension scheme.

I remember the day I arrived in London like it was yesterday. I was not prepared for, and unimpressed by, the extreme weather conditions. I had never before lived away from my family and Aunt Maggie proved to be little more than a stranger to me. I missed the warmth, the sunshine and the freedom I'd left behind and wondered whether I'd made the right decision.

There was little time for self-pity because a lot of people were depending on me. I had been offered an opportunity that few were given, and I had the responsibility to stop complaining and get on with the task at hand. Soon I would find other things to fill the gaping hole, the void I felt, being away from my home and family.

There was no real choice on my part about whether I would become a nurse. My aunt saw this as a means to an end. It seemed to be the natural progression of my life. In her eyes she'd done her part to assist me and, indirectly, her brother and his family; so now it was up to me to make the most of the opportunity I'd been given.

A lovely house, a good car and nice clothes were just a few of the luxuries afforded to my aunt by a well-paid job and a skill for managing her finances. She seemed happy, but had no one to share her life with. She was set in her ways and liked her own space. As a result, she was only too happy that I went away to Scotland to do my nurse training.

During my training I made a few friends and learned to revel in my new found independence, and feelings of sexual liberation. It wasn't until my second year in training that I had the confidence to act on, these feelings. The result was less than rewarding and left me disappointed. His name was Ian and we'd met in a local bar. Thanks to copious amounts of alcohol it was all over in a few minutes.

The next time was magical. So much so, that I chose to remember it as my first. His name was Noel and, since I liked all things Christmas, it wasn't hard to fall for him. Noel was the brother of Gina, one of my colleagues and he lived in London. We met during one of his visits to Glasgow to see his sister.

Our first meeting was uneventful, but our mutual attraction seemed to grow with each visit, and I got to know him better. Gina was very busy with her boyfriend and had little time for Noel, which suited me fine. We took long walks through the city and talked for hours sometimes.

Noel visited over the Christmas holidays but Gina had unwittingly arranged to go to Paris with her boyfriend, which left him to his own devices for the duration. We were on a three-week break from college, I had no intention of spending any of this time visiting Aunt Maggie in London and so I welcomed the idea of spending part of it with Noel.

On the first evening Gina was away, Noel and I went into town for a meal. During the meal he casually asked if I had a girlfriend. I told him that I was single, careful not to mention anything about my sexuality. I felt the natural thing to do was to reciprocate and ask him if he was in a relationship. He said that he was also single but that it was not by choice.

He explained that he had difficulty meeting someone special. I reassured him that it would only be a matter of time before he found the right person. He told me he thought that he'd found that person, but he wasn't sure if they felt the same way about him. I convinced him to tell '*her*' how he felt. He owed it to himself to know for certain if there was a chance for something special.

He took a large gulp of his drink before asking if I felt the same way about him. Initially I was shocked, but later realised that I'd walked right into his seduction. We were both attracted to each other, but it was Noel who felt confident enough to make the first move.

We were inseparable for the next few days, until Gina's return from Paris. Our relationship lasted just over a year, but by the time I graduated from college we began growing apart. We remained friends and he will always have a special place in my heart as my first true lover.

After Noel there were several men, most of whom proved to be disappointments. A few broke my heart, each time I swore never to date again-but that never lasted very long. I tried dating different races, different ages and different classes. The one thing they seemed to have in common, apart from me, was an uncanny ability to break my heart: some more gently than others but wounding me all the same, leaving me a little more jaded for the experience. I was living proof that what didn't kill you certainly made you stronger.

I became more focussed on my personal goals and if a fine man came along then it was all good. If he didn't come into my life then that was OK too. With this new attitude my professional career blossomed and, although I had difficulty replicating a similar success in my love life, I felt good about myself.

2. First impressions

It was a busy morning on the ward. The patients were unsettled and one staff member had called in sick, something of a regular occurrence lately. As the nurse in charge, I was left the unenviable task of trying to manage without adequate staff. This situation was far from ideal, but I had to make do with the available resources.

As I began preparing for the ward meeting, I heard a knock on the door of the nursing station. I looked up, half expecting to see a patient requesting my assistance; instead Dr Richards stood before me. Dr Richards was a senior psychiatrist who often visited the Unit. He was very popular with the female staff, I suspect, in part, because of his handsome Mediterranean features. Six junior doctors, whom he proceeded to introduce, accompanied him.

It was only then that I remembered the memo that had been circulated a few weeks earlier, announcing the start of the rotation for junior doctors. These changes occurred twice yearly, in February and August, causing some disruption to the usually efficient provision of medical cover for the Unit.

There were four male and two female doctors. As Dr Richards introduced his junior colleagues to me, I tried hard not to stare at the very attractive man second from the end. This young man seemed to be just what the doctor ordered!

I played it cool as I waited to be introduced to him. It seemed to take forever for me to get to shake the hand of this Nubian prince. I was unusually nervous but, in a professional yet courteous manner, I shook his hand firmly, remembering to flash him my killer smile.

His name was Dr Ade Sonaike, and you could have slapped me silly when he looked me straight in the eye and held on to my hand just a fraction longer than his colleagues had. His face broke into a broad smile before letting go of my hand. A smile which didn't seem rehearsed, but which I was certain had probably captured a few hearts before. My mind raced with a mixture of excitement and paranoia.

I had a pleasant surprise for the second time that day when it was announced that Dr Sonaike would be working on my ward. He was due to start in a few days. I almost wet myself on hearing this news and contemplated doing a cartwheel down the middle of the ward. The realisation that I would be working closely with the good doctor made my heart beat faster. I had a feeling the next few months were going to be very interesting.

It was difficult to tell whether Dr Sonaike was gay or not. The signs so far were pointing to him being gay, but I'd misread those signs before, resulting in disastrous consequences. This time I planned to be cautious in my endeavour to find out for certain whether he was 'family'.

I didn't believe in romance in the work place; however, on this occasion I was willing to make an exception to that rule. This young man was so fine that he could drive me to distraction, if I allowed him. Gay, straight or anything in-between, I knew I would have my work cut out for me in discovering his hidden depth, but I was up for the challenge.

I was positively giddy for the rest of the day and, surprisingly, the ward seemed a lot more manageable. I performed my duties with renewed energy. This was the effect of a handsome man on me. My friends always said, "The only thing better than good dick, is new dick". One sight of a fine-looking brother and I had dreams of living happily ever after. I was like a runaway train, a man possessed; after all, I was a single, handsome, twenty-something gay man, in search of my soul mate. It seemed as though I'd stumbled on to the next potential candidate for that position.

* * *

The three days I had to wait for Dr Sonaike to join our team seemed to take forever. By the time he showed up for work I had us married with two kids and a golden retriever, living in a little cottage in the countryside. I was out to get my man and if anyone got in my way there would be hell to pay!

Several months later I would realise that I'd lost the plot completely but, at the time, everything seemed plausible to me and it all made sense. It never occurred to me that Dr Sonaike might be heterosexual, possibly married, and with a family. However, going by my track record, he was probably also confused about his sexuality and a complete arsehole. This was not the kind of man that

I would deliberately set out to meet but it seemed, increasingly, to be what I ended up with.

I'd been hurt many times before, yet I had developed a resilience that allowed me to continue believing that, in the end I would find love. The law of averages was on my side as I clung desperately to the hope that next time would be different. All I was asking for was someone who would be honest, kind, gentle; and not turn out to be a disaster like the others. To me this was not an unreasonable request.

I was a desperate man and it wasn't a pretty sight. Dr Sonaike, who preferred to be called by first name Ade, was very charming. He settled into the team well, and was nothing like his predecessor, a stuck up cow named Dr Amanda Harvey-Smith.

Ade was popular with the staff as well as the patients, and seemed to be a genuinely nice guy. He was easy to talk to and, on the few occasions we were alone, his intense gazes made my knees weak. As time went by, I became more convinced that Ade was interested in me romantically. If I was going to make a move towards confirming his status, one way or the other, I would have to act soon.

I arranged it so that most of our shifts coincided as I started carefully laying the groundwork. Ade seemed confident and possessed a lethal combination of intelligence, good looks and good manners. Sometimes when I caught him looking at me he'd quickly look away, like a child caught stealing sweets. I swore there was a hint of a smile appearing before he looked away.

I began to notice he seemed slightly nervous whenever we were alone, which intrigued me. I believed my '*gaydar*' was beginning to focus much more accurately and, unless I was completely off base, I felt pretty certain that I was barking up the right tree. I still had no objective evidence he was a friend of Dorothy but I knew a way to find out.

Gradually he seemed more relaxed and self-assured. I was accustomed to being the predator; being the prey was unfamiliar territory for me. I wondered whether my work colleagues had picked up on the interaction between Ade and myself. I believed that if I had noticed him paying me more attention of a personal nature, then there was a good chance that they would have noticed it too. I was flattered, despite my anxieties, as he seemed to be determined in his pursuit of me.

At nights Ade visited me in my dreams, leaving me drained the next morning. It was an intoxicating feeling. It'd been a long time since I'd felt like this. I wanted the feeling to last forever.

As Ade worked his magic on me, paranoia made its way into my reality and I began to consider that maybe it was all too good to be true. I had a crush on Ade the size of the Titanic and look what happened to that ship.

One evening at work, a couple of colleagues and I were talking about our personal lives. I learned that Ade was born in Birmingham, to Nigerian parents who had separated when he was quite young. His mother, whom he described as emotionally distant and domineering, had, in his mind, abandoned her family when she returned to Lagos.

She was from a wealthy family in Nigeria and decided she didn't like living in England. However, she stayed a few years because her husband had promised they would return to Lagos eventually. That never happened. She decided that if her husband and children wanted to remain in a cold, alien environment, then they would have to do so without her.

Ade's father resented his wife's decision to return to Nigeria, he was adamant that he would remain in England and be the main carer for their three children. She never asked for a divorce because that would have been unheard of in her culture. She was quite content to have an ocean between her and her responsibilities as a wife and mother.

From an early age Ade had known he wanted to be a doctor. He loved to read. While other children were outdoors playing, he could be found at home in his own fantasy world inhabited by words. Initially he missed his mother but, gradually, his feelings of loss turned to resentment. He never understood why a mother would leave her children behind for what, he felt, were purely selfish reasons. He rebelled by not learning to speak his parent's native language, despite spending his school holidays in Nigeria.

I was surprised at how candidly he spoke about his life. It gave me some insight about his identity. He was twenty-nine years old, only three years my senior but it seemed he'd already had much more experience of life.

He said he was single, but getting to an age when he needed to settle down and start having a family. Something didn't ring true about this. It didn't add up, a fact which seemed to take him a step closer to having the words, 'I am gay' tattooed across his forehead.

He was a great catch and could have had the pick of a lot of women. His excuse that his studies had prevented him from marrying and starting a family only served to make me more suspicious about his sexuality. If he had been living in Nigeria he would've been married, and procreating as God intended him to. I smelled something fishy in his story and was eager to get to the bottom of it all.

The rest of my colleagues seemed oblivious to the gaping holes in Ade's story about his romantic life. He asked if I was married. I told him that I was happily married with two small children; I swear the expression on his face was a mixture of surprise and disappointment. My colleagues' laughter reassured him that I was joking and he seemed almost relieved by this news. This convinced me that it was time to move on, to phase-two of my plans.

3. A friend of Dorothy

Kunle and I had been friends for a long time. A few years earlier we'd been in a romantic relationship but it hadn't worked out, instead we settled for friendship. I often wondered whether we would've made a success of our relationship, if cultural traditions and family pressures hadn't got in the way. It had taken me a long time to get over him.

Kunle was born in London, to Nigerian parents. As he approached his twenty-seventh birthday, his family decided to take matters into their own hands. They'd given him sufficient time to find that special person with whom to fall in love and start producing grandchildren. He hadn't managed to do it on his own; so they proceeded to help.

Kunle is as gay as the day is long but he was unable to stand up to his parents. A part of him wanted desperately to be his own man but he was up against an entire culture that had entrusted him with a great deal of responsibility.

We were in love but our love could not withstand such pressure. I was the one who finally confronted the situation, ending the relationship before we began to resent each other. Kunle felt he was being pulled in different directions. It was distressing for me to see him so unhappy. He didn't deserve to be guilt-ridden or in pain because he had to choose between his family, and his lifestyle.

Kunle felt stuck between a rock and a hard place and it was bound to hurt someone, whatever his decision. I needed to be with someone who could love me the way I deserved to be loved. We were both young and would survive this. It was difficult at first but we persevered, successfully, making the transformation from lovers to friends.

Kunle eventually agreed to get married to a nice, quiet girl from Nigeria, called Aduni. It's always the quiet ones you need to look out for. He and Aduni were hitched and set out to procreate as if their lives depended on it.

Kunle didn't grow to love his new wife but he fulfilled his duties as a husband, all the while keeping his eyes on the prize, a child of his own, which would also get his parents off his back. With a new wife in tow and hopefully a child to follow shortly, he would have pleased his family, and society, and would be able to continue dating men.

Aduni's pregnancy was a happy time for Kunle; he was relieved because the frequency of their lovemaking had been reduced significantly. He was also very excited about the impending birth of his first child. His life finally seemed to be making some sense.

The couple's work paid off and they were blessed with a beautiful daughter, whom they named Mercedes. In Kunle's eyes, the new addition to the family assured him that all the sacrifices he'd made had been worthwhile.

After the birth of Mercedes, Aduni's personality changed. Gradually, the quiet, nice girl, from 'back home' had been replaced by a domineering tyrant who exuded a sense of authority, the likes of which Kunle hadn't seen in her before.

Being a mother gave Aduni the ammunition she needed to take control of their home. Her dominance overshadowed Kunle's quiet, retiring, personality. She was continually dissatisfied and disappointed by Kunle and did not spare his feelings in reminding him of his shortcomings, both as a father and as a husband. She was unhappy that they weren't living in the right neighbourhood and felt that he needed to get a better job and more influential friends. He seemed unable to do right by her.

She had become more demanding in bed as well. Kunle tried everything in his power to avoid sex with her including coming in late from work and waiting until she was fast asleep before getting into bed. At times, he would be up at the crack of dawn to leave for work before she woke up.

On the few occasions that he gave into her sexual demands he felt like an impostor and found very little enjoyment in the act itself, only relief that he would not have to repeat the performance anytime soon. When he tried to feign tiredness, she had no sympathy because a good husband would be able to satisfy his wife in every way.

Kunle had to find a way to vent his frustrations, going to the gym seemed the obvious solution. He spent most of his spare time at the local gym where he would work out until he was dog-tired. It helped him maintain his sanity. That, and the love he had for his daughter, kept him going.

He was amazed how this little person had entered his life, changing it completely. He found it difficult to remember a time when Mercedes had not been in his life. Aduni was a different kettle of fish however, and he began to appreciate the enormity of his mistake, of marrying someone with whom he was so incompatible. He wondered how long they would be able to keep up the charade.

His time at the gym was rewarding mentally as well as physically. He developed a well-toned body, which made me see him in a different light. A large part of my attraction to him in the past had been his intellect. We could talk for hours and not run out of things to say to each other. He challenged me mentally, now his physical appearance created another dimension to him. He also had a quiet confidence about him that said he appreciated his physical appearance, without being obsessed about it.

Kunle's attraction to men never waned. There were quite a few fine specimens of the male form at his local gym and opportunities to feast his eyes were plentiful. I asked him once whether he was ever tempted to have a sexual liaison with one of these men. He answered yes but said that he would never actually do anything about it. He believed it would be unfair to Aduni. He took his marriage vows seriously and would never deliberately hurt his family, in any way. His integrity was just another of the many qualities that made him attractive to me. He wanted to be the best father he could be and not to make the same mistakes he felt his parents had made.

Aduni may have been from deepest Africa but she was no fool. She started adding up the clues; it didn't take very long for the penny to drop. She approached her family with her suspicions about her husband and it was all downhill from there.

Kunle had met his wife's brother, Osa, several times before at family events. He knew Osa was gay and, armed with this knowledge, stayed as far away from him as possible. At family functions he kept contact to a minimum because he knew very well that gay men had no trouble identifying other gay men. It was the old adage used in (gay circles) that '*sheep knew sheep*'. He felt, the further the distance between them, the better his chances were of not being found out.

Osa was keen to help when he learned of his sister's suspicions. He was eager to discover all he could about Kunle's sexual preference. Osa knew where to locate the files on Kunle, if indeed they existed. Although his own sexuality had never been discussed openly within the family, it was acknowledged that he would be the right man for the job.

The beans were well and truly spilled when Osa found out, through his sources, that Kunle was a fully paid up member of the club for black men who slept with men. Aduni's family converged in true Mafia-like fashion, to launch a scathing attack on Kunle. They were ruthless in their determination to bring as much shame to Kunle and his family as they thought he'd brought to them. Their reputation was at stake.

The news spread like wildfire throughout the close-knit Nigerian community in London before finally reaching Kunle's family. During this time, Aduni was distant but continued to share the marital home, disclosing nothing of her findings to her husband. As soon as she was certain she had done that which she had set out to, she swiftly started divorce proceedings and moved out of the family home, taking their daughter with her. She claimed that Kunle was an unfit father and set out to further humiliate him by demanding that Social Services supervise all contact between him and his daughter.

Kunle didn't mind the breakdown of his marriage and in some, slightly dysfunctional way, was relieved that it was over. What he was most angry about, was the way in which Aduni had handled the situation. She hadn't considered the effect of her behaviour on their daughter.

Aduni wanted revenge and she was not afraid to use any means at her disposal to make sure she got it, including using their daughter. She felt *she* had fulfilled *her* role in the marriage contract as a dutiful wife and mother; but dick had got in her husband's way when it came to him keeping his end of the bargain.

Kunle had learned several valuable lessons, albeit the hard way. One of the most important lessons was to be true to himself, however difficult the choices he faced in life. He would never again bring a heterosexual woman into 'his world'. Aduni may have turned out to be the wife from hell, but she hadn't deserved to be placed in a situation that was so beyond her control.

Kunle accepted responsibility for his actions and planned to move on with his life. Fortunately his family didn't desert him, despite the fact that their long-held suspicions about his sexuality had been confirmed by Aduni's revelation. They too had kept their eyes on the bigger picture. They had achieved their goal of a grandchild to pass on their genes to future generations and, in their eyes, it had been worth it. Maybe they would have liked more grandchildren, or possibly a different ending to the story, but they felt they'd made the best of a difficult situation.

* * *

I tried to adopt a casual tone when I told Kunle about Ade. I didn't want him to know of my romantic interest. If he knew my motives he would try to warn me about getting emotionally involved with a work colleague. I asked him to do some investigations and was impressed when he responded quickly. It turned out that the good doctor was a distant relative of Aduni.

The verdict was in; Ade was gay. Kunle said he knew this because Ade had called him, shortly after his separation from Aduni, to ask him out on a date. He declined of course; since then, they'd met at a few social events but had never really hit it off as friends. Kunle felt Ade's advances were inappropriate. Ade was also in a relationship with another man at the time.

With this news, I felt like the cat that swallowed the canary. I thought about telling Ade that I knew he was gay, but I wondered if it would only make our situation more awkward. On the other hand, I could do nothing and let nature take its course. However, by doing nothing I could be considered manipulative for withholding this information. I felt like I was in a 'no win' situation.

Kunle had not mentioned anything about Ade's relationship status, so I took this to mean he was available. Of course, it could also have meant that Kunle hadn't said anything because he was unaware of my romantic interest in Ade. I decided to go with my instinct, which was telling me to be patient. It'd been a long time since someone had made me feel the way Ade did-and we hadn't even slept together! Whatever the outcome, I felt ready.

* * *

At work, we seemed to gravitate to each other and began spending more time in each other's company. The chemistry between us was almost palpable. Occasionally I would see him walking forlornly across the lush grounds of the old Victorian hospital and my heart would do a somersault. My feelings for him grew stronger with each passing day.

One cool autumn evening, after a long day at work, I decided to go out to a popular gay bar. The weather was surprisingly good for the time of year and I didn't feel like spending another evening indoors. I seldom ventured out mid-week because of work. I'd also stopped going to bars and clubs because I didn't find those places particularly good for meeting the kind of men I was interested in dating.

On this particular evening I was bored and saw no harm in a little social stimulation. I weighed up my options; of having a quiet night in, or going out to be in the company of men. I decided on the latter. I showered and dressed quickly, before I had time to change my mind. I intended spending only a couple of hours at the club.

When I arrived in Vauxhall I was surprised to find that the club was not very crowded. There were a few familiar faces but I didn't notice anyone I felt particularly interested in approaching. I headed straight for the bar, where I ordered a Barcardi Breezer. I then proceeded to nurse it standing in a darkened corner opposite the club's entrance.

From my position I could observe the punters as they entered. I hadn't had sex in weeks, let alone good sex-and I was hornier than a toad; but by the look of the men entering the club, that situation was not about to change any time soon.

I got the shock of my life when Ade walked into the club. I panicked initially, but soon realised there was nothing for me to be anxious about. I was in a gay club, so what? If he chose to ignore me then that was his problem. He could also forget about telling any of the staff at work about bumping into me because he'd have to explain what he was doing in the club in the first place. I relaxed and waited to see how it would pan out.

I decided to play it cool, leaving the ball firmly in his court. The club was not very large so the likelihood of him not noticing me was remote; even if I was trying to make myself invisible in the darkened corner. This was the last thing I'd expected when I left home. Luckily, I'd made sure I was looking fine because one could never predict when one might run into one's 'prince'.

Ade walked right up to the bar and ordered a drink, then casually strolled over to me as if it was the most natural occurrence in the world. The brother was smooth; he didn't miss a beat. I searched his face for some sign of nerves but there was none. In the meantime, my heart was beating faster than a race horse, from all the excitement.

Our meeting would certainly take care of bringing up the issue of me disclosing my knowledge of his sexuality. He didn't seem the least bit surprised to see me. He flashed me his 'killer' smile and, as I extended my hand to shake his, he drew me into an embrace. It was great to feel the warmth of a man's body. This had all the makings of a fairy tale. Eyes, locked across a crowded room; hearts, beating fast; love in the air. Of course, this could simply be the effect of the one drink I'd had, but the version in my head was the more romantic of the two possibilities.

The club had suddenly become noisier, forcing Ade to lean in close to talk to me. He smelled great and I had difficulty concentrating on what he was saying. Occasionally he would bump into me as we talked. I prayed silently that he'd done it on purpose.

I felt at ease in his company and, after a few more drinks, we were getting on like a house on fire. I had to be up early for work the next day so I decided to cut short our time together. He asked me for a lift home because he hadn't driven to the club. This meant that we'd get to spend a little more time together. I said another silent prayer of thanks to Saint Francis, patron saint of homosexuals.

Ade and I got a few envious looks as we left the club together. I convinced myself they were simply jealous queens who wanted the fine-looking man on my arm. It certainly made a change for me, even if it might all be in my delusional mind.

I could tell that Ade was a little tipsy because his gait was unsteady. We climbed into my 3-series convertible BMW and sped off from the club. He lived about twenty minutes away. As I drove I could see, out of the corners of my eyes that Ade was checking me out. This made me feel sexy, attractive and desirable, all at once. At the rate my head was swelling it wouldn't be long before it exploded.

Before I knew it, we'd arrived outside Ade's flat. A part of me wanted an invitation into his flat for coffee-or anything else for that matter, but another part of me wanted this to be the perfect start to a romance. In my experience sleeping on the first date wasn't usually a recipe for a meaningful long-term relationship. There I was, turning a chance meeting into a first date. What was I like?

I wanted him worse than a crack head wanted his next fix, but I had to be careful with this one. If he was going to be a keeper (all the signs were pointing in that direction), I wanted us to get off to the best possible start. I didn't want him thinking that I was easy.

Ade hesitated briefly before saying, in a slightly slurred voice, "Chris it was really good seeing you tonight, we should do this again, sometime."

He wanted us to go out again! 'First hurdle clear', I thought.

"I had a nice time with you tonight", he said.

"I had fun too and yes I'd certainly like to do it again."

We both sat in silence until he spoke once more to say "Chris, there's something I want to . . ." and before I knew what was happening, he leaned over and gave me a warm, sweet kiss, on my lips.

I was bowled over and my head started spinning. In the distance, I could hear him saying "Good night" as he closed the car door behind him. His actions had taken me by surprise, leaving me speechless.

Dazed, I sat outside his flat for a few seconds before putting the key in the ignition and starting the engine. I felt like I was on cloud sixteen, never mind cloud nine. As I drove home, I wondered whether this was my chance for long-awaited happiness.

* * *

The next day I was so excited about seeing Ade that I got into work twenty five minutes early, a first for me. I knew I had to keep our meeting at the club a secret, but I found it difficult to contain my excitement. What was once only a fantasy before, a dream, now seemed to be a very real possibility.

There was no denying that the kiss we shared was passionate. Sure he'd had a few drinks, but he was the one who had initiated it. I still wasn't absolutely convinced about having an affair at work but only time would tell, whether we would take things further. Again, the ball seemed to have landed in his court.

My heart skipped several beats when I heard Ade's voice. As I turned around to face him I wondered if the previous night had been some wonderful, if cruel, dream. It wasn't; because standing before me was Ade smiling broadly. He winked at me when he thought no one was looking. At least he wasn't a confused brother who was willing to pretend that nothing had happened between us the previous night.

Later that day when we were alone, Ade thanked me for the previous night, saying that he was very serious about us going out soon. I didn't respond; instead I stood there, grinning like the village idiot. It was difficult to take in what was happening-something I'd longed for, but never achieved.

Just as I was leaving work, Ade joined me and together we walked to my car. I sensed that he had something on his mind and wanted to speak privately. We made small talk whilst we were in the building, but once outside I stopped and looked at him before asking what was wrong. I wondered whether he was beginning to have second thoughts about our next date.

"Is something the matter Ade?" I asked.

"Not really, but . . ." he hesitated before continuing. "Maybe it's more of a question I wanted to ask."

I thought 'here it comes'. He probably doesn't know if he's gay and he's had a change of heart. "Why don't you go ahead and ask me the question, I promise to give you an honest answer."

"Does the rest of the staff know you're gay?" he asked.

"As far as I'm aware they don't. I make it a point to keep my private life separate from my professional life. Whomever I choose to sleep with, or date, is none of their business, and that's the way I like to keep it. As a black man in a senior position I already have enough shit to deal with," I said.

He seemed visibly relieved and the playful side of his personality re-emerged. Ade made me promise to go out with him soon. He didn't realise that I was already walking down that aisle, on his arm. We said goodbye as I got into my car.

Although I was fine with the concept of coming out at work, having to deal with it on a daily basis was something I was not yet prepared to do. As a black man living in a predominantly white culture, I already felt under tremendous pressure to dispel the myths about me that were perpetuated by institutional racism. Adding my sexuality to the mix would further complicate my life.

After having my car stopped and searched by the Police several times in the past, it was difficult to think of it as just another coincidence. It was far easier to believe that it might have something to do with the fact that I was a black man driving a nice car.

It was hard, to continually pretend that white women clutching their bags as I passed by was a sign of the times we were living in. When I acknowledged this publicly I was met with the assumption that I had a chip on my shoulder. I agreed; I had a chip the size of Gibraltar on my shoulder, but I wasn't willing to accept all the responsibility for it.

Wearing my sexuality as a banner, I felt, was not an option for me. My black colleagues would probably consider me a sell out, adopting the 'white man's ways'. My white colleagues on the other hand would still see me as a black man first and foremost; and then my sexuality would only be a source of concern if they felt their masculinity was threatened.

The black community would tolerate me but would ultimately see me as a disappointment. A black man who had a university education, a career that did more than just pay the bills and who wasn't taking or selling illicit drugs was an endangered species. It would be the loss of a potential husband, father and role model.

To many straight men, being gay was a contagious condition. They felt that if they spent too much time with a gay man, they could themselves be 'turned' gay. No, coming out at work was definitely not an option for me at this time in my life.

Like a lot of black, gay men who didn't want their sexuality to be public knowledge, Ade was justifiably concerned that fraternising with a known homosexual would immediately cast doubt on his own sexuality. In the black community, if it wasn't pushed in our faces then we didn't have to see it; and if we didn't see it we could pretend it didn't exist.

4. As time goes by

I came alive around Ade and I suspect he was very aware of the effect he had on me. During the short time we'd worked together, I'd found out a lot about him. Since our first meeting outside of work, he was much more open with me and we shared a closeness that became very important to me. He told me about his family and growing up in North London.

I began to build a picture of a man who had a few issues, some of which were unresolved. On the one hand he appeared cold and detached when he spoke about his family but there also seemed to be another side to him-warm, kind and compassionate. It intrigued me that the two co-existed, contrasting each other. This made for an exciting and heady mix, which further fuelled my interest in him. Those big brown eyes belied a deep well of mystery and passion.

Ade's parents became aware of his sexuality when he could no longer postpone getting married. He'd given them every excuse in the book about why he hadn't found a wife. One day his father had asked him outright about his sexuality. Ade had always maintained, that if asked directly, he would always respond truthfully. His father seemed to take the news well. He didn't want this life for Ade, but he loved him enough to allow him to make his own choices.

His mother on the other hand was an entirely different matter. She was angry and hurt that her eldest son would betray her like this. She blamed his father for allowing those white people in London to corrupt her son. She saw this as yet another reason why her husband should have listened to her many years ago and moved the family back to Nigeria, where this sort of thing would never have happened. She couldn't have known that geography would not have made any difference.

His mother remained unrelenting in her views about her son's chosen lifestyle. She felt strongly that he had been corrupted by his environment. No noble African man would know what homosexuality was, let alone engage in such despicable behaviour. Her reaction didn't surprise Ade.

Whenever his father called, he'd ask Ade about his partner and, on a few occasions, he actually spoke with the special man in Ade's life at the time. His mother would not even entertain the idea of speaking to one of her son's lovers. She was determined that Ade would not bring disgrace to the family name and was grateful that he lived so far away.

Ade's willingness to open up to me was very touching. It convinced me that I'd earned his trust and I felt protective toward him. I wanted desperately to show him the love he believed he'd missed growing up. I wanted him to know that he'd found, in me, someone who would love him in return and who would neither disappoint him nor turn their back on him, like others had done in the past.

It was difficult concentrating at work whenever Ade was present. During one particular staff meeting, I looked up to find him staring at me. His face was expressionless but his eyes seemed transfixed, leaving me with no doubt in my mind of his carnal intentions. Sometimes it felt like we were the only two people on the ward.

Occasionally he'd brush up against me as he walked by, leaving me aroused. At other times, when talking, his hand would rest casually on my shoulder as he listened intently to what I said. This also turned me on. Gradually his antics became more outrageous, sometimes I had to excuse myself and go to the bathroom to splash cold water on my face. I liked the attention, the seduction and the thrill of the chase, but eventually something would have to give.

Things almost came to a head one afternoon. During a particularly long and boring meeting at work, I noticed Ade staring at me. This in its self was not unusual until I observed another colleague observing Ade. I closed my eyes briefly but when I opened them again, Ade continued to stare, unaware he was being watched. I panicked but Ade remained calm and a short while after he looked away and began casually writing on a note pad as if nothing had happened.

* * *

It was clear that Ade and I needed to go on our next date soon. I was also up for some great sex and, if Ade looked this good 'in' clothes, I held high expectations about what he'd look like out of them. My patience was wearing thin. There was several months worth of pent up sexual tension that I needed to release-and soon!

All this attention from Ade was making me dizzy and I loved every minute of it. On the third of my four nights, the telephone operator put through a call to the ward. I was pleasantly surprised to hear Ade's voice on the line.

He said that he needed some information to prepare a report, due the next morning. I soon realised this was just an excuse to talk to me because he only asked a few questions about the patient before quizzing me about my night. He hadn't realised that he didn't have to invent a reason to call me.

We agreed on a time for our next date. Before hanging up, he told me that he missed working with me and wished me a good night.

I had another pleasant surprise, on my last night, when I showed up for work to find out that Ade was the Psychiatrist on call for the night. The patients were settled and there was no obvious reason to contact him. I secretly hoped he'd call but, if he didn't, I was prepared to call him.

He didn't keep me waiting long. At about half past midnight, the telephone rang.

"Hi Chris, how's the shift going?" he asked.

"Fine," I said. "It's really nice hearing from you."

"Are the patients settled?" he asked.

"Yes, most of them have gone to bed. A couple are awake in the television room so I'm just catching up on some paper work."

"Can I come over and spend a little time with you?" He asked.

"I'd like that," I said.

"See you in about half an hour then."

My pulse quickened when I heard Ade's footsteps as he entered the ward. I hadn't seen him in three days, it felt like an eternity. As he entered the office, I noticed he was dressed casually, in jeans and a jumper. He was listening to music on his portable CD player and he wanted me to listen to one of his favourite songs. The name of the track was 'On bended knees' by the group Boys II Men. My heart melted as I listened to the words and imagined him dedicating them to me.

"What time are you going on your break?" he asked.

"In about an hour, when my colleague returns from her break," I said.

"I plan to do some reading when I go back to the doctor's quarters, why don't you join me on your break. We could talk some more," he said.

"That sounds really good but we're not allowed to leave the ward for our break."

"That's a pity." he remarked.

"Indeed; but that's the way it is I'm afraid."

"I'm really looking forward to our date. I can hardly wait to have you all to myself again," he said.

"Um, you read my mind."

"Good, then my work here is done. You have yourself a quiet night and don't do anything I wouldn't do," he said.

"I can't offer any guarantees but I'll try," I said, "I'll see you tomorrow."

"It's after midnight," he said looking at his watch, "so that means we'll be dining tonight."

And not a minute too soon I thought.

5. The date

We agreed to meet at a popular restaurant in Southwest London. I could hear the excitement in his voice when we spoke on the telephone to finalise the time. He was pleased that the day had finally come for us to take things to the next level. I had difficulty disguising my excitement as well and wanted to shout the good news at the top of my voice. It was about time my luck changed.

I went shopping for something nice to wear for my first real date in ages. I also had a haircut, because I wanted to look my best. I arranged to meet Tunde, at Balans café in Soho for tea at high noon. We hadn't seen each other in several months and I wanted to find out what he'd been up to lately.

He was already seated and looking at his watch when I arrived. I didn't need to look at the time to know I was late.

"So what time do you call this?" Tunde asked, his voice dripping with sarcasm.

"Bitch, give me a break, you know five minutes late is a record for me," I replied. "On a hot date tonight, so I thought I'd get a quick MOT," I said.

"Who's the lucky man?" asked Tunde.

"A colleague," I said, trying to sound casual.

"No, tell me I didn't hear you right. Did you just say, 'a colleague'? Have you lost your mind?" he asked, with mock surprise in his voice.

"I know what you're thinking. If someone else had said that to me, I'd be calling that bitch crazy, but this brother is 'FINE' as hell-I couldn't let this chance pass me by."

"I can't hate you because I've been dating someone on the down low too. Sometimes a brother has to do what a brother has to do."

"So are you going to tell me who this mystery man is?" I asked.

"I promised to keep my lips sealed with this one," he said.

"That'll be a first," I said.

"Bitch, don't even start with me," he said, smiling.

"But seriously, why can't you tell me who this man is? Is he someone I know?" I asked.

"It's a little complicated. We just want to be sure first, before we tell anyone."

"But I'm not just anyone," I said.

"I know honey-child. I just don't want to jinx it. When the time's right you'll be the first to know babes," he said.

"You promise?" I asked.

"I promise you baby."

We talked about the difficulties of finding a good man in London, both agreeing, that although the city was filled with handsome boys, most of these children were too confused for their own good.

Tunde was about five feet, ten inches, tall, with attractive features. He was slim, but muscular, in build and the brother looked fine in his clothes. He had a warm personality and an infectious laugh. The boy had it going on; but could he find a good man? Hell no! That's a whole other story.

I gave Tunde the example of our own group of friends, all of us fairly attractive, intelligent, solvent black men, but who between us couldn't find a decent man in London if our lives depended on it. He suggested that maybe our standards were too high. Maybe we weren't willing to compromise. My argument was, 'why should we settle for less, when we deserved better?' I refused to buy into that shit. There were good men around; I knew that because I planned to go out with one in a few hours.

Tunde grew up in Peckham and until recently had been looking for that elusive black man who looked and behaved straight, but who was one hundred percent gay. He'd hoped he would casually run into this thug on a bus, or whilst walking along Peckham high street. Their eyes would meet across a crowed street, this hunk would follow him home and they'd get into bed and make hot, passionate, love; repeatedly.

The reality was that any man who followed you home from that area was taking a huge risk, especially since he didn't know you from a can of paint. Come to think of it, you didn't know him either. The evening of romance would include hiding all your valuables and praying, that if indeed you did sleep together, that he wasn't going to beat the shit out of you in his guilt ridden state and still turn around and rob you. After closer inspection, the reality didn't seem all that great compared to the fantasy.

"So how long have you known this 'colleague' Chris?"

"He joined the staff a couple of months ago."

"So you've known him for . . . what? A minute?" he asked.

"Tunde, whatever you're about to tell me, I've already told myself. I know all the arguments and the many reasons I shouldn't be dating a colleague, especially since I'm not out about my sexuality at work."

"As long as you know what you're doing," he said.

"It feels right. In a short time, this man has made me feel like I haven't felt in a long time. He makes me feel special; wanted; beautiful, and the list goes on."

"Honey-child, you don't need a man to make you feel special, that's our job," he said.

"Yes, but you guys can't give me what he can. You know what I'm talking about?" I asked.

"Child, I hear you and I'll say amen to that. Incest isn't attractive."

We both laughed at Tunde's remark.

"I won't lie to you, I like this man a lot-and then some; and we haven't even slept together yet," I said.

"Hold up Bitch! You're thinking about buying the car without taking it for a test drive? Haven't I taught you anything?" he asked.

"I keep telling myself it's just a date, don't get too excited, we're just trying each other on; but it's much more than that. I know this time it's for real."

"Just promise me one thing baby-that you'll be safe," he said.

"You know I always practice safer sex," I said.

"I mean with your heart Christopher! Promise me you won't let him treat you badly-like that last arsehole did."

"I'll try my best." I said weakly, remembering my last relationship.

"That's all I'm asking baby boy."

Tunde and I spent the rest of the time talking about plans for Christmas, which was now only a few short weeks away. We Said good bye and promised to call each other over the holidays.

I headed up Tottenham Court Road towards Oxford Street to get a few items for my big night. As I walked along the busy West End streets, I thought about what Tunde had said. I was diving into this head first; I needed to be careful that I didn't end up getting hurt badly.

After my last relationship ended I promised myself that I'd try to notice the warning signs earlier. I prided myself in not falling so far down that I couldn't get back up again, but even with the strongest will power there were only so many times that I could recover, only so many breaks my heart could withstand.

When I arrived home I took a long, hot bath, using the bath oils I'd bought that afternoon. After my bath, I massaged cocoa butter lotion into my skin, before changing. The weatherman forecasted rain but I'd seen no evidence of this while out earlier. I decided to wear a caramel-coloured pair of trousers with a matching lamb's wool jumper, under a light jacket. I sprayed on a little *'Contradiction for men'* by Calvin Klein-one of my favourite scents, took one last look in the mirror, before leaving the flat for my hot date.

We'd arranged to meet at seven thirty, in the Giraffe restaurant in Battersea. It boasted an exciting menu and was reputed for having a relaxed, informal, ambience, which was just what we were hoping for-cosy and intimate, yet trendy. A friend had recommended it some time ago but the opportunity to try it for myself had not presented itself. My date with Ade provided just such an opportunity.

A few heads turned as I walked in but I only had eyes for one person. Ade was seated at a table in the far corner of the restaurant. He looked up and greeted me with a warm smile. I noticed he was wearing a pair of dark grey, woollen, trousers, with a white cotton shirt under a grey jumper. He looked very handsome. When I got to the table he stood up to shake my hand, his eyes scanned the length of my body before returning to my face. Round one to me I thought as we took our seats.

"You look really nice tonight," he said, looking directly into my eyes.

I felt like saying "I know," but instead said, "Thanks man, that's very kind of you, and you look quite dashing yourself."

"I had to make an effort for a special occasion," he said.

"Special?" I asked.

"Of course, I'm here with you; something tells me it's going to be a *very* special evening."

"Luckily, I happen to share that particular point of view. Did you drive here?" I asked

"No I left my car at home because I want to have some wine with dinner. Did *you* drive?"

"Lucky for you I did," I said, feeling like putty in his hands.

"I know that I'm lucky, to be sitting here with you, like this," he said.

I wanted to tell him that I felt like *I* was the lucky one.

I skipped the appetiser and ordered a main course for myself. Ade followed suit, before ordering some white wine while we waited for our meal to arrive. He commented on my cologne and I complemented him on his attire. As I looked out onto the street I could see the rain, coming down lightly, and I was grateful that I was sitting warm and dry.

When I looked over at Ade, I saw him staring at me so I asked, "Are you enjoying the view?"

He smiled before responding, "You noticed."

"I did," I said.

"The answer to your question is yes, I do like what I see; I like it a lot."

"I'm glad you do. I have one rule for this evening. Let's not talk about work. We're here to relax and have fun," I said.

"You'll have no argument from me," he said.

I started to relax as the wine entered my bloodstream.

"You seem to be very good at getting information out of other people without giving away anything much about yourself," Ade said, teasing.

Without looking up at him I asked, "Do I?"

"Come on, don't try to play me; you know you do," he said.

"What would you like to find out about me?" I asked, putting down my glass and giving him my undivided attention.

As he was about to respond, the waiter arrived with our meal and I thought, 'Saved by the bell."

"You don't get off that easily Mister; you have the rest of the evening to tell me all about yourself," he said.

Ade ordered hot smoked roast salmon with wasabi and green onion rice, toasted sesame seeds and yakiton sauce. I had Thai chicken and a vermacelli noodle salad with snap peas, cucumber, napa cabbage, spring onions, carrots, green chilli and lime. For desert we shared a slice of Swiss mountain chocolate cheesecake.

It was very easy to talk during the date, despite the few pauses in conversation. I felt at ease in Ade's presence, whether I was talking, or just quietly reflecting on the experience.

After desert, Ade ordered a glass of wine for himself and a cappuccino for me. By this time the rain was coming down heavily outside and any thoughts of going into the city were cancelled. Just then Ade reached across the table, to hold my hand. He thanked me for a wonderful evening and for agreeing to come out to dinner with him. His kind gesture left me speechless.

In a situation like this I would usually be concerned with who was looking at us, but this time no one else in the world mattered. I didn't care who'd seen our public display of affection. This was our night. He must have read my mind because, without saying a word to me he asked the waiter for the bill.

As we walked through the rain to my car, parked a few streets away, we fell into a comfortable silence. Earlier in the date I had considered going to a piano bar in the West End, for after dinner drinks, but what I wanted to do to Ade could not be done in a piano bar; not legally anyway. When we got to the car he said we needed to talk.

"Chris, do you think we could go somewhere quiet to talk?"

"We could go back to my place, if you like," I said.

"Are you sure? We could also go to a bar. The night's still young."

"I'm sure, and besides a bar wouldn't be that quiet."

I didn't understand why he was playing hard to get. Earlier, I had the impression that he wanted me just as badly as I wanted him. Now was his big chance and he was pretending not to be all that eager.

Walking into the flat, I turned on the lamp next to the sofa, illuminating the room with a soft yellow glow. I offered Ade a seat before lighting a few scented candles. Once the mood was set I wanted to feel his warm body against mine all night long. I didn't know if I was asking for too much but I believed in aiming high.

"What time do you need to get home?" I asked, praying to St Francis that he wanted to spend the night.

"Anytime is fine with me," he said. "I'm not on call this weekend."

At least he'd left it open. I was looking for a different answer but this would do for now.

"If you want to stay over, you could always use my bed; I'll sleep on the sofa."

"I wouldn't want to put you out," he said.

I was on the verge of becoming desperate.

"You wouldn't be, honest. The sofa opens out to form a comfortable bed. I'd be fine. Anyhow, the offer's there if you want it."

"We'll play it by ear," he said.

"This evening has been magical. It reminds me of a line from one of my favourite movies-Pretty Woman-when Julia Roberts tells Richard Gere that in case she forgets to say it at the end of the evening, she had a great time."

"The evening's not over yet Chris and if I have anything to do with it, we're a long way off from that."

"Would you like a drink, Sir?"

"I'd love one," he answered. "And you can stop calling me Sir as well!"

"I'm just playing with you," I said.

"Now that's more like it!" he replied suggestively.

I expected him to ask for alcohol, but instead he requested a coffee. Maybe he was trying to sober up so he could make his way home. I tried not to jump to any conclusions. I put on a CD before going to the kitchen.

When I returned, Ade was sitting comfortably on the sofa with his shoes off. He looked very relaxed. I gave him his drink and sat in an armchair opposite, deliberately avoiding any physical contact. If anything were to happen between us, it would have to be because we both wanted it, not because I seduced him. We made small talk for a while before he asked me why I was sitting so far away.

"Why don't you join me on the sofa? I hope I'm not scaring you away, because that's the last thing I'd ever want to do," he said.

"I'm not scared," I said, joining him on the sofa.

"Now isn't this a lot better?" he asked

Just then, one of my favourite songs started playing. Anita's Grammy-winning contribution to soul music, 'I apologise' always put me in a romantic mood. Ade sensed what the music was doing to me, and asked me for a dance.

'Well knock me over with a feather', I thought. Was he something special or what?

He stood up with outstretched hands and said; "I'm serious, may I please have this dance?"

"Of course you may," I answered.

My legs felt like jelly as Ade held me close. I could feel each beat of his heart through the walls of his chest and the rhythm was melodic. It was turning out to be the perfect evening.

At the end of the song he whispered "Thank you" in my ear and then we kissed. At first it was gentle, becoming more passionate as our hands explored each other's body. No words were spoken because none were needed.

When we finally unlocked our lips, I looked at Ade, and it was as if I was seeing him for the first time. I couldn't believe my luck. Here was this gorgeous man, standing before me with opened arms, welcoming me into his life. It was something I longed for, but sometimes doubted, would ever happen. I closed my eyes and opened them again quickly, to make sure I wasn't dreaming.

I led Ade by the hand into my bedroom. As I walked over to the large window to draw the curtains, he suggested that I leave then open. The rain was coming down heavily outside, creating a soothing sound, as it beat against the window. It reminded me of stormy nights in the Caribbean. As a child I would lay awake at nights, listening to the sound of the rain drops on the roof. Just then lightening struck, temporarily illuminating the room. I noticed Ade was still wearing his underwear.

Slowly we made our way to the bed. The room was totally dark, apart from the headlights of the occasional passing car. Sitting on the bed opposite each other, Ade took my hand and placed it on his chest. His racing heart confirmed his excitement. I traced the outline of his face with my other hand, until I found his sensual, full lips. I leaned in and gently kissed him. He tasted warm and sweet.

As we weren't able to see each other in a darkened room, we relied heavily on our other senses, to explore and provide pleasure to one another. The sounds, the smells, taste and touch, all heightened the experience. Ade was gentle and graceful in his exploration of my body, taking me to heights that I hadn't been to in a long time.

Christmas was one of my favourite times of the year, because it reminded me of my childhood and the special closeness I felt with my family. It was a time for forgiveness and new beginnings.

* * *

Ade was in Nigeria and though I missed him, I planned to make the most of the situation. I decided I would call a few friends and arrange to meet up over the holidays. I'd left messages for Tunde and Dele. I hadn't spoken to John in a long time so I called him. He picked up the phone on the first ring. About three minutes into the conversation I regretted calling him, as he proceeded to tell me about his troubled relationship with his boyfriend.

John and I met a few years before and had created a friendship out of a failed one-night stand. He was an upper middle class, professional Englishman, who was terminally attracted to black men, usually from Africa. He was a firm believer in the saying, 'the blacker the berry, the sweeter the juice'.

John hadn't been very successful in his relationships. I suspect this was due, in part, to the type of men he dated. He looked for the brothers who were either on social security-known in the gay community as 'giro queens'-or men who were hiding from the immigration authorities.

I believe he sought out these men to feel better about himself. Having someone dependant upon him probably did wonders for his ego. If a decent brother, with a job and an IQ in double digits paid him any attention, he repelled him-like kryptonite repelled Superman. Dating *within* his social class, *or* race, was uncommon for John.

His generosity was often abused by the men he dated. Initially I felt sorry for him, until I realised he was the author of his own destiny. On the few occasions I tried to discuss the matter with him, he became defensive and I realised that he was his own worst enemy.

He needed to take responsibility for his own actions. He and I were once close, but in recent years we had drifted apart. With it being the season of goodwill, I decided a telephone call was appropriate.

Steve was young, black, and ambitious. He was not John's usual type. They met two years earlier, whilst John was on holiday in Jamaica. John was not very forthcoming with details about their meeting but Steve had arrived in London six months later, and the rest as they say, is history.

Steve was, allegedly, fleeing Jamaica to escape a violent ex-partner. There was no question about who would be supporting him, or where he would live. John dropped everything, including his friends, to be at Steve's beck and call. Within a couple months of his arrival in the UK Steve was attending college.

John had a senior position in a public relations company and made good money-which Steve was happy to help him spend. Steve and I barely tolerated each other at first, because I saw right through him. I had no intention of warning John about his new lover. Experience had taught me never to offer relationship advice to anyone who didn't want it.

According to John, it had been Steve's idea for him to have less contact with his friends. Gradually John spent less and less time with his friends, most of whom could not be bothered to sustain the friendships. Steve was firmly in the driver's seat of that relationship. John's friendships were doomed to fizzle out.

As soon as Steve was established, John began to suffer the consequences of giving away control. Steve moved into his own flat, financed by John. His excuse for living on his own was to have his own space. Steve also changed the rules of their relationship, something John was unhappy about-but by then, it was too late.

John had given up so much for Steve that he now had nothing left with which to bargain. Steve felt they should be good friends-who slept together occasionally-as long as John continued to support him financially. John knew he was in an emotionally abusive relationship but, like most victims of abuse, he felt powerless to end it.

To the casual observer, John's relationship was dying a slow and painful death. John was totally consumed by his on-off relationship with Steve. His few remaining friends had to constantly endure the pain of him rehashing the gory details at every opportunity. At times I felt like holding John by the shoulders and shaking some sense into him, hoping that he'd wake up and smell the coffee.

John's invitation, to Steve's New Year's Eve party, was a mere formality. Steve had advised him to bring a friend, making it very clear that they should not be seen as a couple on this occasion. Steve usually got on my last nerve-but the child did know how to organise a party! I'd been to a couple of his parties before and had been impressed. The guests were usually very well selected and not the 'throw backs' one encountered in the gay clubs.

I had no plans for New Year's Eve, since my man was away. I didn't want to be alone on the last night of the year so I accepted John's invitation to accompany him to Steve's party. I hadn't received a card or phone call from Ade over the Christmas holidays so I needed something to lift my spirits. When he returned from his holidays he would have a lot of explaining to do; but for now I was out to have a good time.

* * *

John arrived at my flat at ten fifteen, a few minutes later we were on our way to Brixton. I wore a pair of brown leather trousers and brown, silk, shirt. John wore black trousers with a red turtleneck jumper.

We made the journey in good time, arriving at Steve's flat a little after eleven. The party was in full swing when we walked in. A few heads turned when we entered. Some of those heads remained turned-staring-I felt proud that I still had it going on. It cheered me up and set the tone for the rest of the night.

I was having a good time until I recognised the DJ. He was my ex, and this time the *'ex'* was short for 'excrement'. My newly-found confidence plummeted to the ground as I realised I had to share the same space with Patrick. The thought made me nauseous. I left John and made my way to the kitchen, which served as a bar, to get some alcohol in me.

Patrick and I had dated for about nine months, two years earlier. And it was nine months too long if you asked me. I thought we were fine, until he informed me that he was married. I was a little surprised by his admission. Not because he'd hidden it from me so well, but because a woman could possibly believe that he was straight.

He lived with his wife and two daughters, whom he enjoyed introducing to the men he dated. I finally ended the relationship because, as far as I was concerned, *he* was free to do what *he* wanted to his family, but I didn't want to be a part of the freak show.

Patrick was a very handsome, black, man. He was medium in build and stood just over six feet tall. He regularly shaved his head and sported a neatly groomed goatee beard. Physically, he was certainly my type, but I preferred my men a lot less confused. He was gay one minute, bisexual, straight the next. His sexuality seemed to change quicker than the weather.

Patrick and I were not friends by any stretch of the imagination, especially since he still owed me £500. He had borrowed this money just before the end of our relationship, then refused to repay me. I suspect he knew the relationship was about to end and had decided that once we parted he'd no longer be obligated to honour the debt. Luckily, I had observed the golden rule of money lending-never lend more than you can afford to give away-£500 was never going to bankrupt me.

I'd also learned never to get into the mud with a pig, because I'd only get dirty whilst the pig would enjoy it. I held fast to the belief, that what went around would eventually come right back around; it was only a matter of time before he reaped what he'd sown. Patrick was likely to try that shit on the wrong man one day, exposing him for the fraud that he is.

There he stood, in glorious Technicolor. I could have run away and hidden or I could take back the control I'd given him. I chose to remain and enjoy myself, letting him see just what he let slip through his thieving hands.

Besides, there were some fine-looking brothers at this party and the likes of Patrick were not going to prevent me from enjoying *their* company. There was no law against browsing through the market place, even if I didn't plan on buying anything. For all I knew, Ade was busy having fun with someone else in Nigeria.

As a boyfriend, Patrick was lower than a snake's belly; as a DJ however, he had earned his stripes. The man knew how to get people onto the dance floor and keep them there. It was one of the qualities that had attracted me to him. He mixed up his set with a little old-school and reggae, with a sprinkling of raga for good measure and a few soca tracks before switching to the R&B and slow grind selections. This allowed the men present to get up close and personal.

I spent so much time reminiscing about Patrick, that I didn't notice Kunle arriving at the party. The boy looked fine as hell in a pair of bum-hugging black trousers and black skin-tight shirt that accentuated every muscle of his torso. He walked up and embraced me.

"Fancy meeting you here," he said.

"Small world isn't it? I didn't realise you knew Steve," I said.

"He's a friend of a friend. What about you, how do you know him?" asked Kunle.

"I was invited by Steve's boyfriend," I replied.

"I thought Steve was single," he said.

"He is. Long story; sad too. Maybe I'll tell you about it some day," I said.

"Do I know your friend?" he asked.

I looked around for John but couldn't see him. "I'll introduce you to him later," I said.

"Is Ade still in Nigeria?" Kunle asked. "It must be difficult, being apart over the holidays."

I looked to see if he was making fun of me before responding. "Are we going to stand here all night talking about other people or are you going to get me a drink?"

"By the way you look hot," Kunle said.

"Thanks baby, you look pretty fine yourself. I bet you'll drive these men crazy tonight. Oh what am I saying, these fools are already crazy."

As Kunle walked towards the kitchen I looked at his backside and realised that the boy had it going on. He was working those trousers harder than a part time job. I was still sexually attracted to him, even after all that we'd been through. I had to remind myself that I already had a man, even if he was halfway across the world and not in my good books right then.

No sooner had Kunle returned' than one of our favourite songs began playing. I smiled as I remembered the times we danced to this song, holding on to each other as if adrift at sea. Kunle smiled as well; with outstretched hands, he beckoned me to accompany him on a journey down memory lane. I took his hand and we made our way to the centre of the crowded room. It reminded me of a time when we were both young, naïve, and full of hope for the future.

While dancing with Kunle, I saw John, on the other side of the room with a handsome, young man. Kunle held me so close to him that I could feel the pounding beat of his heart. I could also feel a very obvious bulge between his legs; it embarrassed me initially but I soon began feeling sexually aroused in return.

To my surprise, Kunle pulled me even closer when he realised what was happening. He felt safe and I needed to be held, so I gave in to my feelings, enjoying the company of an attractive man. Kunle's physical reaction to me and my own reaction to him confirmed that there was still some sexual chemistry present between us.

Later, I had an opportunity to introduce Kunle to John. I was surprised by Kunle's reaction, a mixture of indifference and disapproval. This was not like him at all. He was usually warm and pleasant, so I knew something was up. John seemed oblivious to Kunle's reaction and kept looking over his shoulder, at the man I'd seen him talking with earlier. I made a mental note, to find out from Kunle what was going on later when we were alone.

John and I started chatting as Kunle disappeared into the crowd. John proudly announced that Winston, the man he'd been talking to earlier, was a doctor. It seemed they had hit it off and, even though I felt this man was out of John's league, I was pleased for him; especially since he would be dating outside of his comfort zone.

John asked if I could get a lift home from Kunle, because he was planning to take Winston back to his flat. 'A typical gay man's reaction to new dick' I thought. I should have anticipated that John would drop me, like a bad habit, at the sniff of a man. Luckily, Kunle had driven to the party; otherwise I would have been left stranded.

When Kunle returned I quizzed him about John.

"Chris, I've seen that guy before. The last time I saw them together was about three weeks ago."

"What do you mean by '*them*'?" I asked

"He was with Ade at the time."

I felt Kunle was mistaken because, surely, John would've told me he knew Ade when I spoke with him about my new man.

"You must be mistaken," I said.

"Chris, I'm certain it's him. I didn't think much of it at the time, but now I'm sure."

When he noticed the shocked look on my face, he added, "Maybe I'm mistaken, but the person I saw with Ade looked a lot like your friend."

I wanted to ask Kunle a thousand questions which were racing through my head but I didn't because I wasn't prepared for any answers he might have given me. Ade had been spending all of his spare time with me and, surely, John was not that evil to be seeing my boyfriend behind my back. Anyway, who was I kidding? John was capable of anything. My disbelief quickly faded when Kunle gave me accurate details having seen them in the city, near to John's work place.

My shock turned to anger. My heart raced as adrenaline was pumped throughout my body. I tried to keep my cool, not to let Kunle see the effect of the news on me. I told him about the negative comments John had made when he learned that Ade and I were dating.

At the time I didn't think much of it, knowing that single gay men seldom supported each other at the beginning of relationships. Every time I looked across the room at John he would smile back at me. It was hard to resist the temptation to run over and bitch-slap him, wiping that stupid smile off his smug face.

I decided that two could play his little game. I noticed Steve heading my way and approached him, in full view of John, as the DJ started playing a raga track. I asked Steve for a dance, refusing to accept 'No' for an answer. I told him that the host had a responsibility to keep his guests happy. He took little encouragement to start gyrating to the cool, tropical, rhythms.

The rest of the room was oblivious to my little ploy, but I knew that it had been a success when John began paying close attention to what was going on. I could feel the daggers from his stares.

It never failed to amaze me how paranoid gay men became when they felt someone was after their man. John knew that I was not at all interested in Steve romantically, but he couldn't be absolutely sure, and although he had Winston on his arms for the night, he could not stand the thought that I might be going after Steve. I soon got tired of our little game and went in search of Kunle.

As I passed where John was standing, he appeared to be in deep conversation with Winston, his Ghanaian gynaecologist. I didn't know Winston, but Kunle soon supplied the missing pieces of the puzzle.

Winston was notorious on the gay scene for two things-having sex outside of his relationship and having a big dick. Yes, Winston had a boyfriend who often travelled to Ireland to visit family during holidays, leaving Winston behind and free to get up to all sorts.

Winston believed that when the cat was away the mice had a duty to play. He claimed to be committed to his partner, but never let his prospective dates in on that little fact until after he'd taken them to bed. I also learned that Winston was reputed to be very well endowed; and that he used his, not so hidden talent, expertly. I guess Santa had answered one little boy's wishes, albeit a little late.

Patrick slowed the rhythm right down as midnight approached. He announced that we had five minutes left, to grab the person next to us and prepare to bring in the New Year. I was reminded of the words to a Luther Vandross song which suggest; if you couldn't be with the one you loved then you should love the one you're with.

Patrick chose an old Roberta Flack number to welcome in the New Year. As she sang, "the first time ever I saw your face", we were seconds away from midnight. I surveyed the room, looking for Kunle. Everyone seemed to be paired up, even Patrick and his boyfriend held on to each other tightly.

I didn't want to be alone. Nor did I want to be bringing in the New Year with a prefect stranger. I started to walk to a corner of the room as the melodic notes of Roberta's song drifted through the air, like sweet perfume. At least, in a darkened corner, I wouldn't have to face the humiliation of standing alone.

I felt a gentle touch on my elbow and was almost too afraid to turn around. I gathered my courage and turned, to find Kunle standing silently before me, his eyes seemed to look right through me. He held me close and we started moving in time to the music. I rested my head on his shoulder and closed my eyes. I felt relieved-grateful that, once again, Kunle had rescued me.

My year was about to end in a whirlwind of confusion. I missed Ade, despite the anger I felt about him not calling me over the Christmas holidays. I was also angry that he hadn't told me about John. Still, I was dancing with a friend who cared about me and I didn't want the song to end. As the clock struck midnight, several couples were locked in romantic embraces. There was a brief hesitation before Kunle kissed me, softly at first, then more intensely. I struggled with my emotions.

At about one-thirty, John approached me to say goodbye. I saw Winston, standing a short distance away. John asked if I had arranged a lift with Kunle. I felt like saying, "Bitch! Like you give a shit." Instead I told him that I hadn't, but that I'd probably get home, somehow.

"Is your friend going home with you?" he asked.

"That's none of your business," I said dryly.

"I'm only concerned about you getting home safely Chris."

"If you were that concerned, *you'd* be the one taking me home. I don't want to cramp your style so I'll get home how I get home. I just hope you can walk tomorrow."

"What do you mean by that?" he asked suspiciously.

"Give me a call tomorrow and I'll explain it," I said, before turning and walking away.

Kunle and I left the party a short time later. I said goodbye to Steve, and promised to stay in touch. Neither of us meant it; but it felt like the polite thing to say at the time. I held on to Kunle's hand as we left, giving the onlookers material to gossip about the next day. The cool night air woke me up as we walked briskly to Kunle's car. As I sat in the Audi, I realised how tired I was. The party had taken more out of me than I'd expected.

Kunle asked if I wanted to go back to his flat for a drink, after which, he would take me home. He wanted us to spend some quality time together, in quiet reflection. I suggested that we went to my flat instead for that drink, saving him an additional journey. I also suggested that he could sleep over if he was too tired or too drunk to drive home.

When we arrived at my flat Kunle took a seat while I fixed us a couple of Bailey's Irish creams. We talked about our New Year resolutions. He reminded me that he didn't believe in making significant changes only at the beginning of the year. He made them whenever he felt they needed to be made.

We also talked about our failed relationships and where we felt they'd gone wrong.

"Are you happy Chris?"

"What do you mean, happy with a particular aspect of my life, or happy in general?"

"I mean with your love life," he said.

"Until tonight I thought I was, now I'm not so sure," I said.

"Is it because of what I told you earlier, about John and Ade?" Kunle asked.

"Maybe," I said. "But I guess it's a combination of lots of things."

"It could just be a coincidence Chris. A lot of people at the party tonight might have seen *us* together and jumped to the wrong conclusion. Maybe I'm mistaken about Ade and John. It's an easy mistake to make," he pleaded.

"I sometimes wonder whether I'd ever be truly happy again, or maybe my expectations are unrealistic. Do you ever feel like that?" I asked.

"I try to separate fantasy from reality, but sometimes we can't help who we fall in love with. We can't fake it when it's the real thing," he said.

"Have you ever been in love Kunle? I mean truly, deeply, madly in love."

"Yes. Once before," he answered.

"How did you know it was the real thing?" I asked.

"Because it still hurts sometimes," he said. "What about you?"

"You already know all there is to know about me. Don't you know that I tell you everything," I said jokingly. "I think you deserve to be happy again. Wouldn't you like to have someone in your life, to love again?"

"I have and I do, he just doesn't know it yet."

"I'm happy for you Kunle and I hope this guy realises just how lucky he is to have you. Maybe you'll introduce him to me one day, when you're ready, that is," I said.

"Maybe," he said nursing his drink.

Kunle was silent before finally asking me, "were you in love with me when we dated?"

I looked at him before answering; "I'm surprised you have to ask that Kunle. Of course I was in love with you, couldn't you tell? Letting you go was one of the hardest things I've had to do, ever."

"Have you ever thought about where we might be today if we were still lovers?" Kunle asked.

"We'd be in love, I guess; but you and I are in a special place now. We choose to be friends and the love we share for each other is different, but just as important to me. When we were in a relationship we loved each other on a romantic level. Now we love each other on a much deeper, emotional, level; and it's a love that has grown. Our relationship has evolved into something more tangible and is built on trust, love, honesty, tolerance and understanding; qualities that are lacking in many romantic relationships."

As we sat talking, I could feel Kunle moving closer, I felt like a deer caught in headlights. I needed to be held; and Ade was far away. Kunle smelled so good that I had to close my eyes and swallow hard. His lips eventually found my own, and I kissed him back, before abruptly coming to my senses. We were friends; and our friendship was far too important to be ruined by one night of passion.

"Don't you love me Chris, because I still love you," he said.

"I love you Kunle, with all my heart, but as a friend. We can't do this. I'm dating Ade now and *you* have someone special in *your* life. If our circumstances were different, then maybe we could try, but they're not."

"But things *are* different! We still have feelings for each other. Why can't you give us a chance?" he asked.

"What about the special person in your life Kunle?"

"The only person I have ever loved is *you* Chris."

I was speechless as Kunle's words sank in. I knew that there were still residual feelings from our relationship, but I hadn't realised that Kunle was still in love with me. I got up from the sofa to make myself a coffee. It was a lot to handle on the first day of the year; Ade and John were probably having an affair and Kunle was here vowing his undying love for me. I hoped the coffee would help to clear my thoughts so I could make sense of what was happening.

When I returned, Kunle was sitting silently, afraid to look at me. He finally spoke, saying; "Chris, you could do so much better than Ade. He doesn't deserve you."

"That's not the point Kunle," I said.

"What *is* the point then?" he asked obviously upset.

"He may not deserve me, but he's the one I've chosen to be with; the man that I am in love with," I said.

"So where does that leave me?" he asked.

"Kunle, listen. Baby, this is not a competition. No one is going to replace you in my life-ever. You mean a great deal to me, I want you to know that; but, I'm in a relationship with Ade. He and I have a lot of issues to sort out, but he's the one I'm with now, so you and I can't go there. I know that we're still attracted to each other sexually, but you know what, it's OK to have those feelings. We just can't act on them. Are you willing to accept that, because it's all I can offer you right now," I said.

"I'm sorry if I offended you Chris," he said, before dropping his head and sobbing.

"Baby boy, you're my best friend and *nothing* can change that. I wish I could give you what you want, but I can't. All I can be right now is your friend," I said.

Kunle asked if he could spend the night at my flat. We'd both been on an emotional roller coaster ride. Kunle needed a friend and I wasn't about to let him down. Whenever he'd stayed over he usually used the sofa bed but, on this occasion, I held his hand and guided him to my bedroom. We were both drained, emotionally and physically, so the chances of us yielding to temptation were pretty slim. We both needed to be held and to know that we would make it through the storm, somehow.

I turned the lights off before climbing into bed beside Kunle. He wrapped his arms around me and I felt comforted. At that moment I realised just how much I loved Ade. Here I was lying in the arms of a man who, despite all our history, still loved me tremendously. Whose concern for my happiness was unparalleled; and I was giving all that up for a man I obviously didn't know. Just before I drifted off to sleep, Kunle told me that all he wanted was for me to be happy. I told him that I loved him with all my heart and wanted the same for him.

7. Happy New Year!

Kunle and I sat down to a full English breakfast. Talking to him was very easy, a lot easier than talking to Ade. It seemed that we could talk about anything. He was always attentive and ready to offer support and advice when I needed it. We both agreed to leave the events of the previous night in the past and get on with the job of being friends. Kunle had to get home so I walked him to his car and promised to call him later.

After Kunle had left, I listened to the messages from the previous night. The first message was from my mother, who had called to wish me a happy New Year.

The second message was from friends in Hertfordshire. They'd called after their return from midnight mass. I had neither spoken to nor seen them in a long time, so I made a note to return their call soon to arrange a meeting.

The next message was from my friend Dele. The last time I'd heard from him was during the summer. He was in London and wanted to meet up. Although he was based in London, he frequently travelled to Nigeria for business purposes. Dele was a live wire; a true diva. His flamboyance was sometimes hard to take but I knew he meant well.

The fourth message was from my baby. This was the first I'd heard from him since he arrived in Lagos. So he finally remembered he had a boyfriend in London.

He sounded subdued. The telephone connection must have been faulty because I had difficulty understanding exactly what he was saying. From what I could gather, he said he missed me and was looking forward to seeing me soon. My anger toward him was immediately replaced by the excitement of knowing that we would soon be reunited. He was due back in four days, I could hardly wait.

The final message was from Kunle. He must have called soon after leaving my flat. He thanked me for the gift of friendship. He also reminded me that if things didn't work out between Ade and I that he would wait for me, however long it took. This made me feel a little sad. Although I was happy that we were still friends, I was concerned; if he continued to have strong romantic feelings for me, he wouldn't be open to finding a man of his own.

I wondered why I hadn't heard from John-surely his man would have left by that time. The men he dated usually didn't stay long after sex but maybe this time was different. Maybe Winston was different, the thought made me laugh aloud. I knew he'd eventually call and, when he did, I would be ready for him.

* * *

I called Dele a couple of days after receiving his message. He picked up the telephone immediately, as if he'd been expecting a call. He laughed hysterically recognising my voice.

"Bitch you don't know how happy I am to hear your voice. Which hole have you crawled out of?" he asked.

"Miss Thing, I'm not anybody's bitch; and I should be asking you the same question. What, or should I say who, the hell have you been up to?"

"I'm expecting a call from trade so I may have to cut our conversation short," Dele said.

"Bitch, tell me you're not blowing me off for a man," I said, jokingly.

"Baby you know that I love you; but I need me some dick and this man promises to fix me good tonight."

"Just be careful," I said.

"Thanks baby."

Dele gave me a quick update on his love life before asking me about my own.

"So who has been warming your bed lately?" He asked.

"I am officially off the market," I said. "I've found me a good black man and, you'd better believe he's the genuine article."

"What's wrong with this one? Is he missing a leg, or an arm?" Dele said in jest.

"You're just a jealous Ho. He's a decent man I met at work."

"See what I told you, the bitch is crazy. Is he one of your psychiatric patients?" Dele asked.

"Tell me you didn't just go there," I said.

"You know I'm only playing with you, I'm very happy for you baby. Life is short and you have to take happiness anywhere you can get it."

As Dele was about to tell me what he'd been up to, our call was interrupted by the 'call-waiting' signal. Someone else was trying to get through to him so he excused himself briefly, to check who was calling.

"Was that your new man?" I asked when he returned, a few seconds later.

"It was one of my old shags," he said.

"Aren't you going to take him up on his offer? I don't want to spoil your market," I said.

"I already have new dick lined up for tonight so I'll give him a call when I'm desperate. Right now I want to spend some time talking with my friend," he said.

"You were about to tell me what you've been up to," I said.

"Yes I was. Well, you know that I've been travelling a lot, between London and Lagos lately." He said.

"Yes," I replied.

"I've been involved in some business that has really taken off," he said.

"Are you sure there isn't a man involved?" I asked.

"Well there are a few men, but no one special. Just keeping my options open," he replied.

"When did you get back from Nigeria?" I asked.

"Two weeks ago," he replied.

"And, bitch, you only found the time to call me now?"

"Baby I've been busy," he said.

"OK, what's his name?" I asked.

"You know me; places to go, people to screw."

"So how long are you going to be in London for this time?" I asked.

"Six months. I may look sixteen, but this Diva is certainly not as young and energetic as he used to be. I need to rest my tired old ass-and I don't want any remarks about my ass, OK. Just as well really because there was some crazy shit happening in Lagos. If I get into it with you now BT will arrest me for indecency."

Just then the 'call-waiting' signal interrupted our conversation for the second time. Dele said goodbye, hoping it would be his 'bit of trade' calling. He promised to call me back another time, to continue our conversation.

A few minutes later the telephone rang, it was Dele, but now he sounded pissed off.

"Bitch, these idiots wouldn't give me a chance. It's another fool crawling out of the woodwork. You probably thought I wasn't going to call you back," he said.

"You know me too well Dele. So, who is this mystery man that's put a spring in your step? Does he know that we are friends, because I don't want to be stabbed in the back with a rusty ice pick, by one of your crazy-ass men-I am too young, and too fabulous, to get my ass killed over a man," I said.

Dele laughed. "Baby you still crazy, yes. This is not exactly a new man. I'm sure I told you about Peter who was living in Cape Town. He's just returned to London and is a bit sex-starved."

"Well, I don't want to be the one that's keeping the lamb from its slaughter," I said.

"Honey, if you can't beat them, then you have to join them. This isn't the ideal situation for me but good sex is better than no sex at all, and the last time he gave me a working over I could hardly walk for days."

"I don't want to spoil your fun, so you have a good time-and we'll meet up when you can walk again," I said.

Before saying good bye, Dele told me about his New Year's resolution, which involved providing an informal forum for gay men, especially black gay men, to discuss important social issues. He promised it would not be a scheme to meet men for sex, but added that if relationships developed between men in the group, then that was their own business. I thought it was a good idea and told him I was interested. He said he'd keep me informed of developments.

It was only after my conversation with Dele ended that I remembered him telling me about Peter in the past. They'd met in London about three years ago and had a brief affair before Peter left for a work assignment. At that time he worked as a freelance reporter for the BBC world service and his job took him to lots of exciting places, around the world.

Peter's mother was Nigerian and his father was French. He'd spent a significant part of his early childhood in France, a fact which accounted for his sexy French accent. According to Dele, he also had a PhD in sex. The man's appetite for sex was reputed to be insatiable.

Peter was softly spoken and gentle in manner. His dick wasn't the biggest Dele had ever seen-and Dele had seen quite a few dicks in his time. Allegedly, they had marathon sex; the kind that lasted for hours, leaving them both exhausted. There was no romance, nor any expression of emotional feelings. It was, purely and simply, sex. I remembered asking at the time whether Peter was addicted to sex. Dele said he'd bet good money on it.

Dele told me about one occasion, when Peter visited London after spending a few months on assignment in Northern Africa. They'd had a particularly adventurous time. He'd picked Peter up from the airport and taken him back to his flat. Peter was so horny, that neither of them got any sleep that night. Dele was exhausted the next morning and getting to church proved a painful experience. He felt it was a small price to pay for the previous night's pleasures. Peter was asleep in bed when he left.

Dele had seen Jeremy for the first time in church that morning and had known, almost immediately, that he was a friend of Dorothy. It was a clear case of 'sheep recognising sheep'. When Jeremy asked if he could come back to Dele's flat after church, he knew the deal had been sealed. Dele didn't factor into the equation the matter of a naked man asleep in his flat. He'd also forgotten the pain of the previous night's escapades.

When Dele returned with Jeremy, they met Peter, sitting stark naked on the sofa. Dele walked in first and casually introduced the two men; as if expecting to find Peter naked. Jeremy didn't miss a beat and showed no sign of discomfort. Modesty got the better of Peter and he eventually went to the bathroom to get a towel, which he wrapped around himself.

Jeremy was curious about the arrangements and, while Peter was out of the room, asked Dele if they were lovers. Dele felt the question was rhetorical but answered anyway, saying they were friends who had sex occasionally. Dele said he could have sworn he'd seen a twinkle appear in Jeremy's eyes just then. Before long, all three men were naked and engaged in sex. Later that night Dele went to bed, leaving Peter and Jeremy to continue having sex. Dele knew when to leave the buffet.

* * *

Ade called me on the day he returned to London. He wanted to come over, but he was clearly tired from his trip. I felt, that as we'd already waited two weeks, another night would not be impossible to endure. Hearing his voice made my heart leap around inside my chest. So much had happened in the weeks that he'd been away that it seemed as if a lifetime had gone by. After saying goodnight to Ade, I had a shower and went to bed. Surprisingly sleep came easily.

At work the next day I quickly fell into the normal routine. It helped to distract me as I waited for my lover's return. I started work one hour before Ade. As I stood in the adjacent room, my heart skipped several beats when the staff and patients welcomed him. It felt like it'd been a year since we'd seen each other. I resisted the temptation to rush out of the room and into to his arms.

A few minutes later I heard a gentle knock on the door to the linen room, followed quickly by Ade's voice calling my name. I hesitated briefly before opening the door to let him in. He slipped inside, closing the door behind him. We began kissing each other hungrily. I tried to speak but our lips were locked together. How I'd missed my man. I'd missed his smell, his touch, his lips; I'd missed everything about him.

"I missed you baby. Did you miss me?" he asked between kisses.

"What do you think? Of course I missed you. Maybe you'd like me to show you just how much I missed you." I teased.

"You won't have to wait long," he said, "I'll be straight over to yours after work."

He seemed a shade darker in complexion and his shiny black skin had never looked healthier. I also noticed his hair was cut much shorter than usual and instantly I got an erection. He noticed the bulge between my legs and whispered in my ear, "not long to go baby". We adjusted ourselves before leaving the room. Although we'd only been alone for a few short minutes, it seemed much longer. I was grateful that the rest of the ward seemed oblivious to our absence.

The remainder of the morning went smoothly and just before I left work Ade handed me a note, it read; '8:00pm at your flat'. He had certainly got my attention; and I knew the evening would be magical.

I drove home as fast as I could to prepare for our reunion later. I planned to make his favourite meal but would make sure I was going to be the tastiest dish on the menu. I'd been sex-starved for the past two weeks and I fought to contain my excitement. I hoped he wasn't too jet lagged.

I was startled by a sharp knock on the door. He was early. Wearing a pair of red silk boxer shorts and matching robe I opened the door to let him in. Ade's face broke into a broad smile of appreciation. Once inside, his hand appeared from behind his back to produce a dozen red roses, which he gave to me before kissing me lightly on my lips.

He moved across the room like a panther stalking its prey. I felt like a West End star under the glare of the spotlight. I loved the attention.

"Would you like a drink before dinner?" I asked

"I've already eaten," he said.

"I thought we were supposed to have a meal together tonight," I said.

"If you're hungry we can still have something later."

"I guess I can wait," I said.

"It'll be worth your while," he said seductively.

"What about that drink then?" I asked.

"A glass of white wine please."

"Coming right up," I said.

When I returned with the wine, Ade took the glass from me and placed it on the table next to the sofa. I noticed the intensity in his eyes. Without saying a word he kissed my forehead. I felt goose pimples all along the length of my spine. He took a step back and looked at me, shaking his head in appreciation. It was his turn to act as though he was seeing me for the very first time. He opened my robe, inhaling sharply, before pushing the flimsy garment over my shoulders; it fell silently to the floor. I was transfixed.

I stood before Ade in my shorts; feeling emotionally exposed, vulnerable yet sexy. He moved closer and kissed my neck. Ade was still fully clothed as he began to explore my body. His hands found their way over my shoulders, chest, neck, then to my nipples; finally he embraced me tightly. He was very attentive and I responded to his touch. His hands did magical things to me; and I was being played like a musical instrument in the hands of a maestro.

We eventually made our way, to the bedroom and on to the sheets that I'd sprinkled lightly with talcum powder. Ade took his time undressing, stopping briefly to look at me after removing each item of clothing. He was driving me crazy with his teasing. When he finally got down to his underwear, the flimsy, white, material had a difficult time containing his erection.

The light from the bedside lamp seemed to make Ade's skin come alive. The look of hunger and anticipation in his eyes screamed he wanted me just as badly as I wanted him. His fingers found the waist of my boxers and in one fluid movement they were off.

Fantasy became reality as our hands began to explore each other's body. We were hungry for one another and made love like it was going to be the last time. I'd had great sex before, but this time was different. We feel asleep exhausted, in each other's arms.

The next day at work, we both looked like something the cat had dragged in. We'd only managed to sleep for a couple of hours and for the first time I understood what it meant to feel like five pounds of shit, squeezed into a two-pound bag. Ade and I arrived at work together for once, but we were too tired to care about what our colleagues thought.

Ade wasn't too tired to flirt with me throughout the day. I didn't have a clue where he got his energy from. I on the other hand, could hardly wait for the end of my shift when I could go home and collapse into bed, cuddled up next to my man.

8. The other side of the coin

Ade and I were at a good place in our relationship. I felt things were going well, that was at least, until he asked me about how I had spent Christmas. It seemed a strange question since it was almost the end of January. I was a little suspicious but decided not to let my imagination run riot. I told him that I'd worked through most of the holidays.

He seemed unusually inquisitive and eventually, got round to asking me how I had spent the New Year. I suddenly realised where his line of questioning was leading. I told him that I'd had an enjoyable New Year, but deliberately avoided any mention of Steve's party. I knew he was skirting around the real issue but I wasn't going to make it easy for him.

"Did you go out on New Year's eve?" he asked.

"Yes, I did. I went to a house party with a friend."

"Anyone I know?" he asked, casually.

I felt like screaming; 'I went with the same friend you've been screwing behind my back'. "I went with John. You might know him. He lives in Lewisham," I said.

"Yeah, I think I know who you're talking about," he said.

"You think you know?" I asked, with mock surprise in my voice.

"Yes I remember him now. He's a short, stocky, white guy."

"That's the one," I said, sarcastically.

It became increasingly difficult to control my anger.

"Did you have a good time at the party?" he asked.

"Yes, I had a wonderful time," I replied.

"Did you see anyone you knew?" he continued.

"There were a few familiar faces . . . no one important."

"Umm," he mused.

This was the straw that broke the camel's back. I needed to cut to the chase so I stopped the washing up and turned to face him. I was curious to know what he was really after.

The penny finally dropped when he asked; "So did you leave the party with anyone?"

"You need to ask the same person who told you I was at the party." I said.

"Are you saying that you left the party alone?" he asked.

"What I'm saying is that your questions are rhetorical; you're not asking the right ones!"

"What do you mean by that?" he asked.

"I mean that you know I didn't leave the party alone, so why ask me questions you already know the answers to? What you should be asking, is why the hell you couldn't call me on Christmas day, instead of listening to gossip."

"So who was the guy you left the party with?" he asked, ignoring my last statement.

"That's more like it. Now we're getting to the heart of the matter. I left the party with a friend," I said angrily.

"Is he someone I know?" He continued.

"Yes, you know him. As a matter of fact you know him quite well." I said, the anger rising in my voice. "I left the party with Kunle. He was married to Aduni, your cousin. Yes, the same one you tried to date after he and his wife separated. Satisfied now?"

"I didn't know you two were friends," Ade said.

"Small world isn't it?" I said-my voice heavy with sarcasm.

"I didn't mean to . . ."

"Of course you did," I interrupted, "you heard one side of the story, added two and two together and got twenty two!"

"Chris, don't be naive. It's only natural for men to be tempted."

"I'm not an amoeba Ade, I have a brain. However great the temptation, I do have the ability to resist another man. *I* can say no."

"You're an attractive man and I wouldn't blame a guy for trying to . . ."

"Is that something you would do Ade?"

"I deserve that. Look baby, I am sorry. I don't think that anything happened. I just had to find out for myself. Please forgive me? How long have you and Kunle been friends?" he asked.

"A long time," I answered.

"Were you lovers in the past?" he asked.

"Why is that relevant now?" I asked.

"You're avoiding answering the question," he said.

"My past is right where it belongs; in the past! I'm with *you* now. What's the big deal about who I've been with before?"

"So you two were lovers after all." he said.

"Yes, we dated in the past but now we're just good friends," I answered.

"Was it serious?" he asked.

I felt like saying, 'as serious as a heart attack mate', but I remained silent.

"Does he know that you're seeing someone now?" asked Ade.

Again I didn't answer. Ade's questions were winding me up big time and I was trying hard not to let him see the effect he was having on me.

"Did he spend the night Chris?" he asked.

"What if he did? Friends can spend time together can't they?"

"So you're saying that he didn't try anything. Baby, you don't know how these Nigerian men think; if I was in his . . ." he stopped when he realised what he was about to say.

"Go on, if you were in Kunle's shoes you would do what?" I asked angrily, already knowing the answer to the question.

"Baby it's just . . . Well, from what my friends were saying, it seems that he still has feelings for you. I find it hard to believe he didn't try to get you into bed."

"So what does that make me . . . a slut?" I asked indignantly.

"I Just . . ."

"You're just what? Say it! Do you believe that because you can't be trusted to keep your dick in your pants that I can't? Don't make me laugh! Stop deluding yourself baby, some of us have morals. Besides, was your arm broken so you couldn't pick up the phone to call me on Christmas day?"

"Why you keep bringing that up? I told you it was difficult to get away from my relatives. There were a lot of things happening," he said.

"Whatever." I said as I walked out of the kitchen.

"Where the fuck you going?" he asked. "I told you about walking away when we're trying to have a discussion."

I walked back into the kitchen and, in a slightly tremulous voice, asked; "Excuse me, what did you just say?"

"I'm not putting up with this shit anymore Chris."

"*You're* not putting up with *this shit*" I said. "That's rich coming from you. I'm not the one sleeping around am I? If you can't stand the heat, then get the fuck out of the kitchen. I was fine before I met your crazy ass and I'll be fine without you, bitch."

I stood motionless as Ade picked up a vase and hurled it at me. It missed narrowly, smashing against the wall behind me. I'd never seen this side of him before. Almost immediately he began apologising, but it was too late. He'd turned into someone I no longer recognised. I told him he had two minutes in which to leave the flat, or I would get the police to escort him out of my home. He swore under his breath as he slammed the door shut behind him.

After he left I poured myself a drink to calm my nerves. I was convinced that Ade had deliberately picked that fight with me. A lot of people had been at the party, any of them could have told him about me leaving with Kunle. What I couldn't figure out, was what any of them had to gain from telling him; and then there was his reaction to the news. Didn't he trust me?

I hadn't heard from John since the party so I assumed he was still busy playing 'doctor' with Winston. I suspected John was the culprit behind Ade's sudden concerns about my fidelity. I felt like driving over to John's house and cussing him out but I had standards, doing that would bring me down to his level. No, revenge was a dish best served up cold.

John didn't know who he was messing with. That fool had picked on the wrong man. Ade also needed to take responsibility for his own behaviour. His lack of trust convinced me that there was more to this story. I'd been so happy to see him when he returned that I was able to put aside my disappointment about not hearing from him over the holidays. I was even willing to disregard my initial impression that he was sleeping with John. True love meant, trusting your lover and believing he'd do right by you.

My hands were trembling as I dialled Kunle's number. It was past midnight, but I hoped he was still awake. The phone rang for ages, but just as I was preparing to leave a message I heard him say; "hello." A wave of relief swept over me. This was soon replaced by guilt for having disturbed him so late.

"Hi Kunle, did I wake you?"

"I was just drifting off to sleep but I'm awake now. What's up?" he asked.

"I just had a fight with Ade," I managed to say, before breaking down and sobbing. I told him everything.

"Are you all right?" Kunle asked with obvious concern in his voice.

"I'm OK, just a little shaken, that's all," I said.

"Do you want me to come over?" Kunle asked.

"I'll be fine. I just needed someone to talk to," I said.

"I'm glad you called me. Chris you know how I feel about your relationship with Ade. I'm not going to say, 'I told you so,' but you both need to be able to trust each other. Without trust, you'll have nothing."

I knew exactly what Kunle was saying. I had dished out the same advice in the past.

When I met Ade I was at the point of giving up on finding a good man. Finding him was like getting an unexpected treat. I sometimes wondered whether it was too good to be true; but I believed in love. I deserved to be loved and I felt compelled to take a chance on Ade. I knew Kunle didn't approve of our relationship. However, I hoped that in time he'd grow to see Ade was a changed man and, more importantly, that he was the right man for me.

I needed some time on my own to think things through. I thanked Kunle for listening, promising to call him if I changed my mind about his offer. I was surprised by just how supportive Kunle had been. I' expected him to advise me to run as far away from Ade as I could but, instead, he suggested that I follow my heart.

I hadn't returned any of Ade's calls since our fight because I wanted to address the problem when I was ready to do so and not before. He'd be leaving for a new job in a couple of weeks, so there was a light at the end of the tunnel. I planned to take some of my annual leave so I wouldn't have to see much of him.

Before I went on leave I was tempted to take Ade aside, to ask him what the fuck was he thinking. I had my principles though and I knew that if I didn't stand up for something, then I'd fall for anything. As difficult as it was, not having Ade in my life, I needed the time apart to make sense of my situation. However much I loved him, our relationship had become toxic and we couldn't continue as we were. Something had to change.

9. The funeral

Finally curiosity got the better of me and I contacted Kunle to find out what was up between Ade and John. He said they'd dated briefly but were no longer romantically involved. I was still puzzled about why Ade had gone to such great lengths to conceal his friendship with John, especially since it was only supposed to be platonic. I didn't trust John as far as I could throw him because I knew that given the chance, he'd sleep with my man in a heartbeat.

I wasn't in a relationship with John, so he had no responsibility to me. Ade was my man, or so I thought; and I trusted him not to deliberately hurt me. It always took two to tango, and whatever was going on, nothing could happen unless they both allowed it to happen. I got worried when Kunle advised me to have a seat for what he was about to tell me. He hadn't planned on telling me over the phone but he felt I needed to know as soon as possible.

After the room stopped spinning I heard Kunle's voice in the distance, asking if I was OK. I asked him to repeat what he had told me so I'd know that it hadn't been some cruel joke. He said he'd found out that Ade was in a long-term relationship with a man named Michael and that they'd been living together for the last two years. His statement didn't have the same impact the second time around but I was still shocked.

Kunle told me that Michael was a young man from Nigeria, who was training to be a nurse in London. Words floated around in my head but I was afraid to speak for fear of sounding like I'd lost my mind.

It all began to fall into place. I had dropped Ade off at his home several times; but had never been invited in. On a few occasions I had suggested spending the night at his flat, but he always made an excuse and I eventually gave up, thinking that maybe he just liked spending time at my place. Now I knew the reason for his avoidance and it was the last thing I'd expected.

This news took the wind out of my sails and I began wondering how much of my relationship with Ade was true. I knew that gay men were, first and foremost, men; and that men lied, cheated and did just about anything they felt they might get away with. I thought, however, that some men were different-because *I* was different. I thought that what we had was special.

I had been so careful this time in trying to protect my heart yet it had still been broken-maybe this was my fate. I wanted so much to believe the best about Ade that I forgot to consider the worst in him. I was glad that I'd taken time off work because I couldn't bear the humiliation of facing him. I planned to lay low until he left the ward and I had figured out what my next move was going to be.

Ade left several messages when he found out I hadn't been to work. I screened my calls because I was certain he'd try to contact me. I was tempted to call him, to confront him about Michael, but I was done playing games. I was in self-preservation mode and grateful that I was out of that situation in one piece.

* * *

The day after I returned to work I had a distressing call from Kunle. A close friend of his had died. He was very upset so I went over to his flat. All I had to offer was a friendly shoulder to cry on.

James had been diagnosed with a brain tumour three years earlier, soon after migrating to London from Nigeria. His diagnosis was devastating to him and his family. It signalled the end of a promising career as a medical doctor. As a result of surgery and chemotherapy he went into remission and his career flourished for a while.

He and his boyfriend bought a property and moved in together. However, his illness returned and his health had deteriorated rapidly. Although his death was not very sudden, it was still shocking to his family and friends.

"How are you holding up Kunle?"

"I knew James was ill but I just wasn't prepared for this. It's hard to believe he's gone," he managed, before sobbing uncontrollably.

"No one can ever be ready for that kind of loss," I said. "I'm going to stay the night-you shouldn't be alone at a time like this."

"Thanks, but I'll be fine," he said.

"When did James die?" I asked.

"This morning," he said. "He'd been unconscious for a few days."

"When's the funeral?"

"It'll probably be next week-some of his relatives are coming over from Nigeria and the US. I'll get the details from his sister."

"Would you like me to accompany you to the funeral?" I asked.

"Would you Chris? I'd really appreciate that. Thanks man."

I held him as he cried in my arms. I rubbed the back of his neck in an attempt to soothe his pain.

The next day Kunle called with details of the funeral. He asked me if I could sing at the service. The family of the deceased had asked him if he wanted to say a few words. He didn't feel able to so, he suggested asking me to sing. I told him that I'd be honoured. I agreed to sing a hymn James liked, called, 'It is well with my soul'. I learned that the organist was able to accompany me, provided he knew in advance which key I planned to sing in.

I saw Kunle most evenings during the week leading up to the funeral. Ade continued to leave messages, each sounding more desperate than the last. I didn't return any of his calls because I needed to help Kunle through his difficult time before I could concentrate on my own dilemma. A part of me wanted to call Ade and put him out of his misery, but another part of me felt his sorry ass could wait until I was good and ready to deal with him.

* * *

It was one of those winter mornings when the sun shone brilliantly, despite the temperature struggling to rise above freezing. Kunle picked me up at London Bridge around ten thirty, together we headed toward Catford.

When we arrived at the church most of the congregation were already seated. It was a very solemn occasion-I recognised a few faces. The heaviness that permeated the air in the church was almost palpable; a mixture of sadness and resignation.

Kunle and I took our seats, midway up the aisle. I sat nearest the end for easy access when it came time for me to sing. I had intended to meet the organist before the start of the service but the traffic on the way delayed our arrival. Kunle assured me that the organist was very competent.

The congregation stood up as the mahogany coffin entered the church. It was so quiet that you could hear a pin drop. With my head bowed I said a silent prayer; for James' family and friends. I prayed his family would have the strength of the all-mighty, all-knowing, all-powerful God, to guide them through this traumatic experience.

As we took our seats again I squeezed Kunle's hand, as a gesture of support. When I looked over at him his eyes were closed but the tears flowed down his face, I wished I could have done more to ease his pain.

After the opening prayer and a short reading from the bible, I made my way to the front of the congregation. I looked to my right and saw that Simon, the organist, was awaiting my instructions. I nodded to him, signalling the introduction to the hymn. I lowered my eyes as a mark of respect, before belting out the first few lines of the hymn; "When peace like a river attended my way, when sorrows like sea billows roll. Whatever my lot, you have taught me to say, it is well, it is well, with my soul."

As I sang, I saw a few surprised looks in the congregation. I could tell that my vocal talent had impressed a few of the queens present. I didn't expect them to know that I'd spent three years with a voice coach and another two years honing my vocal skills with a gospel choir. However, this was neither the time nor the place to try to impress anyone, so I pushed the Diva in me to one side.

I wanted the congregation to feel what I felt, to know that hope existed through God and that even in their darkest hour; *He* would never leave their side. They didn't have to walk alone, ever. *He* would provide them with shelter from the rains as they passed through the storms of life.

I felt certain that a few of the young men present probably couldn't remember the last time they'd been inside a church. I saw that Kunle's head remained bowed; his pain was transferred to me and reflected in my voice as I sang.

Towards the end of the song I lowered the volume to a mere whisper, before going up an octave and driving the message home. For the last few lines I held the notes for what must have seemed an eternity. The Diva in me returned to enjoy the attention of the captive audience. Simon the organist sat with his back to the congregation and rose to the occasion. I was the only one able to see his smile but it was clear that Simon appreciated the talents of a Diva. I also suspected that Simon was a friend of Dorothy.

On the way back to my seat I noticed Ade sitting at the back of the church. My heart skipped several beats and I struggled to keep my composure. He sat with his eyes closed and head bowed. I quickly took my seat next to Kunle and tried to concentrate on the rest of the service. I didn't tell Kunle that I'd seen Ade.

The rest of the service went smoothly and, at the end, we were all given the opportunity to say goodbye to James. It was difficult listening to his mother as she sobbed loudly. I wasn't a parent and, therefore, couldn't entirely have known what she was experiencing, but parents weren't supposed to bury their children. That to me didn't seem to be the natural order or things. The family's hopes had been pinned on James since he'd been the eldest of her five children. Those hopes were now dashed.

Kunle sat with his hand in mine. He didn't get up to view the coffin. He said he wanted to remember James laughing and reminiscing about old times. Funerals are never happy events but they seem all the more difficult when someone so young dies. With older adults, it's somehow easier to believe that they've gone to a better place after a long and fulfilling life. However, with the young it seemed unfair-like the destruction of a flower in bloom.

Kunle went to say 'hello' to a few friends whilst I headed to the main door of the church. It was very cold outside, but I needed the fresh air. On the way out I went to shake Simon's hand and to thank him for his support. He winked at me; and my suspicions were confirmed.

I stood in the brilliant sunshine while I waited for Kunle. James' mother came up to me and we embraced. I had never met the woman before but this was an occasion that transcended formalities. I searched frantically for some words of comfort I could offer to ease her pain, but couldn't find any. She invited Kunle and I back to her home for refreshments after the burial at Hither Green cemetery.

I saw Ade, a short distance away, smoking a cigarette and staring at me. I decided to put my feelings about our situation aside and went over to offer him my condolences.

"I'm sorry about your loss," I said, "I didn't realise James was a friend."

"We were at medical school together," he said, before looking away. He tried to hide the tears but it was too late. I'd already seen the evidence of his pain. It was difficult seeing him so distressed. My instinct was to comfort him. I rubbed his shoulders until he regained his composure as we began walking away from the church.

Unexpectedly Ade stopped and hugged me, holding on to me like a child about to be taken away from its parent. I told him that everything would be all right, eventually.

"Why haven't you returned any of my calls Chris? I was worried about you."

In an instant, I went from wanting to comfort him to wanting to put a pillow over his face and hold it there.

"We'll talk about that another time Ade," I said.

"I didn't realise you could sing so well Chris. You sang beautifully." He said.

"Thank you. There's a lot you don't know about me Ade. I have to leave now. Once again I'm really sorry about your friend's death. Just remember that things will get easier. We'll talk soon. Bye." I walked away without looking back.

On the drive home Kunle told me he'd seen me walking with Ade. He sat silently, waiting for my response. I spared him the details, telling him I was simply being civil to Ade. The drama between Ade and I could wait for another day. Kunle was surprised that I could be civilised toward Ade after the way he'd treated me. I didn't tell him that seeing Ade crying had stirred feelings in me that I thought I'd laid to rest.

It wasn't until we'd arrived back at Kunle's flat that I realised that he'd taken James' death far worse than I'd initially thought. The kitchen was piled high with dirty dishes and items of clothing were strewn all over the flat. I couldn't change the circumstances that caused his pain but I could help, by providing a little tender loving care and some practical support. I felt it would be therapeutic for him to talk about his friendship with James, especially the good times.

I suggested he take a relaxing bath while I tidied the flat and did the washing up. I also made his favourite meal; corned beef stew with pasta. He pretended not to want me fussing over him, but seemed relieved. After dinner we talked a little more; I waited until he fell asleep before leaving.

When I arrived home there were three messages from Ade on my answer machine, which I ignored. As I got ready for bed the telephone rang, I impulsively picked up the receiver expecting to hear Kunle's voice.

"Hi Chris, I called earlier but you weren't in. I thought you'd have gone straight home after the funeral." Ade said.

"I'm home now Ade, what do you want?" I asked with resignation in my voice.

"I just wanted to hear your voice," he said.

I felt like saying, 'well now that you've heard it, goodbye', but I didn't. Instead I said, "It'd been a stressful day for everyone. Shouldn't you be having an early night?"

He sounded genuinely upset, but by this time I was getting fed up.

"I don't want to be alone Chris," he said.

"You don't have to be alone Ade, you have Michael to keep you company." After I'd said it I wondered whether it was an appropriate time to bring up the subject.

Ade was silent for a long time.

I finally asked, "Are you still there?"

The tone in his voice changed as he said, "I'll be over in twenty minutes," ending the call before I could respond.

I thought about not letting him into my flat but I realised I'd only be postponing the inevitable. It was time to stand up and face the music.

I let the doorbell ring a few times before I let him in. Ade walked straight past me, into the sitting room, where he took a seat. I went to the kitchen to make myself a drink.

When I returned Ade was leaning forward, holding his face in both hands. I didn't get him a drink because I didn't want him to get too comfortable. This was not going to be a social visit. I took a seat in the armchair opposite. He looked up and there were tears in his eyes. I tried to appear cold and uncaring but my resolve was quickly disintegrating.

"Do you believe I love you Chris?"

"Honestly, I don't know what to believe. All I know is that love isn't supposed to hurt like this. I feel betrayed and humiliated," I said.

In one fluid movement Ade was on his knees in front of me, resting his head in my lap and sobbing like a baby.

"I've really fucked up Chris," he said.

I had to agree with him. I struggled with the urge to hold him and tell him it was going to be OK. I didn't, because everything was not OK.

Ade spent the next two hours telling me all about his relationship with Michael. They'd dated for about eighteen months. At the end of their relationship Michael felt rejected, he didn't handle the break up very well. They had continued to live together so that Michael could complete his training to be a nurse and become more financially stable. Michael still had romantic feelings for him but Ade had held on to the belief that in time they could become friends.

I remained silent as Ade continued talking. He said he hadn't told me about Michael before because he was afraid of losing me. He had known that he would have to address the situation at some point but he'd kept on hoping that it would eventually just go away. He also told me about dating John a long time ago. He apologised, for his lack of trust in me and for his violent behaviour when he thought he'd lost me. He begged for my forgiveness.

He said that he thought he'd lost the best thing that had ever happened to him when he heard about me leaving the New Year's Eve party with another man. At the time he had difficulty thinking clearly because he was under a lot of stress. James was very ill and everything seemed to be going wrong.

His friend's death reminded him just how fragile life could be, 'here today, gone tomorrow.' He wanted another chance to prove to me that our relationship could work. He said he realised that things could never be the same but he believed in us and was prepared to wait, for however long it took, to win back my love.

"Why couldn't you have told me all of this earlier?" I asked.

"I wish I knew Chris. I wanted to but when I thought the right time had come, something would happen."

"Lovers are supposed to be able to be honest with each other," I said. "How can I ever trust you again?"

"Yes, I know; and all I can do is, beg for your forgiveness and promise to be more honest with you. If you don't want me being friends with . . ."

"This isn't about who you choose to be friends with, it's about us. You and me," I said interrupting him.

"I know it's a lot to ask for, but I need you," he said.

He was right. It was a lot to ask.

"I realise that I've fucked up big time. I never meant to hurt you. Please believe me. All I'm asking for is a second chance to show you that you're the one for me. The only one for me-we belong together," he said.

"I don't know Ade. I'm confused."

"That's OK baby. Take all the time you need; I'm patient," he said.

"I'll have to think about this," I said.

"That's all I need baby. Please; just think about it."

"If I decide to take you back there'll have to be some changes," I said.

"Whatever you want baby. I'm willing to do anything to get you back. Baby, one more thing please, I really don't want to be on my own tonight. Could I spend the night with you? I promise I won't try anything. I'll even sleep on the sofa if you want me to."

I felt emotionally exhausted. I had no energy left, with which to fight Ade so I granted his request to spend the night, once he understood that sex was out of the question. I gave him a blanket and some pillows so he'd be comfortable on the sofa. Spending the night in my flat was one thing, spending the night in my bed was an entirely different matter. To get back into my bed he'd have to earn my trust and that was not going to be as easy as it seemed.

As I lay in bed that night with Ade a short distance away, I contemplated what to do. Was I setting myself up to fail again? It was a well known fact that all it took, for evil to be perpetrated, was for good men to do nothing. Was I standing idly by to be abused repeatedly? Could I ever completely trust Ade again and were we even meant to be together?

These were all questions to which I had no answers. Maybe I attracted people who would treat me badly. I knew my standards were high but I didn't believe my expectations were unrealistic. Was I being foolish by expecting a leopard to change its spots?

Maybe I was listening to what Ade was telling me and not paying much attention to the evidence. What if he were incapable of change in the same way that an animal could not change which species it belonged to. Was it in my nature to seek out men who would make me unhappy? Men, who would, ultimately hurt me despite their good intentions.

As soon as Ade left the next morning I called Kunle to find out how he was doing? I omitted telling him that Ade had spent the night at my flat. He told me he was doing fine but I had the feeling he was being brave for my benefit. I offered to take him out for a meal and, after a lot of convincing, he accepted. He needed cheering up and I wanted to be distracted from my problems as well.

We arranged to meet at a popular Chinese restaurant in Greenwich. I arrived early and had a diet coke whilst I waited for Kunle. He was punctual and appeared pleased to see me. I ordered a glass of wine as we chatted, before ordering our meals. I decided to have my favourite meal but Kunle only wanted something light, so he ordered soup. He said he didn't have much of an appetite.

It hurt me to see Kunle suffering. I desperately wanted to make him feel better. I suggested going back to my flat after dinner, hoping for a chance to spend more time together. I didn't have to work the following day so we could have stayed up late, watched a movie or listened to music, if he didn't feel like talking. He was also welcomed to spend the night if he wanted to.

I was surprised by Kunle's refusal of my offer. I thought that he would have jumped at the chance for us to spend quality time together. I hadn't realised the full extent of his suffering, until he finally told me that seeing me wasn't helping him.

"I know that you mean well and that you're trying to be supportive, but I think this is something I have to do on my own," Kunle said.

"I only want to help. I hate seeing you suffer like this," I said.

"I don't know how to say this without hurting your feelings Chris, but you being nice, well it's not helping. I want us to be more than just friends and I know that's not something you can offer me right now. James' death has made me think about my own happiness. I know it sounds selfish, but I need to do this for me," he said.

I was speechless as Kunle explained to me that I was no longer part of the solution, but part of the problem. It seemed that he was having a harder time moving on than I'd suspected. I understood what he was saying; I just had difficulty accepting it. He needed time to heal and, as a friend, I was prepared to give him that space. I would miss him but I would be waiting for him until he was ready to resume our friendship.

Kunle's revelation had caught me by surprise. The last thing I wanted to be was a source of additional pain to him. I cared about him a great deal but I was not able to offer him the kind of love he needed. Being apart would be a small sacrifice for me to make to preserve our friendship. I thanked Kunle for his honesty and pledged my support by honouring his wishes. Parting was, indeed, such sweet sorrow.

10. Second chances

Work kept me busy, but I still missed Kunle. At times I was tempted to call him but I respected him too much to disregard his wishes. I couldn't remember a time when I wasn't able to pick up the phone and hear his voice. Things were out of my control and, as much as I wanted it to go back to the way it was, our relationship had changed. It would never again be the same and that was going to take a great deal of adjustment on my part.

Ade and I agreed to rekindle our relationship. We both hoped we'd get it right second time around. My decision to give him another chance was based on my belief, that what we had was too special to throw away after just one attempt. This time there would be new rules. I didn't want to be dependant on someone else for my happiness, so I took back some of that responsibility. I had no intention of making the same mistakes twice.

* * *

One evening at work, a colleague told me about some strange calls she'd received on duty. Initially, the caller didn't speak, but she'd heard heavy breathing on the other end of the phone line. Later, as the calls continued, the caller had begun to talk; his speech was slurred, as though he'd been drinking. Once he had asked for *me* by name; my colleague wondered if it was someone I knew. She assured me she'd followed hospital policy and hadn't disclosed any personal information about me to the caller.

A few days later I received a suspicious call while at work. At first the caller was silent, but I knew he was there because I could hear him, breathing noisily. I instinctively thought it might be an ex-patient, calling to harass me. As I was about to end the call, he mentioned my name but before I could respond I heard the dial tone.

Later, when I reflected on the call, there was a sinister quality about it that resonated within me. I didn't recognise the caller's voice and had no idea why he'd called me. I had no control over this individual's behaviour. I did, however, have the power to not let it upset me. The calls ceased for a few days but, as sure as clockwork, they returned.

The next time I answered the phone he hung up, but called back a few minutes later. I was convinced this was the work of someone with mental health problems. I tried being empathetic but I also wanted to send a very clear message, that I wouldn't tolerate his behaviour. I suggested that he contact his family doctor or Community Mental Health Centre to arrange support. I was met with a barrage of obscenities.

"Where the fuck do you get off telling me I'm mad-you cunt. You're the one who needs to be put out of your fucking misery. You think you can fuck with other people's lives and get away with it, well you'll be sorry, I'll fuck you up, you fucking bitch," he said in a slurred speech.

I was stunned into silence as I listened to him rant. When he was finished, I told him that although I understood he was angry, I was not prepared to tolerate his behaviour and that if he tried that stunt again I'd contact the police.

I'd been verbally abused by patients in the past and was even physically assaulted once at work but this felt different; it felt personal. I couldn't think of anything I'd done to this man to warrant such feelings of hate. For the first time in my career I was worried for my own safety. I considered calling Kunle for advice but he was still taking a hiatus from our friendship. I also thought about contacting the police but since I had no evidence I gave up on that idea. I'd been under a lot of stress lately and decided I'd be fine after a good night's sleep.

* * *

Ade and I decided to take things slowly, once we started dating again. There was a lot of work to be done, bridges to rebuild. We wanted to get it right so there was no need to rush things.

Ade suggested we meet outside of my work place at 5:30pm. I didn't think it was a good idea as we risked being seen by colleagues, so instead we agreed to meet at London Bridge station for 6:30pm. We'd get a train to Charring Cross and then walk up to China Town.

Ade called to let me know he was running late, which gave me time to go home first to get changed.

I arrived at London Bridge station on time. I thought Ade looked very handsome talking to an elegantly dressed female. As I approached the pair, the young lady turned to face me. She was quite attractive. Ade introduced Allison as a colleague and I extended my hand to greet her. I was very surprised when she told me that it was a pleasure to finally meet the man who had captured Ade's heart.

Ade and I said goodbye to Allison and made our way to platform six. I refrained from talking about Allison during the short train journey, even though I was curious about her knowledge of Ade's sexuality, and more importantly, about our relationship.

Sitting in the restaurant reading the menu I said, "On my way to meet you tonight I thought I was being followed."

"Are you sure? Why do you think that?" Ade asked.

"I don't really know. It's just a feeling I guess."

"You're probably tired," he said.

"Maybe, but there's something I just can't put my finger on. Maybe I'm making a mountain out of a mole hill," I said.

"Tell me what exactly happened," he said.

"I'm just stressed, that's all, I said.

"I know what would take your mind off the subject," he said.

"That's so not going to happen tonight," I said, knowing he was talking about sex.

"I know I'm to blame for a lot of the stress you've been under lately, and if there's anything I can do to make it better, I will."

"I'm probably just blowing things out of proportion. You're right, I have been under a great deal of stress recently, so I'll stop thinking about it and enjoy the evening."

"My offer still stands," Ade said smiling. "You need a good soak in the bath followed by a massage and I know just the man for the job."

"And you need to forget about that because it isn't happening," I said.

Later that evening Ade told me that Allison was a medical colleague whom he'd 'come out' to the previous year. He'd told her about me and she'd seemed pleased for him. She knew from experience how difficult it was finding love in a big city like London. Finding sex was like oxygen, it was everywhere. Finding true love and entering the stability of a committed relationship was another kettle of fish. I was impressed by Ade's revelation.

At the end of our meal Ade suggested we drive to Hyde Park, to sit in his car and listen to music. This was one of my favourite spots to hang out with friends. We returned to London Bridge, to retrieve his car, before heading to Hyde Park.

As we sat in his car, overlooking the pond in the middle of Hyde Park, Ade told me that he was sorry for hurting me. He had apologised many times before but this time seemed different. He seemed different. His tone was more intimate. He said he intended to make me fall in love with him all over again. I chose not to tell him that I'd never stopped loving him.

Everything looked so peaceful in the park that it reminded me of the tranquillity I'd once had in my life, and which was now so sorely missed. It was difficult to imagine we were in one of the busiest cities in the world.

As we sat quietly, I reflected on the direction my life had taken. I missed the order I'd once had in my life. Ade's grip on my hand tightened as he turned to look at me. Maybe it had something to do with the strange telephone calls I'd been receiving at work, or perhaps the generally chaotic state of my life, but I suddenly felt very vulnerable.

It was all too much for me. As the tears escaped my eyes I wrestled with my emotions; I wanted to be strong on the one hand whereas on the other, all I wanted was for Ade to hold me close and tell me it would all work out in the end.

I turned up the CD player in the car. The music filled the small space, replacing my apprehension and fears with happier thoughts. Boys II Men were singing about not letting the water in the well run dry. It was up to me to decide whether I would allow our relationship to change so drastically that it lost all of its magic, or whether I was prepared to take Ade as he was; imperfect.

When I thought about it, I realised that it was only us, ourselves, who had placed so many barriers in the way of our happiness. I had to let go, grieve for what had been lost and embrace the new. I would stand up to the challenge and take a second chance on the man I loved, without all the preconditions that my head was telling me were right.

"Baby, please don't cry. I'm really sorry," he said.

He must have thought that I was crying because of the pain he'd caused me. These were tears of resignation-tears of peace and hope for what could be. I had no more tears left to shed for Ade, I had wasted too many of those already. I kissed him passionately. It was his turn to be surprised and he asked me what the kiss meant. I told him it was about taking second chances.

* * *

Dele called me unexpectedly one evening, cursing me for not keeping in touch. He hadn't started the support group just yet, but he felt there was no excuse for us not to meet for a drink. I agreed to go over to his flat the next day.

When I arrived at Dele's flat the first thing I noticed was his weight loss. He told me he'd been under a lot of stress and didn't have much of an appetite. Dele was an attractive black man; at five feet eleven inches tall, with broad shoulders and a slim waist-leading to a pert ass. His skin was dark and smooth, like fine chocolate. He'd always taken good care of his body and it was difficult to believe that he was forty-five years old. He epitomised the saying; 'good black don't crack'.

When we first met we often flirted with each other. He once came out of the bathroom naked and seemed very relaxed with his nudity. I didn't know then that he was an exhibitionist. His dick reached half way down his legs, making it difficult not to stare. He'd caught me staring and boldly asked if I was interested in sampling the goods. I made light of his remark and told him that I didn't fancy being disembowelled. I wanted to be able to walk upright and pain free. He laughed, saying he'd be gentle with me. We never had sex.

Sometime later, Dele told me about his fantasy of sleeping with his friends. He believed it would strengthen the friendships. I knew that he'd slept with a few of our close friends; but that was *before* they had become friends. Our situation was different. I argued that as we were already good friends, sleeping together would not serve to improve what was already excellent. He remained unconvinced even when I explained that I believed our relationship had transcended sex.

Dele had always liked his men young and, annoyingly, never had any trouble maintaining a constant supply of them. It was his unspoken rule never to date anyone over twenty-three. I was curious about what these men were able to offer him, other than great sex.

It had surprised me when he claimed to have been seriously interested in having a relationship with one or more of these men. He hadn't been very successful so far, a fact which I suspected was in part due to the immaturity of the guys he dated. They were too young to take life seriously, and relationships were not a priority for them.

Dating men had always come easy to Dele, but holding on to them was a different matter entirely. Fundamentally, these men wanted different things; but, in his mind, Dele could not distinguish between love and lust.

He hoped to revisit his youth by sleeping with younger men and, like a moth drawn to a flame, Dele was hurt time and time again. Although he was left with the scars, he continued to surround himself with young, virile men, full of stamina, in the hope that some of it would rub off on him.

Seeing Dele in person made me acutely aware of just how much I'd missed him. I missed us spending time together and confiding in each other about our love lives. I could tell him things I didn't feel comfortable telling Kunle because our relationship was different. This reminded me of Kunle. I hoped he was a little closer to resolving his issues-because I missed him dearly. Dele's voice jolted me back to reality.

Our conversation ultimately made its way to talking about men and, more specifically, about the trials of finding a decent man in London. We were both believers in equal opportunity dating.

A few of our friends only dated men of a particular race; but Dele and I wanted to broaden our options, which included dating any man who was gay and emotionally stable, regardless of his race. In the past I occasionally dated bisexual men but soon learned that the label 'bisexual' was sometimes just a substitute for 'confused'.

In principle I had no issues with bisexual men, as long as they made a choice and stuck to it once they decide to enter into a committed relationship. The trouble I had with some of these confused men was that they wore the term 'bisexual' like a designer label, believing that it allowed them to sleep with both sexes simultaneously. They felt that as long as the person they were sleeping with, was of the opposite sex to the person they were in a relationship with it didn't count as being unfaithful.

I took a sip of my drink, then Dele and I prepared to dish the latest dirt. I told him about my relationship with Ade and waited for his response. At the end of my monologue he stood up and, in a dramatic manner, hand on hip, proceeded to warn me about Nigerian men. He said he knew from personal experience, having been down that road many times before. He also knew very well that we couldn't help who we fell in love with, but maintained that we had a responsibility to learn from our mistakes.

"Chris, if I've told you once I've told you a thousand times, these children are confused. They will break your heart in two if you let them," he said, waving his finger at me.

"Dele, you can't help who you fall in love with. This is the person who holds the keys to my heart," I protested.

"I'm not telling you who to fall in love with baby, what I'm saying is that you have to love yourself a little more than you love these men."

"My mind is telling me one thing but my heart feels something else. How am I supposed to get the balance right?" I asked.

"If I knew that, I'd be a happy Ho-and a very rich one at that too. We have to stop giving away so much power to others. We give away the power to make us happy, the power to make us feel like shit, the power to determine our own self worth. We should be holding on to this power with both hands," he said passionately.

Dele's words made a lot of sense; but situations often look different from the outside. He always gave good advice but never took any of it for himself. I asked about his love life and he told me that he'd been very busy with business, so he hadn't been focussing on romance.

I knew him well and there was no business, however important, that would keep him away from 'dick'. He saw the look of disbelief on my face and said he'd met a few men in Lagos. That was more like it, I thought. He described a popular hotel in Lagos which he used as his 'market place'. I knew he seldom went a week without a different young man in his bed.

Dele had given up a promising legal career to pursue his dream of becoming a music producer. His success as a producer was marginal but he didn't let that stop him from living his dream. I admired him for sticking with what made him happy. He'd been a successful Attorney at Law and when he ended that career prematurely he said he'd never felt more fulfilled or happier.

Early on in his career he'd discovered that his heart was not in law but he had persevered because he wanted to please his parents. He felt under tremendous pressure to honour the sacrifices they'd made for him. His decision to give up law had shocked his family. They didn't agree with his choice but understood he needed to do what made him happy, although they secretly hoped he would eventually come to his senses and return to practising law.

He told me about the men he'd met in Nigeria and despite his lack of success in finding a boyfriend, maintained that he was determined to keep looking for 'Mr Right'. He was optimistic about Sheikh, the man he was currently dating. Sheikh lived in London, which seemed a promising start. They'd met over the Internet and Dele had quickly developed strong feelings for Sheikh-whom he described as 'sex on legs'.

On their first meeting, Sheikh had managed to satisfy three of Dele's criteria for a husband. Sheikh was young, had a big dick and a high sex drive. He wasn't very tall at five feet six inches. Dele didn't mind because what Sheikh lacked in height, he more than made up for in bed. He was twenty-two years old and in his second year at university, reading for a degree in biochemistry. His parents were from the Ivory Coast but he was London born and bred.

They'd hit it off almost immediately and, according to Dele, Sheikh's sexual prowess was accompanied by a most amiable disposition. After the first sexual encounter, they were hungry with desire and so arranged to meet regularly.

I didn't want to be the first to cast doubt, but I wondered whether Dele was trying to turn a 'HO' into a housewife. After all, some habits were hard to break; also, the last time I checked, an internet chat room wasn't the most popular place to find a partner for a committed relationship.

Dele was talking like a man in love and, when he told me that Sheikh was a great kisser, I began to wonder whether this guy wasn't just too good to be true. Next he'd be telling me that Sheikh could walk on water. He hadn't introduced Sheikh to his friends because he'd wanted to feel secure in his relationship before doing so.

I was happy for Dele because he deserved some good luck. A small part of me expected Sheikh to have two heads and experience had taught me that if it seemed too good to be true, then it probably was too good to be true. I was certain there'd be room for one more gay man on that river in Egypt, my friends and I usually referred to as 'denial'.

Dele saw the group as a good opportunity to start discussing the real issues relating to black gay men living in London. There was no guarantee we'd be any closer to finding our soulmates by the end of it but, hopefully, we'd be a lot clearer about the relationships we wanted. Separating reality from fantasy in order to take responsibility for our own happiness was an important part of that process.

I agreed to provide light refreshments for the first meeting, which was scheduled to take place in Dele's flat in a couple of weeks. Seven men were invited to the first meeting. As I was leaving, Dele promised to call me a few days before the meeting to remind me about the refreshments.

When I arrived home I was pleasantly surprised to find a telephone message from Kunle. It was his way of telling me that he was doing better. That night, before drifting off to sleep, I said a prayer for my friends and myself; asking that we would find peace and happiness in our lives and would be prepared for, and able to recognise, love, should it come calling.

11. Good friends

Dele contacted me as promised, sounding very excited as he reminded me of my pledge to provide the refreshments for the meeting. He said that I probably wouldn't know any of the other guests. He jokingly suggested that I might meet 'Mr. Right' in the group and I reminded him that I already had the man of my dreams in my life.

Spring was fast approaching and the weather was good enough for me to go out wearing a pair of jeans and a tee shirt. I carried a jumper, just in case it became cooler in the evening.

I arrived at Dele's flat about thirty minutes early. He was in his element as he played the part of 'hostess diva' with his usual flare. Two of the guests, Tunde and Ray, were already seated. Dele was about to introduce me to Tunde when I told him that we already knew each other. We hadn't seen each other since we'd met in the West End for high tea, several months ago.

Dele stood, mouth open, before saying, "bitch you sure do get around."

"Honey you're not the only one with friends," I responded.

Tunde introduced me to Ray, giving no information about how they knew each other. His silence spoke volumes. I made a mental note to find out more.

Tunde and I had been friends for a couple of years after meeting at a nursing conference in Birmingham. We'd gravitated to each other almost instantly, proving that gay men could usually spot each other from a distance.

He was a light-skinned brother, who stood about five feet nine inches tall. We'd cruised each other on the journey to Birmingham and I was surprised to learn we were both headed for the same conference. Within a short time we had worked out that sex wasn't on the cards and agreed to stay in touch as friends, at the end of the two-day conference.

Ray was seriously cute, if a little short at five feet, three inches tall. His skin was the color of peanut butter. His shaved head gave him a masculine edge but by far his best features were his honey-colored eyes, which oozed sex appeal. Just looking into them could make a brother say 'hell yeah'.

We were expecting four other men. Miss Candy spelt like the sweet, was next to arrive-making a flamboyant entrance. We heard him before we actually saw him. When he walked into a room heads turned, usually for no other reason than to see who was making so much noise.

Miss Candy was originally from Ghana, he'd come to the UK age three. His real name was Kofi but his gay friends knew him as Miss Candy. He was as camp as a row of pink tents and despite his overly extrovert personality, he was still easy to like. I felt drawn to him. You either loved Miss Candy or you hated him. He hugged each of us like we were long lost friends.

Next to arrive was Martin. He was from South London and epitomized what was commonly known in gay circles as a 'Dinge Queen'. Martin was a white, middle class man, who exclusively dated much younger black men. He was in his mid-forties if he was a day old, but he dressed and behaved like he was twenty-one. 'Mutton dressing as lamb' had never seemed more appropriate.

It took Martin a few short minutes to let us know that he was a solicitor, owned his own home and drove a BMW. He also mentioned that he was single. We were left with the feeling that Martin wasn't someone who often remained single for very long. Dele knew Martin from his days as an Attorney. They'd dated briefly.

Eric called to cancel because something had some up at the last minute. We all knew exactly what had come up. The power 'dick' held over gay men was amazing. At the prospect of new 'dick' we dropped everything, in a heartbeat. Eric made his apologies and promised to attend the next meeting.

The last person to arrive was Chez. All eyes turned when the brother walked into the room. Baby boy was fine as hell. He looked like he'd just walked off a fashion runway in Europe. At six feet three inches tall, with legs that went on forever and a toned body that looked like he'd spent time in the gym, but wasn't a 'Muscle Mary', he was working it.

His hair was cut short and he wore a diamond stud earring in each ear. His jeans seemed to be painted on and the close-fitting, white, long sleeved tee shirt showed every contour of his finely sculptured body. The brother knew he was fine and didn't mind showing it off, but not in a cocky way. He smiled broadly, showing two rows of perfect white teeth. I'm sure I wasn't the only one left excited.

We took our seats, drinks in hand, as Dele occupied centre stage. He explained the purpose of the meeting and, after agreeing to the ground rules, we each took turns telling a little about ourselves and what we hoped to get out of the evening. The meeting proceeded in a most orderly fashion.

We were all frothing at the mouth when it came to Chez's turn to talk about himself. We learned he was a model; surprise, surprise. He was also a final year, university student, reading for a degree in psychology. He planned on eventually working as a forensic psychologist. He saw modeling as a means to an end. He could pay for his tuition, without having to work at his local fast food restaurant for minimum wage. I was surprised to find that he was neither self-absorbed nor superficial. He seemed refreshingly unaffected by his beauty.

I found myself sexually attracted to Chez, despite having a boyfriend of my very own. I began acting like a lovesick teenager and, judging by the behavior of the others, I wasn't the only one. They were just as captivated as I was. Chez was a conundrum we were all eager to figure out. Here was this very attractive brother, attending a group for people who were, essentially, unlucky in love. Chances were, he'd have men falling over themselves to get to him.

His reasons for being single were different to most of our own. He felt objectified by men whom, he believed, dated him simply because he was a trophy; a possession to be cast aside when they got bored. He believed his opinions were largely ignored and that people were seldom interested in getting to know him as a person. He thought some brothers didn't approach him because they felt someone that handsome and still single, had to be damaged goods.

My difficulties seemed petty compared to the issues Chez was struggling with. It was remarkable that we were attractive, intelligent, solvent men, who for whatever reason had failed to find the right man. Tunde and I were seeing things from a slightly different perspective. I had a man but I doubted whether he was my soulmate. I knew Tunde had been dating a man when we last met and my suspicions led me to the conclusion it was Ray.

Professionally, we were having no such difficulty, each one already climbing the corporate ladder. Romantically, most of us felt we were coated in a repellent that kept away good men. We decided to analyze where we were going wrong as a group.

We broke it down into two main areas so that we could explore our problems more comprehensively. The first area was about our standards. Were we looking for the wrong qualities in men? I had repeatedly asked myself this question in the past and so was eager to find out what the others had to say on the matter.

I often got the qualities I desired in someone I only wanted to shag mixed up with the qualities I wanted in a partner. They were very different things. The people I wanted to screw 'till the sun came up', and the ones I wanted to spend my life with were usually not the same. I hadn't learned how to get the balance right.

The second area was about location. Where were all these fine men located? I'd learned, a long time ago, there was no such thing as a supermarket that stocked up on fine men. Though not impossible, it was unlikely that I would find my life partner in a leather bar. Meeting my soulmate could happen anywhere; but the chance of it happening in that environment was remote. Maybe for someone else it might be appropriate, but not for me.

More importantly, the handsome stud who wanted to have sex all might long, didn't snore and who worshiped the ground I walked on, probably didn't exist outside of my over active imagination. He was a myth; like Big Foot or The Lochness Monster. Even if by some twist of fate he did exist, he'd probably be looking for a brother as fine as himself. What chance did we have?

We all agreed that the 'Gay Bermuda Triangle' was a very real difficulty faced by a lot of gay men. Dele was the one who had coined the term. He believed that a lot of gay men were caught up in a vicious cycle he liked to call the 'Gay Bermuda Triangle'.

We all knew men who were attracted to other men who were unattainable to them. It'd happened to us all. The men we dreamed of having wanted other men whom they were no more capable of having. It seldom worked out that the men of our dreams had us in their dreams, and so we often ended up alone and unhappy.

Ray pointed out that even if we were approached by our soul-mate, would we even recognize him? Maybe we needed to look at our distorted perceptions of 'Mr. Right'.

The six of us relaxed into easy conversation. We all made excellent use of the space to address issues that we felt were important to us.

Time seemed to fly past. Dele was great as a facilitator and kept the conversation flowing while also entertaining us with his tall tales.

It was 10:30pm by the time the group came to a close. We felt we'd begun to get to know each other better. Miss Candy left early for a hot date. Before he left, we all teased him about taking a closer look at his choices in men. He responded by saying the man he was meeting was not husband material, but would do for now. Martin offered Chez a lift to the train station but he declined. The disappointment on Martin's face was a dead giveaway.

Tunde, Ray, Chez and I, stayed behind with Dele for a nightcap. After he finished the washing up, Dele made us a pot of coffee. The weather was warm enough for us to leave the windows ajar.

I sat at the far end of the sofa with Dele's head in my lap as I massaged his tense shoulders. Tunde was in an armchair opposite with his legs curled up under him. Ray was sitting in front of Tunde. Chez sat on the floor, to my left. We listened to the soundtrack from the movie 'Waiting to Exhale', playing softly in the background. Aretha Franklin's voice was full of pain as she asked why love had to hurt so bad-it's like she'd read our minds.

We talked about our past relationships. As I spoke I could feel Chez snuggling up closer to my legs and in a husky voice he asked if he could also have a massage. It seemed fine men were like buses. You waited a long time for one and then three appeared, all at once. I knew for certain that had I been single, I would never have been so popular with these fine men. I was flattered.

I felt close enough to the group of men to tell them about my relationship dilemma. I respected Ade's confidentiality so I didn't mention his name. They all remained silent until I stopped talking. I half-expected them to criticize me, but they didn't. Chez surprised me once again, by telling me that I deserved better and shouldn't settle for less. I should be with someone who only wanted to be with me.

I looked across the room and saw Tunde's hand resting naturally on Ray's shoulder, I continued massaging Chez's shoulders. Touching him felt natural, like touching an old friend. We listened to the music; it was Tony Braxton's turn to advise us to let it flow, everything would work out right in the end.

Tunde and Ray left together. Even though I hadn't managed to get Tunde on his own to ask him about Ray, I was convinced that they were dating. I wondered why he was being so secretive about the man in his life. Maybe he felt uncomfortable about disclosing this in a group situation. As they said goodbye, I promised to give Tunde a call soon.

Chez seemed quite relaxed on Dele's sofa as I got ready to leave. I began to wonder whether he intended spending the night at Dele's flat. Dele hadn't mentioned Sheikh, so I didn't know whether they were still dating. There were no obvious signals of romance between Chez and Dele but that in itself was never an accurate indication of a romantic liaison.

As I said goodnight, Chez asked if he could have a lift to the train station. I kissed Dele good night and left. Arriving at my car, Chez made his surprise that I drove a convertible BMW obvious. I told him we were even. He asked what I meant by that and I explained that he himself had produced a few surprises during the course of the evening. He laughed aloud. Somehow this made him seem even more attractive to me.

Chez was more interesting to talk to on his own, though I suspected that was mostly due to him pouring on the charm. It was well after midnight and quite likely that the last train had already left the station, so I offered to give him a lift to his home. As we drove to Greenwich he told me that he'd been financially successful as a model, so he didn't have to live on campus like many of his colleagues at university.

I asked him if he was truly happy. He was attractive, appeared to be in good health and was more financially stable than most twenty two-year old I knew. There was sadness in his voice when he responded. He said he felt misunderstood.

He disclosed that his last lover had treated him like a fragile porcelain ornament. He felt he wasn't allowed to do anything independently, or go anywhere without his lover, who became insanely jealous if he wasn't involved in every aspect of Chez's life. I pointed out that there must have been some positive qualities about the relationship that helped to sustain it. After all the relationships had lasted three years.

Chez agreed that initially the relationship had been wonderful-he'd been flattered by the attention his partner lavished on him. He had hoped that eventually the novelty would wear off. His partner had begun to use cocaine during the latter stages of their relationship and, although the warning signs had been present earlier, he felt powerless to stop the decline. When his partner eventually died from a drug overdose, Chez felt guilty for not saving him, blaming himself for his partner's untimely death.

His eyes welled up and I squeezed his hand in a gesture of sympathy.

"Chez, you can't be held responsible for your partner's choices. You can only help someone if that person is ready to be helped. Try to think about the good times you shared and keep those memories alive," I said.

"I understand what you're saying Chris. You're a wise man," he said.

"I'm no wiser than anybody else, but I believe that even when we've had bad experiences, there are lessons to be learned. We can learn to make better choices the next time," I said.

"I like you Chris, even though we've only just met."

"I like you too Chez. At first I thought you were just a pretty face but, happily you're not," I said.

"Do you know what I mean when I say 'I like you' Chris?"

"That we get on well and I'm a nice guy?" I asked.

"Yes that too but I'm attracted to you, to your spirit. I know that you're dating someone but it seems to me that he doesn't deserve you."

"That's sweet of you to say. I'm flattered and my self-esteem is soaring now," I said.

"We deserve whatever happiness we can get in life. Remember, if that idiot boyfriend of yours messes up again, you should give me a call," he said.

When I dropped Chez off outside his flat, I had the final surprise of the night. Without warning he kissed me. It was gentle and sweet and, for a minute, he had me rethinking my relationship with Ade. My integrity demanded that I remain faithful to Ade. The grass wasn't always greener on the other side.

12. A happy home

My conversation with Chez boosted my confidence and did wonders for my self-esteem. A fine looking brother like Chez finding me desirable was very self-affirming. Despite the other, maybe better looking, men who'd been at Dele's flat that night, I knew there were different horses for different courses but, by any standard, Chez was a thoroughbred and that thoroughbred had chosen me.

My new found confidence gave me the motivation I needed to work on my relationship with Ade. I wanted to take things to the next level so I arranged a special evening with my man. When I told him about what I had planned for us, he acted like it was the best news he'd heard in a long time.

Two days later the time had come to execute my plans. I paid special attention to every detail, the last thing I wanted to be doing on my special day with Ade was to be slaving over a hot cooker. Ade and I both loved Chinese food, so I ordered a take away meal from one of the local restaurants. The young lady who took my order over the telephone promised me the food would be delivered within the hour.

I ran a bath, put on a CD and sank under the luxurious bubbles. A few seconds later Whitney Houston's voice permeated the entire flat, like a sweet perfume. As I lay in the bath, and the water caressed me, the mixture of aromas from the bath oils and the scented candles made me dizzy. All that was missing was a glass of wine. However I avoided alcohol because I wanted to be alert for the evening's forthcoming events.

The music must have been much louder than I realized, because the deliveryman had to ring the doorbell several times before I heard him. I stepped out of the bath and into a robe. My skin was glistening when I opened the door to find a handsome young man standing before me. His eyes made a slow journey, from my face, to my exposed chest, lingering, before returning to my face. He wore an expression of keen interest.

His cropped hair gave him a thuggish look. His muscular physique was indicative of self-discipline and a love of exercise. At first glance I thought he might be Chinese but, on closer inspection, he appeared to be mixed race, an exotic combination of Caucasian and Oriental background.

The way this young man looked at me left no doubt in my mind that, whatever his heritage, he was kin. Straight men never looked at each other like that. I had never dated an oriental man before but this man had the ability to change that. I quickly remembered the purpose of his visit and realized that I'd opened the door without my wallet. I invited him in, offering him a seat while I went in search of some money.

I returned with the cash and we chatted briefly while I placed the food on the warmer. His name was Kevin. He had a strong, cockney, accent and seemed very relaxed, sitting on my sofa chatting, I wondered whether he had any other customers waiting patiently for deliveries.

During his short visit, Kevin never stopped checking me out. Eventually I ended our pleasant conversation. I told him that I needed to get ready for my guest. He seemed a little disappointed. He gave me his mobile number, just in case I needed another delivery anytime soon. Kenin's handshake told me that he would be happy to deliver more than just food next time.

I took my time dressing. I wore Ade's favorite, a pair of red, silk boxers, which matched the single red rose on the bed. Linen trousers and a lamb's wool jersey, a generous helping of 'Unforgiven' cologne completed my preparation. A quick once-over in the mirror and I was ready for action.

The doorbell rang as I was fastening my gold chain. This time the CD was turned down, so I heard it on the first ring. On my way to the door I stopped briefly to program the CD player. As I opened the door, Whitney Houston's voice belted out the first few notes of the song, 'I will always love you'.

Ade stood in the doorway momentarily, as if waiting to be invited in. As he walked past, his hand emerged from behind his back to produce a bottle of champagne.

"You took your sweet time answering the door," Ade said playfully.

"Was it not worth the wait?" I asked.

He didn't answer me. We kissed passionately; the evening was off to a fabulous start.

I offered Ade a seat before disappearing into the kitchen. When I returned with the two champagne flutes, he was smiling broadly. I asked if he would honour me with a dance, I swear I saw his eyes grow a little misty as he accepted my offer.

"Do you know how long I've waited for this moment?" he asked.

"No I don't know, so you'll have to tell me."

"Let's just say it's been a very long time, and for a while there I thought it might never happen," he said.

"It nearly didn't," I said, "but all that's in the past. Let's dance."

As we embraced, he whispered in my ear the three words I'd been longing to hear. It had been a while since a man had told me 'I love you'. This time I believed he meant it. I told him that I loved him too.

We enjoyed the meal, but agreed to skip dessert so we could move on to more important matters. I was like a rabbit on heat and tonight I planned to be the seducer. Ade never looked sweeter as he sat on the sofa, engulfed by the warm glow of the table lamp. I began to slowly undressed. I knew I had his undivided attention when he began to lick his lips.

With each item of clothing I removed, I moved closer to Ade, making the anticipation build slowly. He fidgeted as he struggled to avoid touching the impressive bulge between his legs, which was growing bigger by the second. It was my turn to practice self-control. I kept the silk boxers on, because I knew he was turned on seeing me in my underwear. I felt like his eyes were burning little holes deep into my skin and I loved it.

Ade stood up abruptly, no longer able to suppress his urges. We kissed hungrily before his mouth moved from my lips to explore the rest of my body. As he worked his magic I had difficulty maintaining my balance. I didn't want him to stop what he was doing, as he drove me closer to the edge. I managed to regain my composure long enough to lead him to my carefully prepared love den.

I sat on the bed as Ade took centre stage. There were several scented candles, strategically placed around the bedroom, a fire hazard I know, but they helped to create a romantic atmosphere.

I needed to touch him to confirm I wasn't dreaming. In panther-like fashion, he crossed the floor space to join me in bed. In a husky voice that barely rose above a whisper, he asked, "do you like what you see?"

My throat was suddenly dry and I had difficulty speaking. Ade took the waistband of my boxers and, using both thumbs, gently pulled them down. The garment fell away from my skin, like leaves falling from a tree in autumn.

Everything seemed to slow down as Ade and I made love. Initially slow and rhythmic, we took turns pleasing each other. He wasn't used to relinquishing control in bed but he adapted quickly. I had been expecting a magical night, full of passion, I wasn't disappointed. Neither of us was able to move for a long time afterwards; we cuddled each other, gently before drifting peacefully off to sleep.

When I finally crawled out of bed the next day I felt muscles aching in my body that I didn't even know I had. I looked on the floor next to the bed and realized we'd used three condoms during the night. Ade was still fast asleep in bed as I made my way into the shower in an attempt to soothe my aching muscles.

* * *

The next few weeks saw spring give way to summer, my favourite time of year. Ade and I spent most nights together, our relationship seemed much better than before. For the first time in a while it felt like we were truly a couple, in every sense of the word. The nights at my flat were spent talking for hours about our future together as a team.

One evening, after a meal in the West End, I suggested going to a bar a short distance away. We'd stayed away from the gay scene since entering into a relationship. There were operas to visit, plays to see, interesting restaurants to sample and lots more to do in London. However, on this occasion I felt like being in the company of other gay men and it seemed a perfect way to end a lovely evening.

We were close to a club called 'The Crypt', which played mainly R&B, hip-hop and pop music. Initially Ade was reluctant, but he eventually agreed because he didn't want to spoil the evening for me. We reached the compromise that we would only stay a short time. I was secretly missing the buzz of the gay nightlife-and I wanted to show off my handsome man.

As we walked down the narrow, winding, stairs into the basement, we could hear the music pumping. The place was packed with hot-looking men and I suddenly felt like I'd been away for a century. Ade tried to convince me that it was too crowded and suggested that we went to another venue. We'd already paid to get in, so I was adamant we were going to get our money's worth.

The atmosphere was groovy, and the vibe, kicking. Ade disappeared briefly to talk to some friends and when he returned he seemed anxious. I thought he might relax with some alcohol on-board and I went to the bar to get us a couple of drinks. He continued to protest about the crowded dance floor, so I reassured him that we'd leave after about an hour. I was hoping he would lighten up soon, because he was really starting to dampen the evening with his mood.

He finally relaxed and stopped looking over his shoulder after a couple of drinks. He was dancing and appeared to be enjoying himself. I had the feeling it didn't get much better than this. One of my favorite songs started playing so I took Ade's hand and led him to the packed dance floor. With my eyes closed I rested my head on his shoulders and we were suddenly alone on a remote, tropical, island.

My tranquility was shattered by a shrill voice, shouting, "Who the fuck is this bitch?"

It took me a few seconds to realize that the question was about me, but directed at Ade. The rest of the patrons started paying closer attention to what was going on. The crowd parted like the Red Sea. Standing in front of me was a young man in his early twenties. His stance suggested that he was ready for action but his gait was unsteady so I knew that he had been drinking.

I thought it was just another queen who couldn't hold her liquor. He continued staring at me menacingly and, when I didn't snap out of it, I realized that this show was on. It was like being in a bad episode of 'Jerry Springer'.

13. Bring it on

In the midst of all the excitement I momentarily forgot that Ade was close by. It took a few more seconds for me to finally figured out the man standing in front of me was Michael. I looked at Ade for some clarification, but there was none.

I had no intention of getting into a confrontation in a club, but I wasn't going to be assaulted by the town drunk either.

His speech was slurred as he shouted, "bitch you better speak up or else."

I thought, 'Miss Thing, you are messing with the wrong man tonight'.

Michael was determined to create a scene and the audience was willing him on to start a fight. By this time the music had been turned down and the crowd seemed to be closing in, expecting to be entertained. I looked across at Ade, standing beside me with a look of embarrassment on his face. Luckily I wasn't expecting him to rescue me, or else I would have been disappointed.

Michael turned his attention to Ade and asked, "Aren't you going to fill your little boyfriend here in on what's going on?"

"Look, I don't know who you think you are, but you're messing with the wrong man tonight. Whatever is going on between you and Ade is between the two of you, so leave me the fuck out of it," I said angrily.

Ade seemed uncomfortable with all the attention and tried desperately to look for a way out.

"What's up with this? Are you trying to embarrass me in front of my friends by bringing your trashy new boyfriend here?" asked Michael.

I thought, 'oh hell no, he didn't just go there. I'll beat this HO like he stole something.'.

"There's no need for this, let's break it up," I heard Ade reply finally.

Michael tried to take a swing at me while I was looking at Ade, but he lost his balance and ended up in a heap on the dance floor.

The crowd dispersed when the security staff arrived and the DJ began playing an upbeat song. The crowd seemed disappointed that the night's entertainment had ended prematurely. Michael was so drunk that the men had to bear the full weight of his body as they took him away. He looked a pathetic sight.

Ade had only managed to say a few words during the entire bizarre episode. As I walked past Michael on my way out of the club, I thought there was no point in upsetting myself more than I already was, because he obviously had a few issues to address, the least of which was Ade's relationship with me.

As I was leaving, Ade mumbled that he would meet me outside. My final image on leaving the club was that of Ade bending over Michael who was slumped, semiconscious, on the floor. At another time and place, that scene would have been funny, but there was nothing humorous about the situation, I just wanted to put the entire, sordid, affair behind me.

I reflected on the night's events as I waited for Ade outside the club. The embarrassment of what had happened hit me like a ton of bricks. I couldn't remember ever having felt that humiliated. Fighting in a club was the last thing I'd expected to happen when I left home. Ade seemed to take forever to join me and I couldn't believe how bad I felt. The evening had turned into a nightmare.

When he finally emerged from the club, he tried to explain Michael's difficulty in coming to terms with the end of their relationship. He told me that after I'd left the club Michael had broken down in tears and apologized. Ade felt Michael was in no fit state to get home on his own, and that he needed his support. I looked at Ade like he was from another planet.

I didn't realize what I'd said until the expression on Ade's face changed.

"What's going on Ade? Who's going to support me? What about my feelings?" I asked.

"Chris, I'm so sorry," he answered looking away.

"Sorry doesn't ease the pain Ade, I wish it did," I said.

It was clear that I had to deal with this all by myself. I wanted to know who was going to offer me support. Who cared about my feelings or how I was dealing with this traumatic experience? It wasn't every day that I was verbally abused and threatened with assault. Ade seemed caught between a rock and a hard place, but I wasn't going to make it easy for him. The sweet, understanding, boyfriend was off duty.

I was in no mood to listen to any excuses. I wanted to get home. The realization that Ade wasn't going be accompanying me, began to sink in as I started walking down Charring Cross Road, towards Leicester Square. His words stung like a slap across my face.

"I wouldn't be able to forgive myself if I let Michael go home alone in this state and he did something stupid," were Ade's final words as I walked away. I needed to clear my head. I wasn't about to have another fight outside the club. I'd had enough humiliation for one night. He offered to get me a cab but I chose to walk instead.

14. After the storm

I had no idea of where I was headed-I just needed to get away. I walked around the West End for about an hour before finally sitting outside a café. I was angry with myself, mostly because I'd placed myself in a position to be embarrassed. I was also angry for handing over the power to make me feel like shit. When would I ever learn?

As I sat drinking my coffee, I heard a gentle voice ask if I was all right. I looked up and it took a few seconds for my tear filled eyes to focus properly. By this time my anger had given way to self-pity. A young man had noticed I was upset and decided not to simply walk on by. I tried to speak but was afraid that I would start crying like a baby. Instead I gave him a half smile. He asked if he could join me.

I nodded, 'yes' even though I wasn't sure I'd be good company. He told me his name was Tore, short for Salvatore. He didn't talk a lot and sat drinking his hot chocolate. Occasionally he looked over at me with a kind expression on his face. He seemed to understand that whatever was bothering me was private, and that I wasn't ready to talk to him about it. It was nice to know that there were still good people left in the world.

When I felt able to talk I told Tore my name and thanked him for sitting with me. I also assured him that I' be fine. He offered to give me a lift home, which I politely declined. He'd already done more than enough. Before leaving he gave me his business card, on which he had also written his mobile number. I promised to call him. In a voice filled with compassion, he said that he'd wait to hear from me.

On the bus journey home I thought about meeting Tore. He seemed to be a very caring person. This was obvious because it would have been easy to do what most other people did, and just ignore someone in distress.

* * *

I didn't take any of Ade's calls for a few days but I soon realized it was pointless trying to avoid him. I felt nervous as I dialed his number. He answered on the first ring and seemed relieved to hear my voice. He said that he'd been going crazy with worry about me. We agreed to meet the following day. After speaking with him I got ready to attend the monthly support group at Dele's flat.

Chez and Tunde were already at the flat by the time I arrived. I kissed Tunde on his each cheek as he playfully squeezed my bum, before I hugged Dele. Finally I embraced Chez and held on to his fine body. Baby boy was still working it. I attempted to kiss him on the cheek, but instead he turned his face to offer me his lips. Luckily, the others were distracted by pictures of naked men on Dele's computer screen and hadn't noticed our minor indiscretion.

Miss Candy arrived next and 'Miss Thing' came in drag. He looked like a winner of Britain's Next Top Model, wearing a black leather miniskirt and candy-pink sweater. The hair of his blonde wig was held away from his face with a black satin ribbon. His make-up was flawless and he had the confidence to carry it off. It was difficult to remember there was a man under all that warpaint and feminine clothes. The transformation was stunning and in the right lighting, it would probably fool any man into thinking he was the genuine article.

Dele informed us that Ray was unable to attend the group because he was under the weather. Miss Candy, in true diva fashion, said that Ray was probably under something, it certainly wasn't the weather. We all laughed at his comment, momentarily forgetting Tunde's presence. I still hadn't found out what was going on between the two of them.

Martin arrived with a friend, Nigel. We all welcomed Nigel, 'the chicken', because if this young man was a day over seventeen, then I was Tyson Beckford's identical twin. Nigel, we learned, was originally from the Cameroon. He was about five feet, five inches tall and had green eyes that didn't fool anyone; the child wasn't fooling anyone with those contact lenses. Martin claimed that he and Nigel were just friends-and the fool actually expected us to believe him.

Dele told us that he was expecting one more person. I joined him in the kitchen, where he was preparing a light snack for the group. I wanted to find out more. The young man's name was Hans and they'd met at his local train station.

Dele was as sharp as a razor when chasing after a gay man he had an interest in. For him it was almost a sixth sense, being able to spot a gay man in a crowd. Nor was he shy about approaching someone he was interested in either. I on the other hand, found it difficult to approach men. I didn't possess the skills to successfully chase men and so accepted my limitations gracefully.

About ten minutes after the meeting was due to start, Hans walked into the flat. This fine Germans specimen of the Arian race was twenty-three years old and a second year law student. Hans liked his men black, with big dicks and lots of energy. He turned out to be a nice guy to talk to, but you were left feeling as though you'd just been interviewed, for the position of his next shag.

We all retired to the living room, took our seats and prepared to bare our souls. We each took a turn to talk about what had happened in our lives the previous month. I wasn't brave enough to go first, so I waited a while before speaking. When the time came for me to speak, I felt unusually nervous, but threw caution to the wind and told them everything. I was careful not to mention any names because I still wanted to keep Ade's identity private, even after all I'd been through. I also mentioned having met Tore.

When I was finished, Dele, who was seated next to Hans, got up and joined me on the sofa. It took all my self-control to hold back the tears which threatened to come gushing out. I'd promised myself I wouldn't cry because I had already wasted too many tears on the men in my life.

Miss Candy broke the ice with his quick wit and said, "We all know that men are dogs-can I hear amen to that?" He suggested that I call Tore to thank him for his concern.

Everyone except Chez felt I should accept Tore's hand in friendship. Chez felt Tore was after something and that in my vulnerable state I couldn't be objective about my situation. I wondered how objective Chez was being. Miss Candy said he felt Tore seemed like a good man, volunteering to take him off my hands if I didn't want him. I needed a friend to talk to, especially since Kunle was still dealing with his own issues.

In an attempt to try and cheer me up, Miss Candy told us about a story that was making the rounds of London's black gay community. He wanted to show me that although my situation was terrible, there were people out there who were far worse off.

His story was about a young man, who was about to get married to please his parents. He intended to go through with the arranged marriage, leaving his bride in Nigeria, while he remained in London with his boyfriend. Sadly, we had all heard about similar stories in the past, but it was never any less shocking to learn that it still went on.

We all gasped in unison when Miss Candy told us the man's boyfriend was going to be the best man at the wedding. The stag night was going to be the black gay event of the year. I had to be grateful that however complicated my situation was, at least it wasn't as bad as the one Miss Candy had described. He didn't know the men involved but we all agreed that it sounded messy.

I was pleasantly surprised by how supportive the group was. Even Hans was able to offer some sound advice. He said I needed to decide whether Ade was worth fighting for. If I believed Ade was the genuine article, then I couldn't choose which battles I wanted to fight. I had to take the rough with the smooth and not give up easily. He went on to say that even good men had weaknesses and faults. If the relationship was going to survive, then I had to find a way past this.

As the meeting came to an end it was clear *we* would not be hanging around Dele's flat because *he* had other plans for Hans. I noticed Tunde hadn't said more than a few words throughout the evening so I offered him a lift. To my disappointment, he took a ride with Martin and Nigel instead. As I kissed Dele goodnight, I urged him to be gentle with Hans. He laughed aloud, causing the others to wonder what was so funny.

I offered Chez a lift home because he too had been unusually quiet during the meeting. On the drive home he told me that the anniversary of his partner's death was approaching. He'd felt uncomfortable about sharing it with the others for fear they'd think he was wallowing in self pity. I touched his hand and he looked out the window.

There I was, being self-absorbed when my friend was having a tough time. I suggested we go for a drink at his local pub but he said he didn't feel like going out. Instead he invited me back to his flat. He seemed to be in a lot of pain.

I was surprised by the tasteful decor of Chez's flat. I still thought of him as an ordinary college student when, in fact, he was by no means ordinary. His flat was not very spacious but, what it lacked in size, it more than made up for in charm. He offered me a seat while he prepared a drink for himself and a coffee for me.

His mood seemed to brighten as he talked about the good times he had shared with his partner and, for the first time that evening, a hint of a smile crept across his face. As I was about to leave, he asked if I wanted to spend the night. Though tempted, I declined. We hugged and I reminded him that I was just a phone call away.

15. The right decision

I called Tore's office the next day and spoke to his secretary because he was in a meeting. I asked her to have him call me when he was free. It was only after I ended the call that I realized, I hadn't left my own number.

I made a second call to Tore later that day, this time his secretary put me straight through to him.

"Hi Christopher, sorry I missed your call earlier. I was with a client."

"No need to be so formal, you can call me Chris. I know that you're a busy man with a lot of people to help," I said.

"I'm glad you called again," he said, "how are you doing?"

"Not yet back to where I need to be, but I'm doing OK," I replied.

"Happy to hear that," he said, "You do sound a lot brighter. Any chance we could meet for a coffee?"

"I take it you want to see for yourself that I am doing fine," I said.

"Hopefully I don't need an excuse to see a friend. I just thought it'd be nice to meet for a chat. The last time we met we didn't really talk much," he said.

I wondered whether Tore was flirting with me.

"I was pretty impressed that you took the time to sit with me when I was upset;" I said, "not many people would have done that."

"I'm always happy to help someone if I can. Anyway, at the time you looked like you needed a friendly ear and, guess what? I'm actually pretty good at listening. Do you know what else I am pretty good at?" he asked.

"Is this a trick question?"

"No it's not. I'm pretty good at noticing when people avoid answering my questions. How about coffee sometime?" he asked.

"That would be nice," I replied.

"Do you have a number I can reach you on? I'm hoping we could meet next week," he said.

Just then our chat was interrupted by the 'call-waiting' signal. Tore apologized for the interruption and, even though I offered to continue the conversation at another time, he insisted I hold on.

We started talking again after a brief silence. He had such a calm manner that I didn't realize we'd been talking for more than half an hour. He laughed when I told him that he really was a good listener. Before ending our conversation we arranged a time to meet the following week. We chose to return to the coffee shop where we'd first met.

After my call to Tore, I felt more certain that he'd been flirting with me. I didn't need another lover; what I needed was a friend, so I put those thoughts right out of my head. My life was complicated enough. He'd proven to me that he was kind, understanding, and caring, someone with integrity; qualities I treasured in a friend.

* * *

I agreed to meet Ade on neutral territory, at a popular wine bar in Greenwich. I arrived early and spent a few anxious minutes on my own before he joined me. He looked handsome in a linen shirt and chino trousers with a pair of brown leather loafers, but seemed a little nervous as he took a seat next to me.

"How are you doing Chris?"

I was tempted to ask him, 'how the hell do you think I'm doing', but I simply replied, "Fine". I deliberately avoided asking him how he was doing. Instead, I thought I'd cut to the chase.

"Did Michael get home safe?" I asked.

He didn't look up as he said, "you know this is killing me, don't you?"

"Now you know how I feel," I said.

"Is this about revenge Chris?"

"You've made it very clear where your priority lies and it's not with me," I said.

"What do you want me to say? I've already apologized for my actions. I love you Chris. I *was* in a relationship with Michael but now we're just friends. I can't help it if Michael is still in love with me. I love him as a friend, but it's you I'm in love with."

"Then you have a funny way of showing it, Ade."

"Would you have preferred that I left Michael at the club, in the state he was in?"

"I just wished for once that you would . . ."

"Would do what Chris? What?"

"I guess it really doesn't matter now. We, or should I say I, need to work out where I go from here," I said.

"Chris let's not make this any harder than it needs to be."

"I think it's a little late for that Ade."

"Can't we get past this? There are going to be rough times but, together, we can work them out. We can't give up every time we get to a hurdle," he pleaded.

"It seems like history is repeating itself and I need to break the pattern," I said.

The waiter returned with our meals, bringing our conversation to a halt. I didn't have much of an appetite and just picked at the food in front of me, while Ade sat looking like a lost puppy. He seemed unwilling to face the inevitable, that maybe we just weren't meant to be. I'd already decided that although love was worth fighting for, there had to be a limit to the pain I would endure.

I wondered whether I was being too logical. We could always start over, but we'd been down that road before and look where it had got us. Surely we couldn't keep hurting each other like this. Ade and I spent the remainder of the meal in silence. The atmosphere was so thick with tension that one would have needed an axe to cut it.

As we left the restaurant Ade asked if he could accompany me home. I didn't trust myself, alone in my flat with him, so I declined. He seemed disappointed, but I reassured him that it didn't mean the end of our relationship. I needed time to think things over; we both did.

We stood outside the restaurant awkwardly to say goodbye. Ade pulled me close, kissing me in full view of the passers-by. Two black men kissing in the streets of Southeast London was not a common sight. I was grateful that I didn't live in that area.

Ade was brave, I had to give him that, but it was the kind of brave that made people tie a rope to their feet and jump off tall bridges for fun. That was something other people did. He must have felt desperate to pull a stunt like that in an attempt to win me back.

I was impressed but then again, sometimes a kiss was simply that; just a kiss.

After my heartbeat returned to its regular rhythm I began to speculate on the true meaning of Ade's public gesture of affection. I looked into his eyes and it didn't matter that we were two men standing in the streets holding on to each other. The clouds gathered overhead threatened to open up and let the heavens pour out. It seemed a fitting metaphor for the state I was in. I felt I was at a crossroads and would have to choose my next move wisely.

A public display of affection from Ade was pretty special. We'd never even held hands in public. Ade was concerned with portraying a masculine image. He held strong views about how black men should behave in public. What they got up to in the privacy of their own bedrooms was one thing but, since the odds were stacked against them in society, there was no mileage to be gained by adding insult to injury.

He felt his sexual identity was separate from the rest of his life and he had worked hard to foster this illusion. This gave a little more credence to Ade's public gesture. The likelihood of being seen in Greenwich by anyone we knew was relatively remote, but it didn't make it any less significant in my eyes and for this I respected him. I didn't change my mind about letting him come back to my flat, but it helped me to appreciate how important our relationship was to him.

I arrived home to find a message from Kunle. He didn't say whether he wanted me to call him back so I hesitated only briefly, before dialing his number. I desperately needed to talk to him. We had neither seen nor spoken to each other for at least a month, for us this was a very long time. Although I was calling for purely selfish reasons, I was hoping it wouldn't put any further strain on our friendship.

The telephone rang a few times before Kunle answered. As he spoke, I listened carefully, to detect from his voice whether he was ready to rekindle our friendship. He seemed pleased to hear from me and, he told me about his efforts to work things out with Aduni, for their daughter's benefit. For a moment I though he meant they were getting back together, but he explained that they needed to be on good terms for the sake of his little girl.

Ade understood that there was still a lot of healing to take place between he and his ex-wife, but he was willing to be patient, to avoid further heartache. He became animated when he spoke about his daughter, Mercedes. He asked me how I was doing, and although I was tempted to update him on the latest drama in my life, I told him that I was doing fine. He knew me well enough to realise by the tone in my voice that I wasn't.

He told me that there were so few opportunities for happiness in life, that if there was even a remote chance of finding it, then we had a responsibility to grab hold and not let go. I told him that I loved him as a friend and that I had missed him, and wanted to let him know that. Our time apart had taught me to cherish the important people in my life and to let them know it. I also told him about Dele's group, but he said that he wasn't brave enough to share his feelings with a group of strangers.

Lying in bed that night, I took a long, hard, look at my situation and wondered whether I would ever be truly happy. I couldn't ignore the common denominator in all of my failed relationships; me. Was there something about me that attracted men who were no good for me? I said yet another prayer to Saint Francis, asking for wisdom to make the right decisions and to be able to live with the consequences of my choices.

16. Tell me it ain't so

My relationship with Ade had become stagnant as I searched my heart to decide what to do. I certainly didn't want to make a decision based entirely on my emotions, nor did I want to let a good man slip through my fingers.

As I was leaving work one evening, I heard someone call out my name. I turned around to see Michael approaching me. My instinct was to get the hell out of the car park, but I knew I needed to sort it out, once and for all. I was not a violent man but *it* was going to end here.

I was sure Michael could probably see that I was anxious as he advanced toward me. He stopped a few meters away and said we needed to talk. I thought we'd done enough talking at the club but I had a feeling that if I didn't allow him to say his piece, then we'd be down this road again, soon.

He looked younger and more vulnerable that I remembered. Dressed in a pair of jeans and tee shirt he looked rough, like he'd slept in his clothes. He suggested we went somewhere quiet to sit and talk. I told him that whatever he had to say could be said there and then. He looked so pathetic, standing before me that I eventually agreed to go somewhere else, away from the prying eyes of my colleagues.

We arranged to meet the following day at 6:30pm, in the local McDonald's restaurant. I told him that I'd wait for fifteen minutes but if he didn't show up, he agreed not to contact me again. After our confrontation at the club I'd worked out that he'd been the one calling me at work.

When I eventually reached my car I was shaking but I couldn't tell if it was due to fear or anger. What was I getting myself into? It felt as though I was caught up in a whirlwind and that I had no control over which direction I would be blown in.

I rang Kunle when I got home, eager to tell him about my second encounter with Michael. There was no answer so I left a message. I felt the need to talk to someone, so I made myself a drink and called Dele.

"Chris, are you seriously considering meeting up with this crazy fool?" Dele asked.

"It seems the only way to get to the bottom of this," I said.

"But what if he puts on another show like he did at the club?"

"Then I'll have to deal with it. If you'd seen him in the car park you'd know he was in a bad way. I think he has a lot of issues and maybe one of them is the fact that he's still in love with Ade. He said he just wants to tell me his side of the story. Everybody deserves a chance to do that, don't they?" I asked.

"Just be careful. I don't want to hear on the news tomorrow that you've been sliced up by that psycho bitch."

"I feel I need to see this through Dele. Hopefully it will make things clearer for me-so I can come to a decision about Ade."

"Whatever you need to get you through this baby; just be safe and promise you'll tell me all about it afterwards. Have to run now; hot date tonight. Talk to you soon." Dele said, ending our call abruptly.

I sat contemplating Dele's advice. Meeting Michael could turn into another disaster but on the other hand it just might offer me some answers. The main complication of meeting with him would be to risk getting further embroiled in that unhealthy love triangle, but it was a risk I was prepared to take. I hoped things would seem clearer after our meeting.

I arrived early to find that Michael was already waiting for me and I wondered how long he'd been sitting there. He was nursing the remains of a strawberry milkshake and offered to get me one. I declined as I took a seat opposite him, making it clear that I wanted to get straight down to business. This was not a social call.

A few minutes later, Michael began telling me about how he'd met Ade. At times he seemed on the brink of tears as he related his story to me. They'd met about four years earlier, shortly after he'd arrived in London as a naive eighteen year old. At the time he was a support worker in a hospital in Brighton, where Ade was a junior doctor.

Michael said it was love at first sight on his part. Ade's dashing good looks and charm had won him over instantly. He didn't act on his feelings straight away because he was too shy. At the time he was going through some sexual identity issues, but his attraction to Ade was so strong that he couldn't ignore it for very long.

After Ade finished his job at that hospital they'd gone their separate ways, before any romantic developments. They met again a few months later, at a mutual friend's party. This time Michael was much more confident and left nothing to chance. He said it was one of the hardest, but most rewarding things he'd ever had to do; disclosing his feelings to Ade. He believed that fate had brought them together a second time, and was pleasantly surprised to learn that Ade was single and interested in dating him.

He had fallen in love with Ade, who was far more experienced and had literally 'charmed the pants off him.' Ade quickly took control of their relationship and they never looked back. Although he had a Muslim background and Ade was Christian, Michael had not allowed their religious differences to get in the way of their relationship. They seemed perfect for each other.

Ade encouraged Michael to train as a nurse and, about six months into their relationship, they moved in together. To their families, they were two friends sharing a flat. To their gay friends, the arrangement was a match made in heaven. They loved each other and made plans for, what promised to be, a very bright future.

At that point Michael burst into tears and I found myself consoling him, not because I felt particularly sorry for him, but because he was starting to draw attention to us and I was beginning to get embarrassed.

After composing himself he continued with his story. The relationship had appeared to be fine, until rumors about Ade sleeping around, had surfaced.

I thought, 'well nothing's changed there.'

At first he had difficulty believing the rumours, mainly because Ade had convinced him that the people spreading them were malicious queens, trying to ruin their relationship. He'd bought Ade's story-because it was easier to do so than face the alternative. There'd been no obvious changes in their relationship and he was still head over heels in love with Ade.

One day he received a call from Yomi, who claimed to have slept with Ade. At first he didn't believe him; but, on closer inspection, Yomi's story seemed credible. He had sensed Michael's reluctance to believe him and had told him details about the couple's bedroom that only someone who'd been there would know.

Michael was stunned by the revelation. Yomi had tried to give the impression that he was being helpful by informing Michael about his cheating boyfriend-but Michael was no fool, he had known what the true motive was.

When Michael confronted Ade, an argument ensued that evolved into a fist fight. Ade later promised to change but things were never the same. Michael became suspicious about Ade and continually questioned their relationship. To him, Ade had been a knight in shining armour, the apple of his eye. He felt betrayed after putting up with a lot, including Ade's marriage.

I hadn't realized that I'd repeated the word "marriage" quite so loudly, until I noticed all eyes were on us. I started coughing and struggled to breathe. My chest felt tight, my heart was racing and my skin suddenly felt clammy. I was having my first panic attack. I couldn't believe what I'd heard.

Michael quickly got me a glass of water, and began apologizing. He thought that I had known about Ade's wedding. It had been the reason for Ade's trip to Nigeria last Christmas. His family had arranged for him to be married in Nigeria, where his wife would remain until the immigration legalities were completed. They planned to have another ceremony in the UK when his bride joined him. In his role of best man, Michael bore the unenviable responsibility of arranging the bachelor party.

Ade planned to continue his relationship with Michael on the down low. It would be relatively easy for Ade to explain the long hours away from home. After all he'd probably have to work longer hours to earn enough to meet his increased financial responsibilities as a husband.

Michael continued talking, but I hardly heard a word he said. I felt like I was drowning and got up to leave. I must have stood up too suddenly, because the next thing I remembered was Michael kneeling over me, asking me if I was ok. Obviously I wasn't. He helped me to my seat and held my head between my knees. Someone brought me a hot drink.

Michael said that when he first found out about me, a few months ago, he'd thought that it wouldn't last. He believed I was only a minor distraction; like all the others. When Ade told him that he was in love with me, he felt his world had collapsed; but he had invested too much in the relationship to let it go without a fight. He refused to believe it was over.

Ade then began spending a lot of time away from home. In the early days, Ade had told him he was working extra shifts to earn some additional cash for the wedding. He had believed him, until he realized it was the same excuse that they'd planned to use with Ade's new bride.

It hadn't been difficult for him to find me, since Ade and I worked together. He had followed me from work more than once and, when he saw us together, it reminded him of what he once had. He'd seen a look in Ade's eyes that confirmed his suspicions. He couldn't compete with love, so he began drowning his sorrows in alcohol, while inventing ways to remain in Ade's life, if only on a platonic basis.

He used alcohol to numb his pain and, after a particularly long binge session, he had attempted to take his own life. At the time he felt he had nothing more to live for, so he took a large overdose of tablets in the hope that he'd go to sleep and never wake up. Ade found him lying unconscious on the kitchen floor. This had been a wake-up call for him; he also thought that he'd dealt with the situation-until he saw us together at the nightclub.

He hadn't meant to create a scene but said that Ade had caused him further embarrassment, by bringing me to the club where several of his friends were present. They were thought of as an ideal couple by most of their friends. Ade had firmly dispelled that myth by turning up at the club with his new lover. He looked away as the tears began to roll down his face.

Having partially recovered from the earlier shock, I found myself trying to find the right words to comfort Michael. After all, we were both inextricably bound together. There were more similarities in our experiences with Ade than there were differences. It was clear that Ade was looking out for number one and it was time that the rest of us followed his example. Michael and I went our separate ways, each of us a little more jaded for the experience. It was clear to me what I had to do.

When I arrived home there were three messages on my answer machine. I deleted them all without finding out who had left them, and ran myself a warm bath. It was time for Ade to pay.

17. Just friends

After careful consideration I decided to keep my appointment with Tore. It had been two days since my meeting with Michael and I hadn't heard from Ade, despite leaving him several messages. I deduced that he must have found out about my little rendezvous and needed time to work out how he'd get out of this one.

I noticed Tore sitting in the corner of the café as I walked in. He was casually dressed and looked relaxed. A broad smile appeared across his face as he rose to shake my outstretched hand. His grip was firm but there was also a sense of intimacy in his touch. As he took a seat, he told me how pleased he was to see me again.

I pretended that everything was fine as Tore tried to put me at ease.

"I've been thinking about you a lot since our first meeting Chris."

"Oh really," I said.

"Surprised?" he asked.

"Surprised that you were thinking about me or surprised that you decided to tell me you were thinking about me?" I asked.

"Do you always answer a question with another question?" he asked, smiling.

"I'm just a bit curious that you were thinking about me."

"You seemed pretty upset and, to tell you the truth, I was a little worried . . ."

"That I'd do something silly," I interrupted.

"No, I guess I was worried that it was something serious. Just wished I could have helped more, that's all."

"Thanks for your concern and, as you can see for yourself, I'm better now," I said hastily.

During the two hours we spent in the café I learned that Tore lived in West London and that he was single, following the end of a difficult relationship. He said that he'd been single for a few months but there was no indication whether his last relationship had been with a man or a woman.

Tore managed to make me forget my disastrous love life for a short time. He continued paying me compliments, treating me with respect and dignity. I felt no sexual pressure from him and quickly relaxed in his company. I was well and truly intrigued by him.

Before leaving, he asked if we could meet again. Before I had a chance to censor my thoughts, I asked, if he was looking for a new project. He seemed genuinely hurt by my insensitive comment. He didn't deserve that. He'd been a decent guy and I was projecting my issues onto him.

My resolve to avoid burdening Tore with my problems melted away and I began to pour out my heart to him. He listened intently to every word I said, and was silent for a long time after I finished talking. So now that he knew I was gay, I searched for a reaction but there was none. I hoped my sexuality was not going to be an obstacle to us becoming friends.

Eventually he spoke, saying that although it felt really bad at present, that it would be less difficult in time. His remark was insightful and empathetic. I felt my eyes begin to sting as the tears threatened to come flooding out. He reached across the table to touch my hand and, in the process, he touched my heart. We agreed to meet again soon.

When I arrived home I felt emotionally exhausted. I pressed the play button on the answer machine and Ade's voice came to life. He apologized, blaming a busy work schedule for not getting back to me sooner. He promised to call again soon.

The next voice on the machine startled me. It was a message from Tore. He said he'd read somewhere that people came into our lives for a reason, a season or a lifetime. When we figured out which it was we would know exactly what to do. He also said that from the little he had seen of me, he believed I had the inner-strength to make the right decisions for me. From the time on the answer machine, he must have called soon after we'd left the café.

I decided to take a leave of absence from work because I needed some time on my own-time to heal and plan my revenge for Ade. I wanted to prevent him from ever doing this to anyone else. That night I cried myself to sleep, but made a promise that it would be the last time I cried for Ade.

18. The blues

After a week of sleepless nights I visited my doctor. Dr Patterson was able to tell that my insomnia was a sign of a much deeper issue. I was struggling to cope with everyday activities, but I felt too humiliated to tell her the full story. How could I explain to her that I had the classic symptoms of a fool in love? Instead, I told her that I'd been under a lot of stress and needed time off work. She gave me a course of sleeping tablets and a 'sicknote' for the next two weeks. I promised to return to see her if my sleep pattern didn't change.

I didn't tell her that I'd lost my appetite, I felt low in mood or that I was crying all the time. I knew the signs of depression, but felt powerless to do anything about it. I felt I was sinking, ever deeper, into an emotional abyss.

The next few days were spent in a dimly-lit flat, with the curtains drawn. I unplugged the telephone and stopped taking an interest in everything, including my personal hygiene. I spent long periods in bed feeling sorry for myself and thinking about going to sleep-never to wake up. On the few occasions that I fell asleep, the peace was short-lived because of the nightmares that plagued me.

I had a recurring dream of running down a street and into a building, several stories high. I didn't recognize who, was pursuing me and, just as I got to the top of the building, my escape would be blocked. I would become desperate, feeling helplessly trapped. I would usually wake up at this point, drenched in sweat and breathing heavily.

After I'd had this dream a few times I didn't need a psychoanalyst to tell me it was about avoidance of something unpleasant. I needed to confront my fears, but I didn't have the will power or the strength, to pick myself up off the floor. Everything seemed like an enormous obstacles.

My mind began playing tricks on me. At times I felt as though I wasn't alone in the flat but, when I went looking, I wouldn't find anyone. I would hear hysterical laughter inside the flat, only to then realize it was coming from me.

It was during these times that fear replaced the hopelessness I felt. I feared that I was truly loosing my mind. My experience as a psychiatric nurse had taught me there was a very fine line between sanity and insanity; I couldn't help thinking that maybe I had crossed it.

Everyday seemed more difficult than the one before. It became increasingly easier to simply let time pass me by. I kept wishing that my pain would ease, but the image of me being taken for a fool was just too difficult to get out of my head.

My fears were gradually replaced by anger at having allowed someone to use me in this way. I didn't deserve to be treated like this. The rage which burned within me fuelled my determination to make Ade pay for what he had done.

One day, I awoke from a particularly distressing dream in which my mother had died. This frightened me, even more than my own demise. I realized, there and then, I could either allow Ade to continue destroying me, or I could take back the control I had relinquished.

Firstly, I needed to stop feeling sorry for myself; I was in a bad situation, sure, but I was stronger than this. I dragged myself out of bed and into the bath. I plugged in the telephone and started dialing. I heard my mother's voice and a wave of relief swept over me. She was ok.

I felt so emotionally overwhelmed upon hearing her voice that I began sobbing uncontrollably. I heard the panic in her voice as she asked me what was wrong. I wanted to tell her everything, so she could make it all better, but I didn't. It wasn't fair to burden her with my troubles.

My mother had long suspected that I was gay and, although we had never talked about it, she had resigned herself to the fact that until men could impregnate one another, she wouldn't be getting any grandchildren from me.

Despite the issue of my sexuality, which might well have distanced most other black parents, she never stopped loving me. This was probably because she felt she had to give me more love, to combat the bigotry I was likely to face in life as a black, gay, man. She once told me, that after ten hours of labor, she took one look at me and fell in love; completely forgetting the pain she'd just endured.

I could hear the genuine concern in her voice as she said, "baby I know you're hurting, I only wish I could be there to make it better."

These words jolted me back to reality. I lied and told her that I'd been under a lot of stress at work. I'm sure she saw right through my story, as she always did, but she didn't challenge me. Instead, she said that whatever was causing my pain would soon be over and she reminded me of one of her favourite sayings; 'and this too shall pass'.

Whilst talking to my mother I heard a knock at the door, followed by my name being called. I put my mother on hold as I answered the door. Standing in front of me were two Police officers. I must have looked like shit; and the flat was a mess. They appeared uneasy as they explained the reason for their presence.

Kunle had contacted them when he was unable to reach me at work or at home. He'd been to the flat to check up on me but had become worried when his key would not work because of the deadbolt. I told the officers that I'd been away for a few days and that my telephone was broken. I reassured them I was fine and promised to call Kunle. They hesitated briefly before leaving.

After they left, I continued my conversation with my mother. She asked who was at the door. I lied again and told her it was a neighbour returning some items he'd borrowed. She asked if I was going to be alright, and I answered "yes" before promising to call her again the next day.

I made two more telephone calls. The first was to Kunle, to let him know I was OK. He apologized for having called the police, but said that he'd been worried about me. We needed to talk further, but that would have to wait until another time.

My next call was to Tore. I breathed a sigh of relief when I realized that he wasn't in his office. Although I had his mobile and home numbers, I left a message with his secretary.

Tore called me back a few minutes later. He didn't sound like his usual calm self. He seemed relieved when I told him I was OK. He'd tried calling me at home several times but, had thought my telephone was out of order. He had no other way of getting in touch and feared he might never hear from me again. I promised to explain further when we next saw each other; we then made plans to meet soon.

While sorting through a pile of unopened mail I came across an envelope with familiar handwriting on the front. It was a letter from Ade. My heart raced as I read his words.

'Dear Chris,

I know I have no right to contact you, but I felt I owed you an explanation. More importantly I owe you an apology. There are no words that I could use to tell you just how sorry I am for hurting you, but I want to try.

I had hoped to apologize to you in person, but there was no answer when I came to your flat recently. I don't blame you for not wanting to see me, but I can't let you carry on thinking that I never loved you.

It was never my intention to hurt you, but it seems like I keep hurting the people who mean the most to me. Whatever you take away from our time together, know that I did, and still do, love you. I always will.

The first day I saw you, I knew you were special. I just didn't know how special you were, or that you would affect my life in such an amazing way. Things between Michael and I died a long time ago but I stayed in that situation because I was a coward. I'm not trying to make any excuses, I do still care about Michael in my own way-I'm just not in love with him anymore.

You helped me believe that relationships between men could work, as well as helping me to face some harsh truths about myself. I know that I'm weak for giving into my parents' wishes, and I don't deserve your forgiveness for being dishonest with you. I just hope you can find it in your heart not to hate me. The guilt I feel for having hurt you so badly will be punishment enough.

You and I come from different cultures, so I don't expect you to fully understand the pressures I have been under, to be the son that my parents expect me to be. Somewhere in the back of my mind I hoped that I could still have you in my life, even though I had to fulfil my obligations to my family.

Chris you have left an impression on my heart that will stay with me forever. I hope in time your pain will ease and you will find it in your heart to forgive me. I know that I might be hoping for too much, but maybe one day we could become friends again.

Chris, I'm sorry I wasn't the man you deserved.

Eternally hopeful and still in love with you,
Ade.'

Even out of sight, Ade was still able to affect me. I started sobbing loudly and felt I was heading right back to where I'd just been. He was right about one thing; he couldn't be the man I deserved to be with. I needed to move on with my life and stop settling for less than I deserved.

19. New beginnings

The telephone rang a few times before I picked up the receiver. There was a tone of concern in Tore's voice. We had been due to meet earlier. It wasn't like me to forget to call him back but I had a lot on my mind. I apologized and told him I couldn't go into it over the telephone, but agreed to meet for coffee the next day.

"Chris, are you sure we can't meet this evening?"

"Something's come up. It's probably just a storm in a tea cup, but tomorrow will be better," I said.

"Call me if you change your mind," he said.

"I'll do that," I said. "And I'll see you tomorrow evening. Good bye Tore."

"See you tomorrow," he said.

When I returned to work, everyone treated me with kid gloves. I'd only been away for two weeks but it seemed longer. They could tell that something was wrong, but no one probed me for details. I didn't volunteer any information. If life threw me lemons, then I was going to make lemonade.

My friend Dele always said; that when a door closed, somewhere a window opened. This was his way of explaining that out of adversity and disappointment, opportunities to grow and learn important lessons could come. I wondered whether Tore was my window of opportunity. What I needed was the love and support of a friend-and that's what he appeared to be offering.

It was mid-week, so the restaurant was relatively quiet. I looked around and noticed there were only a few people eating. As I waited for Tore, I felt excited by the prospect of seeing him again. He was punctual and, noticeably, without his trademark smile. As he approached the table I stood up to shake his hand, which was clammy, and betrayed his cool exterior. He ordered a portion of Bar-B-Que chicken with two side orders. I didn't have much of an appetite so I ordered another drink.

"Aren't you going to have something to eat?" Tore asked.

"I'm not very hungry," I said, "but you can go ahead and order a meal for yourself."

"I had to work through lunch today and my last appointment ran over time. I thought about going home to change, but realized I'd be late if I did," he said. "I didn't want to keep you waiting. I know how I hate to be kept waiting. I could have called but I didn't want to stress you further. I know you've been through a difficult time recently."

Tore was rambling, this was unusual for him.

"Thank you for coming after such a long day at work," I said.

"I'm happy to be here."

The food didn't take long to arrive and Tore ate the tasty-looking chicken with some urgency. Between mouthfuls of food, he asked me about what was on my mind. I felt sufficiently secure with him to tell him the whole story. The only thing I didn't mention was the letter from Ade. I told him that I was convinced that gay men were a special breed of dogs and that I planned to stay as far away from them as I could. I waited for a response to this statement but he continued eating.

When he finished eating, Tore put down the cutlery and looked directly at me. He told me he had a confession to make. As I sat there, trying to work out whether to run or stand still, I hoped it wouldn't jeopardize our friendship. I was a little thin on the ground when it came to dependable friends. He was one of only a few people I felt comfortable talking to about my feelings, especially since Kunle and I were not yet back up to speed.

"You remember I told you about my last relationship and how it ended," he said

I nodded.

"What I didn't tell you was that my partner was male. I could see why you'd think that all gay men are bastards, but I want you to know that there are still a few good ones out there," he said, pointing to himself.

"So what was up with all the secrecy?" I asked.

"Well, it wasn't really a secret. I didn't mention it because it didn't seem important at the time. When we met, I was genuinely concerned about you and simply wanted to help. Then my feelings changed but I felt it was also important that we became friends first."

I remained silent as Tore shared his feelings with me. The tables were turned, and I had assumed the role of listener as he continued.

"When I couldn't get in touch with you I panicked. I knew I had to be honest about my feelings with myself and with you," he said.

The waiter returned to take away the empty plate, causing a brief pause in conversation.

"I realized that my feelings for you are more than just friendship," Tore continued.

Tore must have noticed the panic in my eyes, or maybe my silence spoke volumes, because he added, "I'm not trying to start something with you, but I do owe you honesty. It's my stuff and I'll have to deal with it. I just don't want it to jeopardise our friendship. I'm not asking if you feel the same way about me; because I know you're going through a tough time at present and probably the last thing you need is to start thinking of entering another relationship. Maybe you're not even attracted to me in that way. All I'm saying is that honesty is important in any relationship, platonic or not."

I was confused. It was all too much to take in.

"The last thing I want to do is to add to the pressure you're already under Chris. I'd like us to continue being friends. I know this isn't the reason for meeting today, but I felt the need to be honest with you."

I was speechless when Tore finished speaking. I appreciated his honesty, but this was a lot to deal with. He sat waiting for my response and, for a brief moment, I thought about getting up and running out of the restaurant. My instinct was to get far away from all the confusion in my life. Instead, I chose to be honest with him too. I owed it to him.

"Thank you for being honest with me Tore, and for trusting me with your feelings. My immediate response to what you've just told me is, I don't know how I feel about it all."

"That's OK Chris. All I want is to be whatever you need me to be. I'll understand if you don't feel the same way; I still want to be your friend. But I couldn't continue to do that if I felt unable to be entirely honest with you."

"I appreciate that Tore, but if I was in your place I'd want to know where I stood. What I'm saying, is that I need time to think about all of this."

"So are we still good?" he asked.

"Yeah we're fine," I said, but I couldn't help wondering if things would ever be the same between us.

I never really got a chance to tell him about my disappearance. It didn't matter; we'd had enough drama for one evening.

On my way home I reflected on the evening's events. Sure, my faith in relationships with men had been shaken, but I was gay; and no amount of willing it away would ever change my attraction to men. Just then, however, I needed romance in my life like I needed a bullet to the head. I placed my situation with Tore on the back burner, because I had a much bigger fish to fry.

When I arrived home I called Kunle and arranged to meet him the next day. I wasn't ready to tell him about my plans for revenge, but I planned to sound him out for any information about Ade's wedding. It would prove to be an integral part to the effective execution of my plan. While talking to Kunle, I heard the call-waiting signal and we said, 'goodbye.'

"So what's up with you, bitch?" I heard the caller ask.

Hidden somewhere in Dele's unique brand of humor was genuine concern.

"I thought that maybe you'd found yourself some new trade and the two of you were shacked up with a 'do not disturb' sign on the door."

"I'm sorry you couldn't get hold of me Dele. I was just dealing with some shit; and it took longer than I'd anticipated," I said.

"But what's so important to make you disconnect your telephone line, or did you forget to pay the bill this month again?" he asked.

"It's just a little *man trouble* that I have to sort out," I answered.

"Are you OK now?" he asked.

"Yes I am fine; and thanks for caring about me you crazy bitch. At least now I know you have a heart," I said, laughing.

"So all this time you thought I was heartless?" he asked playfully.

I started to tell Dele all about the meeting with Michael and finding out the truth, or at least another version of it; but I felt that discussing it over the phone wasn't a great idea, so we arranged to meet after the weekend.

* * *

The phone rang and I was surprised to be speaking with John. I hadn't heard from him since the New Year's Eve party, several months ago. I quickly found out the reason for him contacting me, when he began talking about his new boyfriend. I was amazed that he actually thought I gave a shit about his love life.

He announced that he and Fabrice were dating. Fabrice was a French, ballet dancer, barely out of his teens. They'd met in a bar in Soho after work one evening and, according to John, Fabrice was 'absolutely gorgeous', if somewhat temperamental. They had exchanged rings at a private dinner party.

John continued talking, but I'd long lost interest in what he had to say. I realized that the conversation was more for his benefit than it was for mine. He finally got to the point of his conversation. He wanted to introduce Fabrice to his friends and invited me to a dinner party to that end. There were two things wrong with his statement. Firstly, I was no longer his friend and, secondly, I wasn't interested in meeting Fabrice anytime soon.

He told me about an intimate party to celebrate his boyfriend's birthday and I thought, 'you sad fuck'. Not once had he asked how I was doing or how my relationship was going. Of course I was working on the unlikely assumption that he actually cared about anyone but himself. I had no intention of going to his party in this, or any other, lifetime. I told him I'd think about it, before ending the conversation abruptly.

* * *

The countdown had begun. All those who trespassed against me were about to pay; and pay dearly they would. I had surprised myself by turning into a bitter, cynical, old man, who was set on revenge. I'd heard that revenge was a dish best served cold and I intended to find out for myself if it was true.

I was excited to see Kunle. So much had happened in my life and, maybe, in his as well, that it seemed much longer than a few weeks since I'd laid eyes on him. I noticed he'd gained a little weight and had grown a goatee beard, it suited him.

After greeting each other we changed plans and headed for somewhere less noisy, where it would be easier to talk. The weather was lovely and it was still early enough to have a few hours of daylight. I hadn't invited Kunle to my flat because I felt it would've been awkward, for the both of us.

We drove to Richmond Park, one of my favorite places to hang out. It didn't take us long to fall right back into our old routine. The sun was setting when we arrived at the park. The leaves had begun to change colour and the light from the setting sun cast a golden hue over the entire park. We got out of the car and walked toward the open landscape. There were reindeers grazing leisurely in the distance; it was a beautiful scene.

I asked Kunle how he was doing and he told me he was hanging in there. I searched for some comforting words.

"Kunle, I want you to know that God never gives us more than we can bear. Even when it seems too much, He'll see us through," I said, eventually.

"I understand what you're saying Chris, but surely, God knows that I am only human," he said smiling weakly.

It was Kunle's turn to find out how I was doing as we stopped walking and sat beneath a huge tree.

"So, tell me what's happening with you," he said.

"I'm on the mend. It'll take some time, but eventually the wounds will heal. I believe that the worst is over."

"I've been consumed by my own problems lately, but I want you to know, that I'm here for you," he said.

"I know and I'm grateful for your support," I said.

We continued talking and I told him about Ade's letter. I had come through the fire and I was still standing. Kunle was impressed by my new found confidence. I hadn't mentioned to him that after reading Ade's letter I felt like someone had plunged a knife into my heart and drained all the blood. Or that I was filled with a rage so fierce that it could consume the park we were in with flames.

I needed to find out more about Ade's wedding but knew I'd have to approach the topic cautiously. A look of surprise appeared across his face when I asked about the wedding. I quickly reassured him that I wished Ade only the best and that I had no intentions of standing in the way of his happiness. He told me the wedding was scheduled to take place in seven weeks. I didn't want to risk arousing his suspicion by probing further, so I changed the topic of conversation. I only had a short time to execute my plan.

* * *

Getting information from Kunle about Ade's wedding was turning into a painfully slow process, and I didn't have much time to play with. I decided to speed things up and go directly to the source.

Ade answered the phone just as I was about to hang up. There was a brief silence before I heard that familiar voice. A part of me wanted to abandon the call, but I'd come too far to give up now. He seemed surprised to hear from me and was, momentarily, speechless.

I took a deep breath before asking him how he was doing. I needed to find a way to convince him that I was willing to put the past behind me. For my plan to work, I had to make him believe that I wasn't yet totally over him but, also, that I wasn't bitter about our relationship. I told him that I'd done a lot of introspection and had realized that if I continued carrying around all that hate, the person who would be most affected by it would be me.

He asked if I had forgiven him for hurting me. I swallowed hard and told him that I knew that causing me pain had not been his intention. The tears stung my eyes as the words escaped my lips. We'd both been in a difficult place and, although the situation could have been handled differently, there was no point crying over spilled milk. I urged him to strive for happiness, reassuring him that he deserved it.

I wished him every success and suggested that he forgive himself, so he could move on with his life. Oh Lord, I was turning into Oprah. He remained silent as I continued talking. I was far from believing the crap I was spouting. When I thought he'd had enough I changed the subject, asking him if he was excited about his wedding.

I wondered whether I'd gone too far when I heard him go quiet. I quickly followed up by saying that I hoped that now he was getting married, he wouldn't feel under so much pressure from his parents. I suggested meeting for lunch, when he felt ready. The line was thrown; all I had to do now was wait to see if he would take the bait.

I ran the risk of making Ade suspicious but was gambling on him still having feelings for me. After a brief hesitation, he agreed that it might be a good idea to meet. He said it would give him an opportunity to apologize to me in person. A wave of relief swept over me but this was soon replaced by anxiety. Talking over the telephone was one thing, meeting him in person was an entirely different matter.

I didn't have to wait long. Two days later Ade and I were meeting for lunch. I was already seated at a table in the restaurant when Ade joined me. He looked as handsome as ever, wearing a pair of bum-hugging jeans and a designer T-shirt under a sports jacket. He shook my hand before sitting down. He still managed to excite me-even after all I'd been through. I avoided looking at him, because I was sure that if I held his stare too long, he'd read my thoughts.

Ade needed to be sufficiently relaxed to let his guard down so I ordered some wine with our lunch. We talked about his new job and I brought him up to speed on the latest gossip from the hospital where I worked. After his second glass of wine Ade began to relax and I was poised to start reeling-in the fishing line. I took advantage of the fact that he was never one to hold his liquor. I played it cool, waiting for the right opportunity to make my next move.

It didn't take long for Ade's charm to surface. He began smiling more and started flirting openly with me. It amazed me, that he still sent my pulse racing. This realisation saddened me a little; it was further evidence of his hold on me and it was obvious that I was not yet over him. A frightening thought crossed my mind; was I really that weak?

I gently guided the conversation to his wedding. The change in him was sudden and unmistakable. His guard went up and with every word I uttered I felt a stabbing pain in my side, but still I persevered. I asked whether he was looking forward to the big day. The tone in his voice changed from happy to anxious as he responded, telling me everything was taken care of. I had to think quickly, I needed to throw him off the scent. I told him that I had started dating; it had the desired effect.

After a period of deafening silence, he asked, "Is it Kunle?"

"No. You don't know this person," I said.

"Is he Nigerian?" he asked.

My earlier emotions were replaced by anger as I answered, "No he's not."

"Is he white then?"

"Does that really matter? He's a nice guy and I like him a lot," I said.

"But do you love him?" he asked.

"His father is Italian and his mother is African," I answered.

"You didn't answer my question?"

"I know," I said.

"Let's make a toast to each other's future," he said.

"To happiness," I added.

"Are you really happy for me Chris, or are you just saying so to be nice?" he asked.

I looked at him and said, "I'm happy now and if there's a chance for you to find happiness as well, then I say you should grab hold of it with both hands."

A look of sadness appeared across his face and for a brief moment I thought he would start crying. He looked away as he apologized for hurting me. A few minutes later I excused myself and made my way to the bathroom where I burst into tears. These were tears of sadness *and* anger. Sadness; because somewhere deep in my heart I still loved Ade. Anger; because I'd promised myself that I wouldn't shed any more tears over him.

When I rejoined Ade he could tell that I'd been crying. I reassured him that I still loved him, but knew deep down that we were not meant to be together. What we shared was over and I would cherish the memories. The funny thing was that some of what I was saying was actually true. He reached across the table to touch my hand. I knew that if he believed I still had feelings for him, then he would think that I was incapable of revenge.

After leaving the restaurant he walked me to my car, which was parked a few streets away. We hugged before saying goodbye. He said he was glad he'd seen me, and wished me happiness. My performance had been so convincing that I'd begun to believe it myself. He started to walk away but stopped, abruptly, and turned to face me.

"Chris I have something to ask you. You don't have to if you don't want to, but I was wondering if you'd come to the wedding."

I resisted the temptation to respond immediately and let a few seconds pass by before saying, "thanks for the invite Ade, but I'll need to check it out with my boyfriend and get back to you."

"That's cool. It was really great seeing you Chris."

The plan had worked but I couldn't rejoice. There was a lot more work to be done. Driving home, I thought about how sorry Ade was going to be. I had to be brutal if my plan was going to succeed, and I wondered if I had it in me to be that devious. Everyone would remember that day for a long time, not least of all Ade.

20. Someone to watch over me

Tore and I had arranged to meet in the West End to see a movie. On the way to meet him, I reflected on the night we first met; it was an amazing turn of fate. I'd been lied to, cheated on and treated badly by men so many times that it seemed a natural state of existence for me. I was still attracted to them, sexually but it was like a diabetic who liked sweets; they just weren't good for me.

Two positive things happened to me the night I met Tore. The first was the realization that Ade was not the one for me. I would never find Mr. Right if I was still holding on to Mr. Wrong. The confrontation in the nightclub provided me with the confidence I needed to take control of my love life. It forced me to take a long, hard look at my situation so that I could change it.

The second positive thing to happen to me that fateful night was meeting Tore. He'd restored some of my faith in men. It would've been easy to walk on by but he hadn't and that made a world of difference. Kunle was still my best friend, but he couldn't be there for me in the way I needed him to be.

Tore was already waiting for me when I arrived in Leicester Square. He suggested we have a coffee before the movie. I told him that it was a beautiful autumn day and seemed a pity to spend it in a cinema, especially when we really needed to talk. He agreed and said he knew just the place; a little Italian restaurant outside of London.

We chatted as we headed toward the southwestern part of the city. I asked him for details about the restaurant, instead he invited me to relax and enjoy the ride. Tore talked about his hobbies and dreams. It was the first time that he'd divulged so much information about himself. Usually he was the one listening to me, going on about my endless problems. It felt nice to have the roles reversed.

When I realised we were approaching the city limits, I assumed we were close to the restaurant. I was surprised, therefore, when we found ourselves on the motorway heading towards Brighton. Tore eventually told me that the restaurant, which belonged to a relative, was in Brighton. He also wanted to prove to me that his cousin's restaurant served the best Spaghetti Cabonara I'd ever tasted.

The weather was great for the time of year; the sun shone brilliantly in the cloudless sky. It took us less than an hour to reach Brighton.

There were a lot of people strolling along the promenade, it made for a carnival atmosphere that seemed to be infectious. It appeared we weren't the only ones taking advantage of the fine weather. It was too early to have dinner so, after parking the car we walked along the beach, just as the wind started to pick up.

Brighton was only a few minutes outside of London, yet it seemed to be a totally different place. It also helped that a large part of the population in Brighton was gay-there was a sense of safety in numbers.

After about half an hour, Tore stopped walking and turned to me. He hesitated briefly, before asking me if I'd given much thought to what he'd said the last time we met. I told him that I had, but that I was unsure of exactly what he wanted from me. I was attracted to him but I was coming out of a bad situation, the last thing I needed was another boyfriend.

We couldn't go back to the way things were. I valued Tore's presence in my life. His body language told me he felt rejected, so I made a decision and followed my heart-which was telling me to give love another chance.

The words had scarcely left my mouth when Tore embraced me. As we held on to each other, he told me that he'd already fallen in love with me and was prepared to wait, however long it took, for me to feel the same way about him. He felt confident that he could restore my faith in love.

He wanted to kiss me and, in a slightly startled voice, I asked, "right here?" He told me that he couldn't think of a better way to celebrate the happiest day of his life. Without waiting for my answer, and in the middle of the busy promenade, we kissed passionately. I let go of my inhibitions and surrendered to the moment.

I was almost afraid that I was tempting fate, by allowing myself to believe that I'd met Mr. Right. Look how things turned out the last time I did. How many chances did we have of finding true love? I had no answers to this question, but I remained hopeful that I was capable of loving more than one person in my lifetime.

Tore and I had an intimate meal in his cousin's restaurant and he was right, the food was great. There seemed to be a glow about him, whilst I remained cautiously optimistic about the future. I'd been down that road before, where I thought nothing could go wrong. That false sense of security had cost me dearly but I hoped that I'd learned my lesson. As we sat looking out onto the seafront, I allowed myself to believe that I could be happy in a relationship with a man once again.

* * *

Tore and I had spoken most days, after returning from Brighton, but hadn't seen each other. I didn't feel like being on my own and so asked him if he wanted some company too. He perked up immediately, inviting me to his flat. I packed an overnight bag before leaving for his place.

Tore greeted me at the door, wearing just a vest and a pair of pajama bottoms. He was more muscular than I'd imagined. I entered his flat and we hugged. It felt great. As we embraced I inhaled his manly scent, which left me feeling slightly intoxicated.

He disappeared briefly before joining me on the sofa, carrying a hot drink for each of us. We talked about our respective days, but I had difficulty getting our earlier conversation out of my head.

"Tore, I'm sorry about my behavior earlier. I didn't mean to offend you," I said.

"I understand what you meant to say. I was just a little surprised that you thought I'd see this as an opportunity to take advantage of you. I thought you knew me better than that," he said.

"I do want to make love to you, but I want it to happen when the time is right. I didn't want you thinking I had orchestrated this to have my way with you," I said.

"You can have your way with me anytime," he laughed. "I'm ready whenever you are; and, when it finally happens, it will be at the right time-whether that time is tonight, or sometime in the future. You're worth waiting for."

We enjoyed the rest of the evening watching one of my favourite films-Pretty Woman-all the while, Tore lay on the sofa with his head in my lap. When we eventually retired to bed, I realized that I'd never before been in his bedroom. I was pleasantly surprised to find that it was large, and nicely decorated. There was a masculine feel to the décor from good use of a black and white theme.

When I walked back into the bedroom from the en suite bathroom, I noticed that Tore had packed my things away in a drawer. As I got ready to join him, I wondered whether I'd be able to stand up to the challenge of sharing a bed with a half-naked, fine-looking brother, like Tore, without giving into temptation.

I climbed into bed and snuggled up close to him. He had a mischievous grin on his face; I soon found out why. Tore didn't try to hide his erection, which tented his loose-fitting pajama bottoms. He'd taken off the vest, to reveal a smooth, muscular, chest.

Most nights I slept naked, but on this occasion I demonstrated a little modesty by keeping on my underwear. I rested my head on Tore's chest and listened to him. The sound of his voice, resonating in his chest, was comforting. We talked for a long time and he told me about his dream of sharing his life with someone special, someone like me.

I too dreamed of finding love, but I'd learned that sometimes love hurt. Tore said that he understood that I'd been hurt before and promised never to intentionally hurt me. I was spooning him when he turned around to face me, saying, "Chris you deserve to be loved, and don't let anyone tell you differently. You're a beautiful man and I love you. Sometimes love hurts, but sometimes it can be amazing as well."

I desperately wanted to believe him. I knew that I deserved to be loved by someone who was capable of loving only me. After all, I was willing to offer the same to someone. I needed a man who respected me as a person, and who didn't feel threatened by me. So far it seemed that I'd found these qualities in Tore. The last thing I heard before drifting peacefully off to sleep that night was Tore, telling me how much he was going to enjoy loving me.

The next morning I woke up lazily. I instinctively looked over to the other side of the bed, it was empty. I heard music coming from the kitchen and recognised Tore's voice singing along to the radio. A few moments later, he appeared at the bedroom door. There was no offer of breakfast in bed, but the sight of a hot man, inviting me to follow him to the kitchen, was the next best thing.

Over breakfast, Tore told me that he planned to work from home.

"Would you do me the honour of spending the day with me young man?" he asked.

"I'd love to, but I'm not sure you'd get much work done," I said.

"That's a chance I'm willing to take, and besides, spending time with my man is more important to me right now than any paperwork."

"Well don't say I didn't warn you when you get very little done," I said.

"Come here baby," he said, opening his arms to welcome me. "You can distract me any day of the week and twice on Sundays. As long as you're with me nothing else matters. Did you have any plans for today?" he asked.

"I need to get some food shopping done and after that I'm all yours-to do with as you wish," I said.

"Be careful," he said, "I just might take you up on that offer."

I contemplated telling Tore about Ade's wedding, but decided against it. Things were about to get messy and he didn't deserve to be placed in a difficult position. At times I was surprised that I could feel warmth and love for Tore, whilst still holding on to the feelings of resentment towards Ade.

Tore changed his plans to catch up on his paperwork and instead we went to IKEA to get a few things for his office. I noticed that there were a lot of cute gay couples shopping. Tore told me he had a surprise planned for the evening. My mind raced with anticipation.

The day passed quickly and before we knew it we were back at his flat, making out on the sofa. I knew that we couldn't go all day without physically demonstrating our affection for each other. He lit some scented candles in the bathroom and filled the bath with bubbles. At first I thought the bath was for him, so I offered to wash his back. He told me that wasn't what he had in mind.

He placed a towel on the carpet in front of the sofa and turned on the CD player, causing Erykah Badu's sensual voice to come to life. He asked me to remove my clothes, as he was preparing to give me a massage. I was out of my clothes quicker than a super hero.

Tore put some oils on a tray next to him and instructed me to lie face down. He behaved like an expert, confirming my suspicions when he later disclosed that he'd done a course in massage therapy. I knew he was an articulate man and could probably talk his way out of anything, but his hands and fingers also spoke-to my muscles-in very relaxing tones. The tension in my body seemed to disappear.

He started with my neck, before making his way slowly down my back. I was happy to relinquish control to him. The smell of the oils and the scented candles helped to relax me further. As he made his way towards my buttocks, I felt my dick come alive. A gentle moan unexpectedly escaped my lips, encouraging Tore to continue. He gently pushed the towel down from my buttocks and continued massaging the area.

My gasps grew louder as my breathing quickened. He asked me to turn over so he could massage my chest. I rolled over slowly, revealing my raging erection. Tore remained very professional and continued as though, oblivious to my state of sexual arousal. He took his time and seemed to genuinely enjoy giving me pleasure. When he was finished he leaned over and kissed me warmly.

I was so turned on that I wanted to screw his brains out right there and then. However, he showed remarkable restraint by simply lying next to me without trying to take things further. I asked him if the massage was the surprise he had planned for me, because I was already won over. To my delight, he said the surprise was still to come.

Tore joined me in the bath and sat between my legs, with the back of his head resting on my chest. I trickled warm water over his chest and circled his nipples with bubbles. I stopped trying to figure out what the surprise was and relaxed, happily enjoying the company of this gorgeous man.

Tore and I never seemed to run out of things to talk about. He told me about his childhood and his parents' separation. He also talked, with great emotion, about the happier times in his life when he had lived with both parents in Italy before moving to London with his mother after the separation. His father followed shortly afterwards. His parents were much better at being friends than they were as a couple. He asked me how I felt about meeting his parents sometime, and I told him I'd honored. When Tore invited me to join his father and him for dinner that evening, I was speechless.

I was indeed surprised and since I'd already said I would be happy to meet his parents, I couldn't very well go back on my word. I accepted his invitation and he smiled broadly. He admitted that he'd already told his father he was bringing a friend. He was confident I wouldn't decline his offer.

I went back to my flat to get a change of clothing; Tore picked me up on the way to his father's home in St John's Wood. I was a little nervous about meeting his father, but if he were anything like Tore I knew I would adore him. What I was really worried about, was whether his father would like me. He told me that one 'Moriarty' was already in love with me-and that was the one that counted.

By the time we arrived at his father's home I had more than a few butterflies in my stomach but I bit the bullet and forged ahead, ready to face whatever was in store that night. Tore greeted his father with kisses on both cheeks. I felt like a member of his family when Tore's father kissed me on both sides of my face.

Franco appeared much younger than I'd thought he would, and his cherubic features made him look more like Tore's older brother than his father. He had warm green eyes and shinny black hair that set off his olive complexion. He was an attractive man; it was obvious where Tore got his handsome features and green coloured eyes from.

Franco's home was modestly furnished and had a heavy, Italian, influence. During the first, tentative, moments of our meeting I looked for some indication that Franco knew the nature of my relationship with his son. There was none.

Tore was right, because his father and I got on great. Franco made us a couple of drinks while we waited for dinner. Tore and I sat on the luxurious, leather, sofa with Franco positioned opposite, in an armchair. It was the first time that I'd heard Tore speaking fluent Italian. However, his father soon reminded him of his manners. Tore apologized and they continued the conversation in English, so I wouldn't feel left out. Tore casually placed a hand on my knee while talking to his father, who seemed oblivious to this affectionate gesture. I was so anxious that it was difficult to concentrate.

Franco left to set the table for dinner and I gave Tore a look that said, 'bitch, what are you doing?' I asked him if his father was aware of his sexuality. His father knew he was gay but he'd only told Franco he was bringing a friend to dinner. He was sure that his father knew the score.

We sat down to a delicious dinner of Spaghetti Cabonara-my favorite. I told Franco how impressed I was with his cooking and he smiled, politely, thanking me for the compliment. Tore reached under the table and gently squeezed my knee to show his appreciation of my efforts. I felt more relaxed after my first glass of wine.

After dinner we retired to the sitting room to have coffee, opera was playing softly in the background. Tore sat next to me and held my hand, acting like it was the most natural thing in the world to do. I knew a lot of people who claimed not to have an issue with homosexuality, only so long as it didn't affect them directly. Once it was on their doorstep the rules changed.

Franco's next words surprised me. "So I finally get to meet the man who's put a smile back on my baby's face."

I don't know why I was surprised that he knew about Tore's last relationship. When he'd noticed Tore looking brighter in recent weeks, he knew that love was in the air. He was pleased to finally meet the person responsible for that improvement in his son's mood. Tore seemed unaffected by his father's disclosure.

I was speechless and not for the first time that evening. I held on, to Tore's hand, to stop myself from fainting. This was all a little too real for me. Sensing my re-emerging discomfort, Tore changed the topic of conversation to his father's law practice. The rest of the evening went without any further surprises. Before we left, Franco told me, he was looking forward to seeing me again soon.

On our way home I told Tore that I was impressed by his linguistic abilities. He informed me that he also spoke a little Yoruba. When we stopped at a set of traffic lights I leaned over and gently kissed his lips. He looked at me with an expression that said, 'what was that for'? I smiled to myself, because I'd finally realized the time was right.

The moment we walked into his flat I took his hand, guiding him into the bedroom. He quickly realized what was about to happen and willingly complied. We stood still for a few seconds, as our eyes adjusted to the dimly-lit room. I fumbled initially as I began undressing him. When he was naked from the waist up I started kissing him, gently, gradually becoming more passionate.

Tore reciprocated, kissing each of my eyelids and the tip of my nose, before biting into my neck like he was a vampire. Instantly my head fell back and I felt a burning sensation spread through my body, as though I was on fire. I moaned loudly when his tongue reached my left nipple. He was a responsive lover and, although I wanted to regain control of the situation, I felt almost paralyzed-a pray at the mercy of its captor.

Eventually we finished undressing, the air was heavy with anticipation. The silence was deafening as we stood, naked, in front of each other, not moving for fear of breaking the spell we both felt under. I tried moving toward him but my legs wouldn't carry me forward. The boy was fine. I remembered the last time I felt like this, but I quickly erased the image of Ade from my mind.

Tore never took his eyes off mines the entire time and; I heard him swallow hard. In one fluid move he bridged the gap between us and we kissed, this time with more urgency. I couldn't get enough of him. His taste, his smell, his touch; he drove me crazy.

He began nibbling my ear while playing with my nipples and I was pushed ever closer to sweet release. Tore had figured out that my nipples were like a remote control for my dick. Play with them and my dick responded favorably.

He made a trail with his tongue down my body, until he was kneeling before me. I had to hold on to his shoulder and close my eyes to maintain my balance. He worked me over like an ice cream cone, and I loved every minute of it. I was keen to return the favour and I gently pulled him up to his feet.

I positioned him on the bed, holding his hands above his head. I nibbled each ear and he let out an encouraging moan, but that wasn't it. I moved down to his nipples and he liked it, but that wasn't it either. I had one last idea, so I released his hands and moved down his body. I paused to give him love bites to the inside of his leg and just between his thighs, I hit the jackpot. I could feel the muscles in his body tensing; he looked like he was about to have an epileptic seizure.

I was turned on by seeing him so excited. I stopped momentarily, before going in for the prize. I started slowly, building up momentum. At times he seemed to lift his entire body off the bed. His hands found the back of my head as he began building a steady rhythm. His moans grew louder and I knew he was close to exploding. I didn't want it to be over just then, so I quickly changed positions.

Our lovemaking went on for several hours as we continued exploring each other's bodies. There were hands and fingers and mouths everywhere. I was sure his neighbours could hear what we got up to. As we surged towards the final of many climaxes we were both dripping with sweat, like two thoroughbred horses at the end of a long, hard race. Every nerve in my body tingled and Tore was breathing heavily.

When Tore eventually spoke, his voice was barely above a whisper. He told me that he loved me and, without taking time to censor my thoughts, I told him I loved him too. After lying a while longer holding on to each other, we decided to have a shower together. While lathering Tore's body, I noticed his erection. Neither of us had ever made love in the shower, nor could we imagine a better time for doing so.

21. Meeting my friends

Dele called unexpectedly one evening to invite me to his birthday party. He claimed it would be a quiet evening, spent with a few close friends. I knew that Dele's parties were rarely quiet. They usually turned out to be nothing short of an orgy of fun. He told me I could bring a friend and I felt it was the perfect opportunity to introduce Tore to the gang.

Since meeting Franco, I'd been thinking of a way to involve Tore more in my life. I checked with him, to see if he would be free that night; he said that he'd love to meet my friends. I joked that he might wish to reserve judgement for after he'd met them.

When I picked Tore up outside his flat he looked handsome. He wore a white cotton shirt and jeans. 'Simple, yet elegant,' was the phrase that sprung to my mind when I saw my baby; but in my eyes he was already a supermodel. I wore a pair of black jeans and a black linen shirt. He got into the car and we kissed, before speeding off into the night.

As I'd suspected, there was nothing small about Dele's party. Tunde answered the door and we greeted each other with a hug before I introduced Tore. There were about two dozen people, most of whom I'd met before. I went in search of Dele and gave him the gift which Tore had thoughtfully bought for him on our behalf. Dele whispered in my ear that he was impressed with Tore, but advised me to watch out for the sisters who'd be on him quicker than flies on shit.

"Miss Thing, are you calling my man shit?" I asked jokingly.

"No honey, I'm just telling you to keep an eye out for the vultures," Dele said. "These children will jump your man faster than you can say what the fuck just happened!"

"And you know that I'll have to get nasty on these bitches if that happens," I said.

Tore stood behind us, laughing heartily. This was a side of me he hadn't seen before. Dele looked past me and said to Tore, "welcome to the whore's den."

"And he means that literally," I added.

"You both have my blessings. Not that you need it of course, but this one looks like a keeper," said Dele motioning to Tore.

Tore was beaming with pride at Dele's approval. I would have been quite happy to spend the entire evening at Tore's side but he suggested that I catch up with my friends.

When Dele left us, he headed toward a tall, handsome man, standing in the corner. I found out his name was Tokunbo. He looked like a tall, cool, drink, of some exotic nectar. I gave Dele a look that told him I needed details later. As I went looking for the others I saw Tore, deep in conversation with some of Dele's guests and I felt less guilty about abandoning him.

I found Miss Candy talking to Ray and we greeted each other with hugs. Miss Candy was working it, wearing a pair of leather trousers. He asked me to point out Tore, before giving his nod of approval.

"Have you heard from the arsehole lately?" Miss Candy asked.

"I had lunch with him recently," I said, trying to sound casual.

"No Miss Thing, tell me you didn't, have you lost the plot completely?" Miss Candy asked dramatically.

"He invited me to his wedding and I plan to go," I said.

"Oh hell no, I don't believe this shit. Tell me aliens abducted your ass, or that you decided to have a sex change, anything but this," Miss Candy said as he guided me into Dele's bedroom. Tunde and Ray were fast on our heels.

"Bitch is you crazy?" Miss Candy asked with obvious concern.

"You sound like I just told you we were getting back together. It's nothing like that. I just feel we need to be civil to each other so we can move on with our lives," I said, trying to convince them I wasn't insane.

"I'm not listening to this shit. Are we talking about the same person? Earth to Chris; are you there? This is the same man that ripped your heart out, before pouring salt into the opened wound!" Miss Candy said, "Could someone please get me the real Chris?"

We heard a knock on the door and were joined by Chez and Dele, who had seen us heading into the bedroom.

"What's up guys?" asked Chez.

"We're having an intervention up in here. This crazy child, sitting here, wants to go to Ade's wedding," said Miss Candy.

I'd already told Chez about my plans to attend the wedding and, although he wasn't convinced it was a good idea, he was supportive of me if it meant I could get closure on my relationship with Ade.

Chez looked at me before answering, "I know, he told me."

"And you agree that he should go to the arsehole's wedding?" asked Miss Candy.

"Chris is an adult and is capable of making up his own mind. He has his reasons for wanting to do this," Chez responded.

"Oh hell no, we need to call an ambulance, because another bitch just went crazy!" said Miss Candy.

The others looked at me as though I'd grown another head, so I decided to put them out of their misery and told them about my plan. He was going to pay for what he'd done to me.

"Now this is more like the Chris I know and love," Miss Candy said, "but honey-child, you know you still have to be careful you don't get hurt again. This is some dangerous shit, and I still think you shouldn't have anything to do with that man. You have moved on and you're with someone else now."

I looked across to Chez in time to see the look of surprise mixed with disappointment on his face, just before he left the room. The others were perplexed by his behavior. They'd long suspected that he had a crush on me. I went after him.

I found Chez standing outside, smoking a cigarette.

"Let's go back inside. It's cold out here and we'll both catch our deaths of pneumonia," I said.

"Then you should get back inside," he said coldly.

"Chez I'm sorry. I didn't mean for you to find out like this. I was going to tell you but the time just didn't seem right."

"I don't mind that you're seeing someone else. Actually I do mind, but not as much as you not telling me about it. I thought we were friends Chris?"

"We are friends," I said.

"Friends don't keep secrets from each other, especially the important stuff," he said.

"You're right. I should have told you before tonight and I apologize for not having done so; will you forgive me?" I asked.

"Chris, too many gay men take friendships lightly. I need your friendship. We may never have the kind of relationship that I'd like us to have, but I thought we had honesty. I want you to be honest with me, even if you feel I might be hurt by the truth."

"I understand; and it won't happen again, I promise. So, are we friends again?" I asked playfully.

"Yes friends," he replied as we hugged.

"Now let's get out of the bloody cold before we freeze to death," I said.

Chez went to the kitchen to fix himself a drink and I rejoined the others in Dele's bedroom. I told them that Chez was fine. They didn't pry any further.

Tunde asked Dele about his new man. Ray and I both said that he looked like the black lead actor from the popular Stephen Spielberg movie-the one about a slave ship that had ended up in the wrong place.

"What's the name of the movie, anyone?" Miss Candy asked.

"The Armistad," Chez said as he entered the room.

"So now supermodels have brains too," said Miss Candy.

"You better believe that shit," said Chez, snapping his fingers. We all laughed.

Tokunbo was sexy as hell. He looked like the sort of man who was cool without trying. At six foot, five inches tall, he couldn't fade into the background but you could tell from a glance that he didn't like being the centre of attention. A few of us would have gladly given up most of our worldly possessions to spend an evening with a man like that. Miss Candy noticed the size of Tokunbo's feet and asked us what we thought it meant. We all knew what he was getting at and I said, "It only means that he wears large shoes."

He responded, "And I bet that's not all that's large."

Chez asked about Tore and Miss Candy interjected that I was foolish to leave such a fine looking man on his own with the sharks circling. I told them that Tore was a good swimmer and was more than capable of dealing with predators.

I was tempted to give my friends the low-down on our lovemaking but I respected Tore too much for that, and besides, I didn't want to offend Chez. We all laughed when Miss Candy said that after talking about fine men he needed to find him some 'new dick' at the party.

We all emerged from Dele's bedroom to join the other guests. I saw Tore talking to two, gorgeous women. He looked across and smiled at me. Heather and Carla looked stunning in their matching designer outfits. They were an attractive lesbian couple whom I'd met at one of Dele's parties. Tore winked at me, signalling his need to be rescued from his new friends. I approached the trio and asked the ladies if I could have a dance with my man. They smiled as I took Tore's hand.

I held Tore close and his body felt good next to mine, like it belonged there. As we moved in time to the music, he thanked me for rescuing him. I whispered in his ear that I was only returning the favour. I felt like the luckiest man in the room.

Before leaving the party I managed to get Dele alone, to find out more about his handsome date. It was unusual for him to be so secretive about the men he dated. He usually couldn't wait to tell everything about them; from graphic descriptions of their anatomy, to their sexual prowess.

He told me they'd met in his local supermarket. He began cruising Tokunbo refusing to believe that he might be straight, or simply not interested. His persistence eventually paid off. By the time Dele left the supermarket he had Tokumbo's number and it was a done deal. Dele had read him like a book.

Dele had warned me that prolonged handshakes, and/or stares, were a dead giveaway of a man's interest in another man. Straight men never looked at each other the same way that gay men did.

On their first date, they didn't have sex because Tokunbo had insisted they get to know each other better before becoming intimate. Dele maintained that he only kept their relationship under wraps because Tokunbo was a very private person. He felt Tokumbo was the real deal; it was difficult for me to share his optimism. I hoped for his sake, that his boyfriend wasn't a player, but as my mother always told me, if it walked like a duck and quacked like a duck, it probably was a duck.

22. From a distance

I'd left four telephone messages for Kunle before he eventually returned my calls. He told me that he'd been busy. I remembered a time when he was never too busy to make time for me. He told me that things seemed to be working out between him and Aduni. I was happy for him, if a little confused.

He said he wasn't planning to get back together with Aduni, despite her hints of wanting to have another child. The length some women were willing to go to was astonishing. He felt that a better relationship with Aduni would facilitate a better relationship with his daughter. He asked me what I'd been up to and I hesitated before telling him about Tore. I didn't sense any resentment on his part, he even seemed happy for me.

He asked me if I had resolved my issues with Ade. I told him that we'd started talking and were a little closer to friendship. I told him that I'd even considered attending his wedding.

"Chris, are you sure that's such a good idea?" Kunle asked.

"It's what I plan to do and I'll really like your support as a friend."

"I do support you Chris, but I also have to be honest with you about my feelings. I think that's always been an important part of our friendship," he said.

"Ade was the one who invited me and he even suggested that I bring a friend along," I said.

"So, you've seen him," he said.

"We had lunch recently."

"I'm your friend Chris; and I will support you, regardless of your decision, but mark my words, this will end in tears."

He hadn't realised just how close he was getting to finding out about my true motive for attending Ade's wedding.

"It's going to be fine Kunle, trust me," I said.

"So are you taking your new man to the wedding?" he asked.

"No. I was hoping *you* would go with me," I said.

"I don't know that I want to be a part of this charade Chris. Supporting you is one thing; attending the wedding is an entirely different matter."

I changed the topic of conversation and told Kunle that I wanted him to meet Tore. I hoped that by meeting Tore he'd realize how happy I was, and move on with his own love life. Kunle wasn't exactly thrilled about the idea, but promised to consider it and get back to me.

I loved Kunle. Talking to him made me realize just how much I'd missed him in recent weeks. So much had happened in my life and it pained me that I hadn't been able to share it with him. I told him that I needed to see him and I wouldn't take 'no' for an answer. He didn't try to make excuses-instead he agreed that it was a good idea to meet.

As soon as I put down the telephone, I received a call from John. He never called unless he wanted something from me, or wanted to gloat about some new man in his life. He told me that he'd met another young man, with whom he was now in love. I thought of asking him about Fabrice, but that would have been cruel since we both knew he couldn't keep a man for very long.

His new man's name was Toks. They'd met a couple of weeks earlier. Toks worked as a junior Doctor at a West London hospital. He'd been working in the A&E department when John attended with 'a friend.' He hadn't given any details, which made me wonder whether 'the friend' had been constructed for my benefit.

I asked if there wasn't some Hippocratic Oath that prevented doctors from sleeping with their patients. He responded, curtly, that Toks was not *his* doctor, so that rule didn't apply; anyway, they were now very much in love. He was adamant that he felt he'd found his Mr. Right. I struggled to avoid making an insensitive remark.

I allowed John to ride his magic carpet a little longer because I knew that, all too soon, he would be plummeting to earth, where the rest of us lived. He suggested meeting so he could introduce me to Toks. I agreed to get back to him on that. Even as I said the words, I knew I had no intention of ever calling him.

I had very little time in my life for people who had no respect for me. Meeting the new man in John's life was therefore, simply not on my list of priorities. I was amused though, that John would think that I'd ever be interested in his love life. Sadly, it has taken me a while to come to the realization that he'd never been my friend.

Kunle and I met at a café near Charring Cross station. I ordered a slice of chocolate cake and a fruit drink. Kunle had strawberry cheese cake and an iced coffee. Seeing him was like coming across an oasis after a long journey though the desert. Since I'd seen him last, he'd started shaving his head-which brought out his strong, ethnic, features and made him appear even more rugged and ultimately more handsome than I'd remembered. He was wearing a light blue jumper and a pair of jeans.

I asked about Mercedes. He told me he suspected Aduni's willingness to cooperate with him was, in part, due to her search for the father of her next child. She'd started dating soon after the divorce and had hoped to get married and continue having children almost immediately; but, after a couple years and no sign of a child on the way, she'd started looking elsewhere.

There was no mention of any romantic prospects on the horizon for him. We were definitely experiencing the 'pink elephant in the room' syndrome. We were both avoiding any mention of his feelings for me. The tension was building; one of us needed to address the issue.

"So, are you seeing anyone special Kunle?"

"I've been too busy with work and Mercedes to find time to date," he said.

"I'm concerned that we don't seem to be as close as we once were, and I miss that-I miss you," I said.

"I'm trying to put things into perspective. You know how I feel about you Chris. I can't just switch my feelings off," he said.

"I don't expect you to Kunle."

"I know you mean well, but this is something I have to work out on my own," he said.

"I guess I'm just being selfish because I need you in my life. I can't help feeling things have changed between us. I don't know what else I can do to let you know how much you mean to me," I said, feeling exasperated.

"Chris I love you and I probably always will. I just need to figure out how I can deal with this. Your friendship is one of the most important things in my life, but I need to learn how to love you without getting hurt myself."

"But can't I be in your life while you figure it out?" I asked.

"I hope so Chris. I truly hope so."

"You deserve someone who can give you what you need. You have a beautiful daughter, who means the world to you, but you're an adult and you have adult feelings and emotions that a child, however important she may be, is not able to provide. You deserve more."

"I know; and maybe one day I'll find it," he said unconvincingly.

I had suddenly lost my appetite.

"Are you still planning on going to Ade's wedding?" he asked.

"I am. Have you decided yet whether you're coming with me?" I asked.

"That depends." he said.

"Depends on what?" I asked.

"It depends on you being totally honest with me," he said.

"What makes you think that I'm not being honest with you?" I asked.

"Now I'm even more certain that you're not being honest with me, or else you wouldn't be avoiding the question," he said.

"What are you getting at Kunle?"

"I think there's more to this than you're telling me Chris. I don't believe that you and Ade have suddenly become best friends. Remember, I know how bad he hurt you. That kind of hurt takes a long time to heal."

"Healing is a slow process; I can't put my life on hold while I wait for it to happen."

"Chris this is me you're talking to; I don't buy that explanation for one minute."

I hesitated briefly, before saying, "You're right. You can see right through me-always have. There is another reason for attending Ade's wedding."

"Just as I thought, what is it?" he asked.

"I need Ade to feel some of the pain he's caused me. I've moved on with my life, but the thought of Ade being free to do this to someone else eats away at me. I've tried to ignore it, but I can't," I said. "I just can't".

Kunle listened quietly until I was finished. There was a look of sheer horror on his face by the time I was through telling him the story. I couldn't figure out whether he was simply disgusted with me, or if he thought I'd lost my mind.

"Aren't you going to say something?" I asked.

"Chris, I think you've said it all. I would never have believed that you could be so spiteful, but maybe I underestimated just how much pain you're in."

"I need to do this to get some closure," I said.

"And you think *this* is the way to get closure?" he asked, "How is this going to help ease your pain?"

"I don't know; but I need to do this. I don't *expect* you to help me, but, as my friend, I want you . . . no, I need you, to be in my corner," I said.

"Of course I'm here for you; as much as I can be Chris, but this is madness-utter madness."

"So now that you know everything, will you come with me?" I asked.

"I'll have to now, to make sure you don't get yourself killed. Hopefully I'll be able to talk you out of this craziness before the big day arrives."

"That would mean that you'd have to spend a lot of time with me. Are you sure you're up to it?" I asked.

"Does Tore know, about this plan of yours?" Kunle asked.

"I haven't told him anything about it. I don't like being dishonest with him, but I feel this is between Ade and me. This all happened before I met him. I guess I'll talk to him about it when the time is right."

23. The way to a man's heart

It had been two days since Tore and I discussed my plans to attend Ade's wedding. He was initially apprehensive about me going, but I managed to persuade him that it would help me to get some closure on the issue. I was surprised by his reaction when I mentioned that Kunle would accompany me to the wedding.

Tore reacted like I'd told him I planned to blow up Tower Bridge. I'd never seen him angry before and it unsettled me. He didn't seem threatened by the fact that I planned to attend the wedding of my ex-boyfriend. Instead, he had difficulty dealing with me spending so much time with Kunle. I began to wonder whether it had been such a good idea to tell him about Kunle's feelings for me.

I loved both of them in different ways and was slowly starting to loose my patience with Tore's attitude. I hadn't given him any reason to feel insecure about my feelings for him. I loved Kunle, but was *in love* with Tore. If *he* couldn't tell the difference then it was his issue to sort out. Kunle and I shared a history that Tore was not a part of, and I couldn't change that fact. He needed to deal with it as an adult.

When Tore's secretary answered the telephone and asked me to hold for a minute, I became suspicious. A few seconds later she informed me that he was with a client. She asked if I wanted to leave a message; I told her to have him call me as soon as he was free. I was having none of his childish behaviour.

When he finally returned my call I asked him if he was avoiding me. He didn't try to make up any excuses. He said he needed some time alone. I had just been through this with my best friend and so, didn't relish repeating the experience with my lover. I told him to do whatever he needed to, to get through this; and that he could call me when he felt ready to discuss things rationally. He apologized immediately and asked if he could come over to my flat.

I was excited about spending the evening with my man. I prepared a meal of baked salmon with seasonal vegetables. I got his favorite wine and desert. I strategically placed a few scented candles, to create an ambience of romance. I planned to convince Tore, once and for all, that my heart was his.

The doorbell rang and when I answered it, Tore looked handsome, wearing a black turtleneck jumper and jeans. The charming smile he usually wore was missing, but I didn't let that spoil my plans for a special evening. We hugged each other and I told him how happy I was to see him before I disappeared to the kitchen to get him a glass of wine.

When I returned with his drink he was seated in the armchair. I knelt between his opened legs and told him, for the second time that evening, how much I'd missed him. He seemed uncomfortable so I decided that we needed to resolve this issue if we were going to have a pleasant evening. I looked deep into his beautiful green eyes and asked, "Do you trust me Tore?"

"Of course I do. I'm not sure if I trust Kunle, that's all," he said.

"But you don't know him." I said.

"You're right I don't know him, but I know that he's still in love with you."

"We both know that it takes two to tango. Kunle can't act on his feelings if I don't allow him to. He's a very special friend, and that's all he is," I said.

"I know it's irrational but I'm afraid of loosing you," he said.

"You won't loose me. I'm yours and no one else can change that."

His eyes became moist as I held him close. Without trust, our relationship would never survive. I suddenly remembered the salmon in the oven and I broke our tender embrace to race to the kitchen. I turned around when I heard Tore's voice behind me, asking if there was anything I needed help with. I told him that I needed to know we were OK. He walked over and kissed me.

Tore complimented me on my culinary skills and said I'd finally found a way to his heart, via his stomach. I replied that I thought I'd already claimed his heart. We hadn't yet made love in the lounge. Tore thought it was about time that we ticked that box. Our love making was deliberately slow. We took out time enjoying each other.

Later that night, while we were in bed, Tore told me he couldn't imagine not having me in his life. His insecurities about our relationship seemed to stem from traumatic experiences in his past. I reassured him that I would not let anything come between us. We had our entire lives ahead of us. I couldn't remove the demons from his past, but now he didn't have to fight them alone. I would rescue him, just as he'd saved me.

24. Supermarket sweep

It was a lazy Saturday, made even lazier by morning sex. Regrettably, I had to get out of bed to run a few errands. I managed to coax Tore out of bed by promising to spend the entire weekend together. After breakfast we ended up in the shower together. It was one of the best showers I've ever had-we got pretty dirty before we were through.

After getting dressed we headed to the local supermarket, which always seemed to be a pick up joint for gay men on Saturday afternoons. The supermarket had more queens in it than the Royal family. In true couple style, Tore pushed the trolley while I scanned the heavily-stocked shelves for the items I needed.

I heard my name being called and turned around to see John, standing next to an attractive black man. I introduced Tore to John, who was eyeing my man as though I wasn't right there. I waited to be introduced to John's friend but it never happened.

The handsome young man, who now stood a few feet away, looked a little uncomfortable. That wasn't unusual because a lot of black men who are insecure about their sexuality can be a little unsettled in the company of other black people, straight or gay. That situation was made even more complicated when the gay couple was interracial.

In the past, whenever I'd dated Caucasian men, I felt like I was in a 'no win' scenario. In predominantly white clubs I would be ignored and my man would be looked down upon, for dating me. When we went to a predominantly black club, he'd receive nasty looks. In the end I settled for the man who made me happy, regardless of his colour. With this in mind, I made allowances for the brother's behaviour.

John and I were both on the arms of gorgeous men. I had to admit though, Toks was fine as hell. He was tall, handsome, and graceful. His shaven head and goatee beard were certainly amongst his best features, but they competed for attention with his beautiful white teeth and full, sensuous, lips.

This brother looked to be high maintenance. I smiled, to myself, when I thought of John trying to hold on to him. The supermarket was very busy and we were causing congestion in the aisle. We agreed to meet soon after for a drink, even though we both knew *that* would never happen. We said goodbye; Tore and I headed to the checkout, while John and his companion continued shopping.

As we were getting into the car, Tore asked me if I recognised the man with John-I didn't. Tore reminded me that we'd seen the handsome stranger at Dele's party.

It took me a few seconds, but eventually the penny dropped. I think I was slow to catch on because on neither occasion had I actually been introduced to this man. Maybe it wasn't that the brother had an issue with his fellow black gay men, perhaps he had an issue with dating several people at once. I couldn't wait to get home and call Dele.

I smiled when Tore explained that 'Toks' was an abbreviated form of the name 'Tokumbo.' So, the idiot didn't even think about using an alias. I wondered just how many other men he was seeing at the same time. I knew Dele could be a 'Ho;' but once he gave his heart to someone, it was serious business. They didn't call John 'The woodcutter' for nothing. When it came to 'dick', John was an overachiever.

Toks must have recognized us from Dele's party, which would explain his shyness. I remembered Dele telling me that Tokumbo wanted to keep things under wraps. He must have figured out that he could continue with his deceptions if he didn't get too involved in his lovers' lives.

I believe a burden shared is a burden halved. I had to tell someone. I knew Tore would disapprove so I waited until he went back to his flat to get some stuff.

Half way through dialing Dele's number, I stopped. I knew that had I been in his position, I would want to know if the man I loved was being unfaithful. Hell, it wasn't too long ago that I *was* in Dele's position; and yes, as painful as it was; I needed to know the truth. I knew Dele thought Tokumbo was 'the one', so it was easy to assume the news would be painful.

I decided to call Chez first to get some advice on how best to handle the situation. He asked me if I was certain, I told him that both Tore and I were positive it was the same man. Chez reminded me that we'd only ever seen the man from a distance and may have mistaken his identity. I admitted there was a possibility that he could be right, but I owed it to Dele to tell him about my suspicions. As we continued talking, Chez became more convinced that our suspicions were well founded.

Chez warned me to consider the effect this revelation might have on my friendship with Dele. Not telling him about my suspicions was not an option for me. What I needed to figure out was how I could break the news to him in a way that didn't seem malicious. The longer I waited before telling him, the more difficult it would've become. Bad news was never easy to deliver, but I had a duty as a friend and that was far more important than my own discomfort with the issue.

I was a little nervous as I dialled Dele's number. There was no turning back. He answered the telephone in a cheerful manner. There was no easy way to break the bad news so I got straight to the point.

"Dele, I ran into Tokumbo while out shopping with Tore today."

"Oh really, did you say hello to him?" Dele asked.

"No I didn't get a chance to, because he was with someone," I said.

"What are you getting at Chris?" Dele asked, the tone in his voice changing dramatically.

"Dele he was with John-the guy I went to the New Year's Eve party with. You must remember me telling you about him."

"Yes, I remember you telling me about him," he said.

"John gave me the impression they were an item. He told me his new man's name was Toks; and I know that your boyfriend's name is Tokumbo."

"Where is this going Chris?"

"There's no easy way to say this Dele. I think the man John claims is his boyfriend is the man you're dating."

"I know all about it Chris."

I was stunned into silence. I could hardly believe my ears. Dele knew his boyfriend was cheating on him and actually seemed OK with it. I would've been sharpening a knife to kill that bitch had I been in his shoes. This wasn't the Dele I knew.

"What are you saying Dele? You know this man is cheating on you? Why are you putting up with this?"

"I love him Chris. You don't understand," he said.

"You're right about that, I don't understand," I said.

"Chris, I've been dating confused men for most of my adult life. I'm tired of sleeping around and I think it's time that I settled down."

"You know I love you and I'm here for you, but have you lost your mind? You're always telling us we should love ourselves a little more than we love these crazy-ass men," I said.

"You're so lucky Chris, you don't just have one-you have three men in love with you. I have great sex, but sometimes that's not enough. At times I feel so empty inside, but I don't let anyone else see that part of me. I appear confident and in control, but all I really want is someone to love me, even if I'm not the only one he loves," Dele lamented.

"People treat us the way we allow them to. You're worth so much more than this. You've told me this so many time babes. Doesn't the same rule apply to you?" I asked.

The line went silent. I had to ask if he was still there before he answered, "Yeah, I'm still here. Tokumbo and I have an open relationship. Well, I'm not seeing anyone else, but he wants to see other people. He says that although he doesn't really love the other person, he doesn't want to hurt him either."

"But in the meantime *you're* getting hurt," I said. "Someone always gets hurt in situations like that."

"I know that I should probably give him up, but I really do love him," he said.

It was the first time that I'd ever seen this vulnerable side of Dele. He began crying. I felt bad for him, but he needed to wake up and smell the coffee.

Between sobs he said, "I wish I had the will power to give him up Chris, but I don't. Tokumbo is the first man who treats me like I'm special."

I felt like saying, "baby you need to check the dictionary because the last time I checked, what you're describing isn't special", but I didn't.

"He's never treated me like a piece of meat. At first I was prepared for just sex, but he gave me so much more. He wanted to get to know me and he showed a genuine interest in what I liked and what I thought. No one had ever done that before-apart from you guys, of course."

I had difficulty understanding why Dele felt he had to settle for less than he deserved. It seemed as though he thought that he couldn't do any better. Despite my views I needed to support *him* as a friend would. He asked me not to mention this to any of the others and I didn't have the heart to tell him that I already had. I couldn't change the past, but I could tell Chez not to tell anyone else.

I could trust Tore not to talk about it, because he was a therapist. When he returned I told him about my call to Dele. He was surprised to learn that Dele knew about Tokumbo and John. I couldn't come down very hard on Dele because I'd been where he was. I was living testimony to the shit some people were prepared to put up with, all in the name of love.

Tore and I began an interesting conversation about open relationships. I told him that I felt open relationships were fine, for some people, but I was certain they weren't for me. He said he felt the same way. He believed that it was up to the individuals involved to create the type of relationship they wanted, but all too often the rules were changed by one partner, to the detriment of the other person.

Over the course of the weekend we talked further about relationships, which brought us back to the topic of our relationship. Tore wanted to know about my feelings for Kunle. I wondered whether he could handle the information. I wasn't convinced it was a good idea to be talking, to my current boyfriend, about my past boyfriends in any detail, so I kept the information to a minimum.

What Kunle and I shared in the past had been sweet and magical, while it lasted. I did hope it would have lasted longer, but it didn't. We settled for friendship because we wanted to be in each other's lives. The chemistry still existed but we were in a new place, a different place.

My relationship with Kunle had not been a typical one for me, for two important reasons. Firstly, I was the one who ended the relationship, by pointing out to Kunle, what was obvious to me at the time. He was under a lot of pressure, from both his family and his culture. There was no room for anything else. Secondly, we had salvaged a valuable friendship from the ruins. Most of my relationships before Kunle had ended badly, so this was the exception.

Tore asked me about my current feelings for Kunle, I said that I loved him, as a friend. A small part of me was still attracted to Kunle, but I didn't tell Tore that. He also asked if I knew Kunle's feeling about me being in a relationship. He seemed pleasantly surprised when I told him about Kunle being happy for us. I wondered whether his perception of Kunle had changed after hearing this news.

I knew that Tore's insecurities ran much deeper than just his fears about Kunle. This became much clearer when he explained that his last partner had been unfaithful with one of their friends. He was distraught at the time because there were no signs of relationship difficulties. He'd felt betrayed by his friend, but even more so by his lover. When the relationship ended, his self-confidence was so damaged that he found it difficult to trust men.

I knew there was nothing I could say to change Tore's views. This was about his pain and I trusted that, in time, he would see I was different, that not all men were the same and, more importantly, that I wouldn't hurt him. It was going to take time for him to realise how much I loved him, but I was prepared to wait because he was worth it. In the meantime, I would continue loving him with all my heart.

The moment I said it, I knew that it was wrong but I'd called his bluff. I promised not to attend Ade's wedding if he didn't want me to. He told me that if he prevented me from going to the wedding, I would resent him later. We needed to be able to trust each other, or else our relationship would be doomed to fail. I considered not attending Ade's wedding, but Tore was right. At some point in the future, maybe not right away, but in time, I would end up resenting him.

* * *

The telephone rang several times before Dele answered. He told me that Tokumbo had just left his flat, after spending the night.

"Chris, the sex is absolutely brilliant and you know I ought to know," he said.

"Honey, I'll take your word for it. Is Tokumbo still seeing John?" I asked.

"I think so, but I know one day soon he'll see how much I love him and I'll be enough for him. Between you and me Chris, it isn't easy, but I love him and I can't just love the easy bits and leave the difficult bits alone. I have to love him for who he is-all of him."

"Dele, you're contradicting yourself. You say you love him as he is but, you expect that he'll change and date only you. To place those expectations on him is unfair to both of you," I said.

"I look around at our group, of intelligent, beautiful, people; but most of us are single Chris! We're good people who are alone. I'm tired of being alone. I'm not getting any younger and I'll soon run out of twenty year old men who are interested in me," he said.

"Since when did being on your own equate to having a plague? I remember a time when you were content with your life and if you had a man, then that was OK-but it was also OK if you didn't have one."

"And *I did* feel that way at the time, but now I feel differently," he said.

"Dele, I just want what's best for you. I may not agree with you, but I love you and support you all the same."

"Thanks Chris, that means a lot to me. I didn't expect you to understand because you're not in my situation, but I was hoping you would support me-and you do. Wait until you get to my age and the future doesn't seem that bright-then maybe you'll understand."

I knew exactly what he meant. Gay culture was built around youth and beauty. I had no idea that Dele had been so unhappy. He always seemed to be the life and soul of the party. I guess we all need to be loved, and at the end of the day where we get that love isn't as important as getting it.

* * *

A few days later I telephoned John, to tell him about his new boyfriend. He wasted no time in bringing me up to speed on his love life. I hesitated only briefly before I went in for the kill. I told him that I'd met Toks before-at his boyfriend's birthday party. He was silent.

He tried to explain that I had my facts wrong, that it must have been a case of mistaken identity. So 'Toks' or 'Tukunbo' hadn't been entirely honest with him. This was going to be more rewarding than I'd imagined. I told John that I was only being a friend, that I wanted him to know all the facts.

John became abusive, accusing me of being jealous of his relationship. I told him I was only keeping it real and that since he was so happy to dish it out, he'd best get used to taking it. What kind of friend would I be if I didn't have his back? His last words to me were, "fuck off, you spiteful bitch." I guess it didn't seem all that funny to him once the shoe was on the other foot.

25. The wedding

I hadn't seen Tore for a few days and had just about given up trying to contact him. He was screening his calls at home and when I tried to get him at work he was either with a client or in a meeting. I tried hard not to overreact but I was slowly becoming impatient. I left several messages and waited for him to get back to me.

Tore returned my calls at times he thought I'd probably be out. He had my mobile number but chose not to use it. I wanted to hold Tore and reassure him that I loved him with every fiber of my being. His avoidance was getting to me, but I felt helpless to do anything about it. I waited patiently for him to come to realize that, despite all that was going on, I loved him.

I was a little distracted, to say the least, because of Ade's wedding, which was only two days away. There were still a few things I needed to get done before the big day. Kunle tried to convince me to wear an Agbada, but I chose to go with something less conspicuous. I decided to get the wedding couple a gift from both Kunle and myself.

As the big day approached and I grew increasingly doubtful about whether I should go through with my plans for revenge. This was going to be an ideal opportunity for Ade to be taught an important lesson and I was the man to do it. I had a responsibility to make sure he thought twice before treating someone else the way he'd treated me.

Kunle abandoned his plan to try and persuade me to change my mind. His arguments, although valid, were no match for my determination to stop Ade in his tracks.

We agreed to meet outside the church in Blackheath. It was a beautiful day. Although it was a cold day the sun shone brilliantly, perched high above a cloudless sky. I recognized Kunle immediately, standing near the entrance to the church. He looked splendid, dressed in traditional costume of white and gold brocade. He wore a Fila and Buba and matching Sokoto, all of which gave him a regal appearance.

The beautiful church, strategically located on a hill in Blackheath, stood out against the skyline and was immediately recognizable by its huge steeple, which pierced the bright blue sky. The lush greenery seemed to stretch for miles, adding to the picturesque setting. It was an impressive landmark and an ideal setting for a wedding.

I extended a hand to greet Kunle, instead he pulled me close to him in an embrace before making our way into the beautifully decorated church. There was still plenty of room so we took seats half way up the aisle, and waited for the other guests to arrive. Kunle kept me entertained with tales of previous weddings he'd attended. I laughed when he told me he had to be careful not to get sexually aroused by the fine men present, since he was wearing very loose-fitting underwear.

The church was decorated with dozens of candles of different sizes, the warmth from which added further to the general ambiance. A beautiful bouquet of dark red and white roses hung at the end of each pew. There were several other large bouquets of flowers, strategically placed around the church to give a feeling of being in a garden, maybe even the Garden of Eden.

The sunlight coming through the stained glass windows added to the fairy tale quality, creating a kaleidoscope of colours which bounced off the brightly-dressed guests. It was clear that a lot of thought and planning had gone into making the day special, I felt a slight twinge of guilt about ruining such a perfect day. However, I had to do what needed to be done-a lot of people would remember this day for a long time to come.

The church slowly filled with guests as Kunle and I talked. I was under no elusion that the wedding would start on time. I looked up and saw the back of Ade's head, my heart skipped several beats. He looked handsome, as he sat patiently waiting for his bride. Sitting next to him was Michael.

I could tell Ade was nervous, even without seeing his face, because he always played with the lobe of his ear when he was anxious about something. Occasionally Michael would lean towards Ade and whisper to him. I could only assume these were words of comfort. Suddenly Ade looked back and his eyes locked on to mine; I had to look away. Kunle saw this and gently squeezed my hand to let me know I was not going through this alone.

The bride was two hours late. I knew tradition dictated that she should be fashionably late but two hours was taking tradition a little too far. Just when the guests began to get noticeably restless, news of her arrival spread through the congregation, like a bush fire on an African plane. The official photographers got into position as Ade stood up, with his groomsmen, to welcome his bride.

He looked splendid in an Ivory-coloured suit and matching shirt, with ruffles at the front. His bow tie was the colour of red wine and he had a carnation on the lapel of his suit. The groomsmen wore burgundy-coloured suite with cream shirts and ties.

The congregation arose. Moments before the organist started playing the bridal march an announcement had been made asking guests to refrain from taking any photos during the ceremony. We were assured there would be time enough later to take photos.

My pulse quickened and my breathing became shallow when the wedding march began playing. Two of the bridesmaids walked elegantly up the aisle of the church one behind the other, carrying baskets of red rose petals, which they dispersed along the path of the following bride. The bridesmaids wore burgundy-coloured, full-length, form fitting, velvet dresses with plunging necklines. As they arrived at the altar they were each met by a groomsman who handed them a single white lily before taking their respective positions.

A distinguished-looking gentleman who was dressed in gold and blue escorted the bride up the aisle. I assumed, by the look of sheer joy on his face, that he was the proud father of the bride. She looked stunning. She was tall and slender, with skin the color of milk chocolate. She looked like a top model in her long sleeved, ivory-coloured dress, made of fine lace.

The dress, which seemed to be painted on her, started at her long, graceful, neck. It hugged her body closely, accentuating all her womanly curves, until just below her knees, from where it flared out into a beautiful train. The chief bridesmaid did a wonderful job of making sure the bride's journey to the altar was flawless.

As she made her way to join her new husband at the altar her eyes remained downcast, underneath a short veil. Her face was lightly made up and her hair was held back in a bun. She wore simple peal earrings and matching necklace. In her hands she held a bouquet of tightly-packed, white, roses. When she arrived at the altar her father presented her to Ade before taking his seat. We all bowed our heads in prayer.

Kunle had told me about the bachelor party, which had been attended by most of the black gay men in London, and beyond. I had to admit that a small part of me felt jealous that I hadn't been invited. However, another part of me was relieved that I'd been spared the experience. Kunle had turned down his invitation to the party.

A young man made his way to the front of the congregation and informed us that the song Ade had chosen to dedicate to his new bride was called, "This is our day". He sang beautifully and I mused that in another time and place I could have been the one doing his job.

By now I was sweating from nerves because I knew the time was getting near for me to play my part in this memorable day. Kunle was also very nervous but didn't attempt to stop me.

Ade wore an uneasy smile on his face and Michael looked like something the cat had dragged in the night before. The bachelor party two nights ago had taken its toll on its participants. At least Michael would get some rest while his man was away on the honeymoon.

Everything went like clockwork until it was time for the question "if anyone here has any objection to this man . . ." This was my cue. In most weddings it was merely a formality but on this occasion, things would be different.

Suddenly the walls of the church appeared to be closing in on me. I had trouble focusing my sight and time seemed to stand still. I had a feeling of being submerged in water so everything seemed to be happening in slow motion. I looked around and saw that all eyes were on me as I slowly rose to my feet.

There was a sharp intake of breath from the congregation in anticipation of what was about to happen. The minister looked at me expectantly. I swallowed hard and looked directly at Ade, who wore a scared expression, like he'd just been given terrible news. His bride looked to him for an explanation about what was happening. His eyes pleaded with mine.

What seemed an eternity was merely a matter of seconds; I glanced to my left and saw that Kunle had his eyes closed and seemed to be muttering under his breath. I tried to speak but no words came out. It felt like I had a huge ball of cotton in my mouth and everyone continued to stare. The air was heavy with trepidation-I felt my head would explode. My legs felt like they'd been replaced by two wooden pegs and were nailed to the floor.

I heard a voice saying, "no Chris no". It was Kunle's feeble attempt to stop the madness. I looked to the far corner of the church and saw a familiar figure. The realization of what I was about to do hit me. All the pent-up emotions I'd held on to came to the surface, like the activation of a dormant volcano. In that moment I knew I was incapable of hurting Ade the way he'd hurt me. As tempting as it was, I couldn't go through with my plans to announce Ade's sexuality to everyone who was important to him. I ran out of the church, tears blurring my vision.

As I stood in the cool air, sobbing, I felt a gentle hand on my shoulder. I was afraid to turn around. Afraid to confront my deepest fears, I turned around and collapsed into Kunle's arms. I was sobbing so hard that I couldn't even speak. I agreed, when he suggested that I go and sit in the car until I had regained my composure.

Kunle and I sat in the back seat of my car-I rested my head on his shoulder. I was calmer now but my mind was still racing with unanswered questions. Instinctively I looked into his eyes, which were visibly moist with fresh tears. I'd been so consumed by my own feelings that I hadn't, even for one minute, stopped to think about the effect of my behaviour on him. In that instant he seemed pure and sweet and caring and loving and unselfish and all the things that I'd fallen in love with so long ago. I kissed him gently and thanked him for being such a good friend.

I looked out of the window and there he stood, watching me. I didn't know how long he'd been there but surely it'd been long enough. So it was *him* in the church when I thought my mind had been playing tricks on me. As I struggled to get past Kunle and out of the car, Tore began walking away. His brisk walk soon turned into a jog and he began to run away from me. The image of that look of betrayal on his face was permanently etched into my mind. This wasn't the ending I'd planned for the day. Instead of achieving closure, I found myself spiraling out of control.

As I walked, slowly back to the car, I realized the full impact of the consequences of my actions. Kunle had his face buried in his hands. He apologized for the kiss. He had been the perfect friend, and once again I had fucked up. Wherever I found myself, disaster seemed to follow shortly. I was all cried out; and it was me who had kissed him first. I needed to get back to my flat so I could call Tore and at least try to explain what had happened. Kunle volunteered to accompany me home but I persuaded him I'd be fine and promised to call him later that evening.

Guests were strolling out of the church as I drove off. On the journey home I called Tore's mobile and wasn't surprised when I was put straight through to his voicemail. I left a message, pleading with him to call me so I could explain-apologise. I also left a message at his flat and contemplated calling his father but realized that would have been extreme.

When I arrived home I checked my answer machine to see if he had called but there were no messages from my baby. I ran a warm bath in which to drown my sorrows. While lying in the bath I replayed the events of the day. I hoped, deep down, that Tore would call me so we could work through this. For the first time in a long while I felt as though a great weight had been taken from me.

Later the phone rang and I answered hoping that it was Tore. It was Kunle, calling to find out how I was feeling. He wanted to come over to keep me company but I thought it wouldn't be a good idea, especially since I was hoping to work things out with Tore. I asked him if he planned on attending the wedding reception, he said he wasn't sure-he'd wait and see how he felt and decide a bit later. Just then I heard the 'call waiting' sound and I told him good bye before ended our conversation.

I was shocked to hear Ade's voice. He was the last person I expected to hear from, the day was getting more bizarre by the minute. He'd called to see if I was feeling any better. Kunle had found him and said that I had run out of the church, distressed, because I wasn't feeling well. He said that he knew attending his wedding was probably difficult for me, but he was grateful that he got to share the experience with me. He ended the conversation by suggesting that if I felt better he'd love to see me at the reception.

After I got off the phone with Ade, I called Kunle.

"You wouldn't believe who just called me," I said.

"Tore?" he asked.

"No." I answered.

"Then who was it?"

"It was Ade, calling to find out how I was doing. He was actually worried about me on his wedding day. Can you believe that shit?"

"It's not so hard to believe that he still cares a great deal about you," he said.

"Yes but I'd have thought he would have more important things to think about on his wedding day. He said you told him I wasn't feeling well. Thanks for that. Once again, you've saved me. I owe you big time."

"I told him it had all been too much for you. It wasn't difficult convincing him of that, thanks to his oversized ego."

"But surely someone would have wondered what the hell was going on when I stood up," I said.

"It may have seemed long to you but it was only a few seconds and, after you left, the ceremony continued as if nothing had happened. Chris, I want to apologize again for what happened earlier today."

"Remember, it was me who kissed you. I need to apologize to you for so many things. Today has made me see that I haven't treated you the way you deserve to be treated. I take full responsibility for all the crap I've been sending your way and the drama my life has turned into."

"Chris, it's no big deal, that's what friends are for."

"It is a big deal Kunle. You keep rescuing me, and I keep expecting you to. It's time I take some responsibility for my own actions and fight some of those battles myself. I want to thank you for being a tower of strength recently, even while you were wrestling with your own demons. If Tore has a problem with you and I being friends that's something he and I will have to work on, but in the meantime stop blaming yourself. You should go to the reception since you weren't able to stay until the end of the ceremony," I suggested.

After talking to Kunle I contemplated my next move. I could sit at home waiting for Tore to call me or I could get on with my life. I decided upon the latter. I called and arranged for a cab-I intended to leave my relationship troubles behind me for the night, they'd be right there waiting for me the next day.

* * *

Ade had spared no expense when he booked the banquet room of a top London Hotel on Park Lane, for the wedding reception. The room, with its very high ceiling, was tastefully decorated. There were lots of gold fittings and the tables were beautifully laid with fine cutlery and dishes of all descriptions. Most of the guests wore traditional African outfits and it looked like a scene from the movie 'Coming to America'. The bride and groom continued to change into matching outfits throughout the night. I was reliably informed that this was supposed to be a sign of the family's wealth.

When I walked into the room a few pairs of eyes turned to see who was entering. One pair of these belonged to Ade who, at the time, was busy talking to a relative. I thought I noticed a smile creep over his face when he saw me, but I quickly found a seat from which to take in the spectacle.

I sat in an inconspicuous corner of the spacious room, watching the sea of colour come to life, as the DJ played mainly traditional West African music. Some of the guests were on the dance floor, beckoning the new couple to join them. Ade, accompanied by his wife, started dancing, to the cheers of everyone. As the happy couple danced, individuals sprayed them with money, another of the many traditions reserved for important occasions.

I looked around for the best man and noticed Michael heading towards the far side of the room. Ade tried to escape the dance floor feigning tiredness. His guests insisted that he remained and entertained them. As I surveyed the room I saw Kunle at the far corner staring silently at me. He looked like he'd seen a ghost. Neither of us broke our gaze, nor did we get up to move toward each other.

When I eventually looked away I felt exposed, like Kunle had peeled away the layers and had seen deep inside of me. I went in search of my first drink of the night, to try and erase this feeling. I would need more than one drink to erase the guilt I felt, about my treatment of Kunle. It would take a miracle-the burning bush kind.

Kunle joined me a few minutes later and said that he couldn't believe his eyes. I told him that I'd changed my mind at the last minute about attending the reception. I tried calling him but there was no answer. Michael interrupted to offer us a drink. We already had drinks so he agreed to bring us some food instead.

Kunle remained by my side throughout the evening. Whenever he did make it onto the dance floor, he kept looking over in my direction to make sure I was OK. Michael returned to where I was sitting several times throughout the night to ask if I needed anything. During one of his visits I squeezed his hand gently to reassure him that I knew it was a difficult time for him. He had a look of resignation on his face.

Later that evening Ade made his way over to where I was sitting, to thank me for coming to the party. In his familiar, charming, manner, he said that the evening would not have been complete without my presence. His guests tried to persuade him to return to the dance floor but he told them he was tired and wanted some fresh air, motioning for me to join him on the balcony.

In a darkened corner of the balcony he pulled me close and his lips found mine. He asked for my forgiveness for having hurt me. I told him that he needed to consider forgiving himself. I was surprised enough that he would try to kiss me at his own wedding reception, but even more so by the fact that my legs neither went weak, nor did my heart start racing from his kiss. It seemed that I was finally over him.

We rejoined the party. Ade managed to get me on to the dance floor but I kept looking for Kunle to rescue me. He was nowhere to be found. The two drinks I had loosened my limbs and I gave into the exotic rhythms.

Kunle suddenly appeared as if from nowhere, smiling, as he moved rhythmically to the sweet sounds of the dark Continent. After a gruelling ten minutes, he and I went out on to the balcony. I stood quietly beside him for a while before sharing my thoughts. I told him about my conversation with Ade and that I'd finally put it all behind me. I stopped him when he started to ask if I'd heard from Tore. This was my night to enjoy. I'd deal with Tore later.

I looked at my watch and it was 2:30am. It was time for me to leave. I said goodbye to Ade and his bride, who had changed into yet another outfit, before Kunle walked me to the front of the hotel. After we left the party I told Kunle of my suspicions that Ade's wife knew the score. He thought I was just being paranoid. As we stood in the cold, waiting for my taxi, Kunle again volunteered to take me home. I told him that I'd be fine and suggested he return to enjoy the rest of the party.

When the taxi arrived I said good bye and agreed to call him when I got home. He said he believed that Tore and I would sort things out. I told him that I hoped so too. We hugged before I climbed into the Taxi. On the drive home I wondered what was going through the taxi driver's mind when he saw two black men hugging each other in the streets.

* * *

Several days had passed before Tore called to say he'd received my letter.

Dear Tore,

I love you very much but I know that sometimes love alone is not enough to sustain a relationship. Whatever you decide, I want you to know that I need you in my life. I can't do this without you.

I know you're hurting right now but, please believe me when I say that it was never my intention to hurt you. Lately, I seem to be hurting those close to me, even if unintentionally. Please let me know if there is anything I can do to ease your pain, because I'm ready to do whatever it takes to make this work-to make us work.

You are a truly beautiful person who has a special place in my heart. There are issues, which needs resolving; but Tore, I can't do it alone. These are my issues, but I need your help so that I can be a better man for myself and for you. I don't know what I would do without you in my life.

If you truly love me, as I believe you do, then we need to talk so we can give ourselves a chance to get past this. We deserve it. Call me; even if you feel we can't go on I need to hear from you. Please baby, call me.

Yours and with all my love
Chris.

I'd sent the letter to his office the day after Ade's wedding. He had received it when his secretary forwarded his office mail to his mother's address in Crawley. He said he needed a few days to clear his mind. This offered me a glimmer of hope.

He apologized for running away and I apologized for disrespecting him by kissing another man. I told him that I meant what I'd said in my letter and that, whatever he decided, he must know that I loved him. He said that he couldn't imagine not loving me. That night I dreamed of living happily ever after with my Prince Charming.

26. A time for healing

Dele called to ask if what he'd heard about the wedding was true. I filled in the details. He could hear the pain in my voice so he didn't make fun of the situation. He told me that my friends were worried about me and wanted to know that I was OK. I promised to attend the next group meeting in a few days, so they could all see for themselves that I'd made it through the storm.

When I arrived at Dele's flat, Miss Candy, Tunde and Chez were already present. They seemed a little uncomfortable until I broke the ice by telling them that the diva in me had to upstage that wedding. They began to relax and make light of the situation. Chez held my hand and asked how I was *really* coping.

"It's all behind me. I'm free to move on with the rest of my life," I said.

"Now Bitch, I did warn you about going to this wedding," Dele said.

"Are you sure you're alright baby boy?" asked Tunde.

"Thanks babes, I'm fine," I said.

We laughed about the incident after a few drinks. They wanted to know how things were between Tore and I; I told them we were working through our difficulties. He planned to spend some time with his mother and, since Christmas was only a few days away, he'd return to London to spend the New Year with me.

This sparked a serious debate about finding a soulmate. We all agreed that the deck was stacked against us, when it came to finding and holding on to partners. At times it seemed an insurmountable task, so when there was a chance of love, despite all these set backs, it was worth holding on to-fighting tooth and nail for.

Heterosexual couples had a head start on us, and even with centuries of experience, they still hadn't figured it out. For most of us there were very few role models of successful gay relationships in our lives. In a sense we were pioneers with an opportunity to shape the way for those to follow.

Miss Candy strongly believed there was only one true love for everyone. I disagreed, because I had been in love with three men in my life and, although I now felt differently about each of these men, I knew that each time it had been love.

I was under no illusion that relationships were like fairy tales; they took work, and sometimes a lot of work. It had always surprised me, how willing we were to work hard at our careers; or other aspects of our lives but when it came to relationships we closed our eyes, crossed our fingers and hoped for the best.

"I'm as romantic as the next person," I said "but there has to be more than one chance at love in a lifetime."

"Who was your first love Chris?" asked Chez.

"Kunle was the first man I gave my heart to," I said.

"And did you ever get over him?" asked Chez.

"Of course he got over Kunle-the real question is, did that crazy bitch ever get over him," replied Dele.

"Would 'Miss Thing' please allow me to answer the question, thank you very much. We're good friends and we do have feelings for each other, we just choose not to act on them. Our friendship is much too important to be jeopardized because of something we had in the past." I said.

"Chris the heartbreaker," said Miss Candy playfully.

Miss Candy believed that he fell a little in love with everybody he went to bed with. We all laughed when Dele commented that he 'certainly had a lot of love to give.' Miss Candy flashed Dele a look that spoke volumes.

Miss Candy told us about someone he'd met recently. He felt this young man was different than the men he'd dated in the past. He believed there was a strong possibility this time things would work out for him. Dele bravely asked if they had slept together, knowing that the question was rhetorical.

"Have you been in contact with this man since you slept together?" asked Dele.

"No, it's only been two days-but I have a good feeling about this," he said.

"Honey-child, feelings are fine but you need to get with the program. I bet the number he gave you is either fake, or he plans on ignoring your calls." Dele responded.

"You need to stop being the prophet of doom and gloom Dele. If there is even a small chance of happiness then I say you go Miss

Candy. Grab it with both hands and don't stop until the ride is over," I said.

"It's like the lottery—you have to be in it to win it. I may have to kiss a few frogs before I meet Mr. Right, but he will come along one day," said Miss Candy.

"Fools in love will do the exact same thing, in exactly the same way, time and time again; expecting different results. When will we realize that this shit just isn't working? I know what you'll say 'Miss Chris', and before you do, I include myself in that group," said Dele.

We knew that Miss Candy's ego wouldn't allow him to accept what Dele had said, but we'd all been down that scary road before and, once again, when he fell, we'd be right there to catch him.

Dele brought the topic of conversation back to Kunle and I, in an attempt to find out what was really going on between us. For the first time I admitted openly that I had unresolved issues with Kunle which confused me at times, but which I was ready to deal with. They were gentle with me and wished me good luck.

The evening flew by quickly but, before we left Dele's flat, I managed to get him on his own to ask about Tokumbo. He said that they were still working on their relationship and he was hopeful things would change. I was pleased for him and proud that despite his challenges, he remained optimistic. My Christmas wish for him was inner peace; and wisdom in the decisions that lay before him. I wished the same for myself.

* * *

The next time we spoke Tore seemed brighter in his mood, he was excited about spending Christmas with his mother and younger sister. He felt the time apart would give us a chance to heal, but he also recognized the importance of keeping the channels of communication open.

He said he was ready for us to move to a better place as a couple. I was pleased, that he was no longer talking from a place of anger and hurt and now seemed more positive about our future together. We decided that honesty was the best policy, despite the natural instinct to spare each other pain. It always hurt worse, in the long run, when important issues were shrouded in lies and deceit.

I told him that I missed him, so much, it hurt. He fell silent before eventually saying, in a sad voice, that he missed me too and couldn't wait to be in my arms again. I asked if he'd spoken with his father and he said yes. He'd told him about our temporary separation. His father knew from experience that perseverance paid off, and encouraged Tore not to give up on our relationship. He added that his father thought the world of me and had seen how happy we were together.

Before ending the call I asked what his mother thought about his lifestyle. He said that her traditional, African and religious, values meant that she wasn't happy about him being gay, but that her love for him outweighed the difficulties she had dealing with his sexuality. She made him promise that he'd be safe. I told him that she sounded like a courageous woman and that I looked forward to meeting her 'someday.' That night I dreamed Tore was in my arms.

27. Still waters run deep

Kunle and I arranged to meet for a meal. There were a number of things we needed to discuss. He was initially reluctant to meet, but I convinced him it was necessary. He still blamed himself for what had happened at the wedding. I saw this as an opportunity to spend time with my friend and to take back some of the responsibility I had so easily entrusted to him.

We met at a restaurant called 'The Giraffe.' The last time I'd been there was with Ade. I walked into the familiar surroundings and located a quiet area where I took a seat to wait for Kunle. I ordered a glass of white wine spritzer, which I sipped anxiously until he arrived. I stood, to shake his hand, he greeted me with a warm embrace. He smelled nice and I complimented him on how good he looked.

Kunle sat opposite me before motioning to the waiter. He seldom drank alcohol but, on this occasion, he ordered a brandy. I could tell he was nervous. I tried my best to get him to loosen up a bit by talking about his daughter. He seemed to visibly relax when I asked about Mercedes.

After about twenty minutes of catching up, I brought up the topic of us. I wanted to address the matter of where we were headed as friends. We had skirted around the issue for some time and needed to talk about our feelings for each other. I felt the tension in the air increase as Kunle searched for the right words to express what was on his mind. He said that my friendship was very important to him, and that he'd been reluctant to join me for dinner because he thought I was about to end it. He smiled weakly when I reassured him that was not the case.

I told him that he had the unique position of being my first love and nothing could ever change that. If I hadn't fallen in love with Tore there would be no issue about taking our relationship to another place but, as things stood, I was seeing someone else, who had my heart. I knew this was difficult for him to hear but I felt he needed to hear it from me.

Kunle listened quietly before responding. He said that he'd been in love with me from the moment we first met-even during his marriage. He hadn't told me this because he was ashamed of being unfair to his wife. He couldn't give her the one thing she wanted more than anything, his heart, because it belonged to someone else.

He never regretted having his daughter, but sometimes wondered why he hadn't stood up to his family, instead of succumbing to the pressure to wed. He said that the arrival of Mercedes in his life had taught him that he could love again, and it didn't have to end in pain.

He also knew, from the moment we met that we would be in each other's lives for a very long time. When our romantic relationship ended he eagerly accepted my offer of friendship. He silently waited in the hope that one day, I would give him another chance-give us another chance. Many nights he dreamed of holding me in his arms and never letting me go. He'd learned his lesson the first time and vowed, if given the opportunity, never to let love slip away again.

He had been prepared to wait for me, that was, until I fell in love with Tore. He knew then that he didn't stand a chance. He hadn't been threatened by my love for Ade because, as painful as it was for me to appreciate at the time, that relationship was doomed to fail, he'd seen the end-long before I had. Tore, on the other hand, was a different matter. Being around the object of his desire and seeing another man capture my heart had proved too much. He understood that I couldn't reciprocate those feelings. He knew that my principles wouldn't allow me to play with his feelings. I respected him for that.

I reassured him that he had impressed me from the start and had continued to impress me throughout the years that we'd known each other. I thanked him for his honesty and reminded him, that although boyfriends came and went in our lives, true friendship was a lot more reliable. If I had anything to do with it, we'd be friends for the rest of our lives.

I felt a little sad because I couldn't give Kunle what he wanted, but he said he was happy as long as he was somewhere in my life. He knew that he would love again eventually, but he had resigned himself to the fact that I would have been the first and most special love of all. I reached across the table and touched his hand, which felt cold. He said that I could depend on him and that he would not ask for anything in return-expect that I should create a place for him in my life. I vowed to value the precious gift of his friendship, and never again take it for granted. Secretly, I hoped that he found a love of his own soon.

I'd come to dinner half-expecting Kunle to say that it was all or nothing. I felt our meeting had been a success. We were a lot clearer about the boundaries. We enjoyed the rest of the meal and he talked about Mercedes some more; like every proud father he showed me the photographs of her, which he carried around in his wallet. My world felt a lot better with Kunle firmly in it.

28. Coming home

There was only space in my life for one lover and Tore had filled the vacancy. Talking with Kunle had re-established our special friendship and my life seemed to be back on track once again. Christmas day had been just like any other day because Tore wasn't with me.

Kunle was visiting his family for Christmas dinner and invited me along. I declined his offer and instead agreed to see him before the start of the New Year. Turning up at his family's home with Kunle would have created drama, which I could have done without. Even if he had mentioned to his family that we were just friends, I'm sure their overactive imaginations would have come up with a much more exciting version.

Tore planned to return to London the day after Boxing Day so we could start the New Year together. It'd been two weeks since we'd seen each other and I was longing to hold my baby in my arms. I was excited to see him again.

It was a beautiful winter's day, made even more special by the fact that my baby was coming home. Tore called me early that morning to find out if everything was in place for his arrival, he'd arranged for his cousin to drive him to London that evening. I wanted everything to be perfect and, spent the early part of the day tidying the flat.

During one of our telephone conversations Tore had brought up the idea of moving in together as a couple. It was something we'd discussed, albeit superficially, in the past. Back then neither of us felt ready to take such a big step. Tore believed the time was now right and I agreed with him, despite a few reservations about sharing my space with another person-even one as handsome and charming as him. I was finally prepared to let go of my insecurities.

Tore planned to come directly over to my flat. We agreed that he would lease his flat for six months before deciding whether to put it up for sale; it made sense. In the unlikely event that living together didn't work out he'd be able to return to his flat.

I didn't hear the phone ringing, due to the noise from the Hoover. When I noticed I had a missed call I dialed 1471. To my surprise,

Dele's number was read out to me by the automated voice. I made myself a cup of tea before sitting down to return the call.

Dele sounded unusually optimistic for that early in the day. He said he had a huge favour to ask me. He'd been invited to an important dinner party and needed me to accompany him. He told me that Tokumbo wasn't able to make it due to a prior engagement. We both knew what the prior engagement was likely to be, although neither of us mentioned it.

I told Dele about Tore's plan to return to London later that evening but agreed to his request on the condition that I could return home in time to welcome my man. He asked what time Tore was expected back in London and I told him, around 10:30pm. He promised that we'd be back in plenty of time. I said I'd need to run it past my man and get back to him to confirm arrangements.

I called Tore after speaking with Dele and he was fine with the slight change of plans. He said we would meet back at '*our home*.' It sounded very natural when he mentioned the words, "our home". In that moment I realized just how fortunate I was to be spending all my time with my man. I told him to hurry up and get his fine black ass back to London as soon as possible. He promised to call me when he was on his way.

Dele was delighted when I told him the news, that I was free to join him that evening. He said I wouldn't regret accompanying him because the men at the party would be fine. I reminded him that I was practically a married man, to which he replied, 'there's no harm in window shopping as long as you don't buy anything.' I told him that I wouldn't have done this for anyone else and, in his customarily jovial manner, he responded, "Miss Thing, come on you know you love me."

I replied, "Yes, I do; and my name is not Miss Thing. Just make sure I get home on time."

Dele arrived at my flat at 5:30pm so we could have drinks before going to the dinner party. At the wine bar I had a sherry but, in the same timescale, Dele had three brandies. I told him that at the rate he was guzzling down his drinks, I'd be booking him into the Priory Clinic pretty soon. He said he was nervous because he felt Tokumbo was getting closer to making a commitment.

There were only a few people at the bar and I suspect this was because most people were probably away, visiting relatives and friends over the Christmas holidays. I was concerned by the hold that Tokumbo seemed to have on Dele, and so enquired further.

"I know that you don't approve of Toks, and Chris, it's not only about the sex. Don't get me wrong, the sex is great. The brother has skills that have surprised even me. He is kind to me Chris, plain and simple. He is a gentleman in every sense of the word."

There were a million responses going through my mind, but this was neither the time of place to challenge Dele, so I said, "I'll get used to it Dele, I promise. I just need a little more time to get my head around it."

"I know sweetheart, and I love you for that. I've been through a lot in the past and I wouldn't do anything to deliberately harm myself," Dele said.

I wondered what he was getting at. It started raining gently. I secretly hoped it would snow. Dele looked past me and outside at the falling rain, his eyes becoming teary. I reached across and held his hand.

"Chris I've never told anyone about this; and I am only telling you because I trust you with my life."

I squeezed his hand, gently, to reassure him his trust was not misplaced.

"The first guy I ever fell in love with committed suicide," Dele said as he looked up to see the stunned look on my face.

I didn't know what to say, so I remained silent.

"His name was Ife, it means 'love'. He was a year older than me and we met during my first year at university in Lagos. We didn't act on our mutual attraction initially because neither of us knew how the other one felt. And child, you know being gay wasn't something you ran screaming down the streets. For a long time I believed that I was the only one who felt the way I did."

"I know the feeling baby," I interjected.

He paused briefly before continuing. "Eventually, we fell in love and spent a lot of time together. I knew that he had experienced episodes of depression before, and that it had been successfully treated with medication, but we were in love, so all that didn't matter."

I sat captivated as Dele continued talking.

"It happened just before Christmas. A friend called me to ask if I'd heard about the boy at university who'd killed himself. When I eventually found out I was devastated and blamed myself. I wondered whether there'd been signs that I'd missed and if there was anything I could've done to save him. I was certain that together we could have handled anything. I wasn't prepared for that."

"Dele, look at me. We can't save everybody. What he did was not your fault. Maybe if he'd told you about his thoughts and plans, things may have turned out differently, but we'll never know. Blaming helps no one."

"I know Chris, but at the time I felt betrayed because we were very close and I believed we could talk about anything. Why couldn't he talk to me about this? I would have understood."

"That was his decision to make and, as painful as it is to accept, he had that right," I said.

"You might look at me and think that I'm a strong person, who makes fun of everything and everyone, but I've experienced pain too. I need to be loved, just like everybody else. Look at me, crying like a big baby! We're supposed to be going to a party tonight and here I am, acting like it's a funeral."

"We don't have to go to this party if you don't feel up to it," I said. "We could stay here for a while; or go back to my place, if you want to talk some more."

"You're not getting off that easy mister. We're going to this party and we're going to have a fabulous time," Dele said, before finishing his drink and getting up.

"How do I look?" He asked.

"Like a million pounds," I answered.

"Right answer," he said, regaining his composure. "Now let's go."

"One last question," I said, "is he the one?"

"Are we talking about Tokunbo?" he asked.

"Yeah," I replied.

"I think so," he replied.

I thought about telling Dele that Tore and I planned to move in together, but I didn't want to steal his thunder, this was his night. I looked at him and saw that beneath the brave façade he was still upset.

"Dele we don't have to do this."

"I'll be OK, just point me in the direction of those fine men," he said.

The event turned out to be very pleasant and Dele was right, there were some fine-looking men present. When I was single, fine men stayed away from me like Superman stayed away from kryptonite. Now that I was happily hitched, decent men were everywhere. Men who were emotionally stable and capable of relationships probably emitted a different aura.

Most of the men I spoke with at the party seemed intelligent and articulate and were capable of holding a conversation without any mention of what they liked to do in bed. I was impressed. They seemed comfortable in their skins and celebrated their blackness. The fact that they chose to sleep with men was simply another dimension to their lives. It was refreshing to find that not everything had to be reduced to dick size or sexual prowess.

I was surprised how quickly the evening went by and soon it was time for Dele and I to leave the party. I hadn't heard from Tore but I assumed that he'd been delayed-probably due to the rain that was now falling heavily. Dele and I headed back to my flat. I thanked him for a wonderful evening.

On the way home I asked Dele if he'd found any of the men at the party attractive. He said the men were fine but that none had come even close to Tokumbo. It was difficult standing idly by, watching Dele go down the same road from which I had recently escaped, but it was a journey he needed to make for himself, so he could get to where he needed to be.

We walked into the flat and Dele was instantly impressed by my efforts to tidy up for Tore's arrival. I jokingly told him that it'd been the maid's day off so I had to do some work for a change. I'd gone into the kitchen to fix us a couple of nightcaps when Dele shouted out that my answer machine was flashing. I told him to play the message. It was probably Tore calling to say he was delayed-my mobile reception was generally poor in bad weather.

I returned to the living room to find Dele with a look of concern on his face. I asked him what was wrong; he suggested that I sit down and listen to the message myself. I thought he was being his overly dramatic self, and pressed the 'play' button on the answer phone. I was surprised to hear Franco's voice on the machine, asking me to contact him urgently. The message had been left at 8:20pm.

In my state of panic I had trouble locating Franco's number but Dele reminded me that I could dial '1471' to get the number of the last caller. He asked if I needed privacy to make the call. I answered-rather abruptly “no”. He sat next to me as I nervously made the call. I thought I had the wrong number when a child answered. I apologized but, just before I hung up I heard Franco’s voice.

He explained that Tore’s sister had answered the phone, because he wasn’t allowed to take the calls in the Intensive Care Unit. My head started spinning. Tore and his cousin had been in a road traffic accident just outside of Crawley. His cousin sustained several fractures but was expected to make a full recovery. Tore was unconscious. I asked for directions to the hospital in Crawley, but Franco said that they were preparing to take him to St George’s Hospital in London. Tore’s condition was more serious than I first thought.

I started sobbing uncontrollably. Dele took the telephone from me and continued talking to Franco. I felt like my world had been turned upside down. I kept replaying my final conversation with Tore. When Dele got off the phone, he told me that Franco was concerned about me. Dele reassured him that he’d stay with me until I was calm. Franco promised to call when they arrived in London.

There were no words to ease the pain caused by what had happened so Dele sat next to me, holding me as I sobbed silently. I felt like I was in a daze. Dele made me a cup of tea. I kept telling myself that Tore would be fine, that he would regain consciousness and I would look after him. We had the rest of our lives together.

Dele went to the bedroom and returned with a couple of blankets and pillows, which he positioned on the floor. He thoughtfully put on some soft background music. I began to hear the soothing tones of Mahalia Jackson. I was surprised when Dele suggested that we pray for Tore. He must have known that I needed it.

29. Saying goodbye

I didn't know I had drifted off to sleep until I woke up around 4:00am. My eyes were swollen and felt sore from crying. For a brief moment I wondered whether it had all been a bad dream. Dele was lying a short distance away, snoring gently. I went to the bathroom before making myself a strong cup of black coffee. I needed to get my wits about me. I had to be strong for Tore.

I decided not to wait for Franco's call and started getting ready to leave for St George's Hospital. Dele woke up while I was in the shower. He noticed that I was more composed, but volunteered to accompany me to the hospital anyway. I thanked him and said it was something I had to do alone. He smiled weakly before saying that he was only a phone call away if I needed anything.

The journey to the hospital was long, but it provided me with some distraction from my difficult situation. I got off the train at Tooting Broadway underground station and caught a bus to the hospital.

The walk from the hospital entrance to the Intensive Care Unit filled me with dread. I felt like a prisoner making his way to the gas chamber for his own execution. I'd been a nurse for many years and as such was accustomed to hospitals, but nothing in my experience had prepared me for this. I had no control over this situation.

I noticed Franco sitting in the corridor, talking to an attractive black woman whom, I guessed, was Tore's mother. He stood to greet me when he saw me approaching. I extended my hands to shake his but instead he pulled me into a comforting embrace. He introduced me to Tore's mother, who greeted me just as courteously.

Franco updated me on Tore's condition. It was far worst that I'd expected. Just then the doctor approached us, asking to speak with a family member. I felt honored when Franco suggested that I see the doctor on my own. He and his ex-wife had already been updated.

Dr Santiago took me to an adjacent room where he inquired about the nature of my relationship with Tore. I told him that we were lovers. He said that Tore's injuries were very serious and, should he regain consciousness, that he would probably need to have both legs amputated. His brain was so traumatized that the life support machine was the only thing keeping him alive.

The medical team had already discussed the possibility of turning off the life support machine, with the rest of the family but Franco insisted that they wait until my arrival before making the final decision. I didn't hear anything else after Dr Santiago uttered those words. My heart was racing and I had difficulty breathing. This time I knew I was experiencing a panic attack. The next thing I remembered was Dr Santiago offering me a hot drink.

The words, 'turning off the life support machine' kept replaying in my mind like a broken record. I knew things were dismal when I left home earlier that day, but never had it occurred to me that this would be the day that Tore might die. I asked if I could see my baby and Dr Santiago took me to him.

I held my breath as I entered Tore's room. He looked so frail, hooked up to all those machines. There were tubes everywhere and his eyes were closed and covered with a gel-like substance. I shut the door behind me and stood next to his bed for a long time, half expecting him to sit up and ask what all the fuss was about. But he didn't.

I reached out to hold his hands and found they were surprisingly warm to the touch. I guess he looked so bruised and lifeless that I thought they'd be cold. I held on to his hands while I closed my eyes and prayed silently. The tears were streaming down my face and I found it difficult to concentrate. I felt it was important that I had this time with him.

After praying for courage I opened my eyes, expecting a miracle, but he was still asleep. I talked to him about finally meeting his mother and about the dinner party I'd attended with Dele the previous night. I was stalling for time, putting off the inevitable.

I asked the nurse to page Dr Santiago and spoke with him about turning off the life support machine. I had to put my personal views aside and think about what Tore would have wanted. He would not have wanted to live like this. It was time to say good bye to my angel.

Dr Santiago remained professionally dispassionate as he explained the process. The machine that was regulating Tore's heart function would be switched off but he would continue to have assistance with his breathing. The machine that was helping him breathe would remain functioning until his heart stopped beating.

Tore's parents and sister were in his hospital room when I returned from talking with Dr Santiago. A look of resignation came across Franco's face at the realization of what was about to happen. This was the day he would say goodbye to his only child. He turned to face the wall and I could see his shoulder moving up and down as he began to sob. I wanted to go over and comfort him, but my legs wouldn't carry me.

After turning off the machine, we were left alone with Tore. His heart began to beat on its own. With every beat there was hope that the outcome could be different-that the miracle would finally happen. His breathing continued to be regulated by the machine, and every minute that his heart continued to pump blood around his frail body was a small victory.

About forty minutes later his heart began to fail. Our brief reprieve was over as the monitor showed that the gaps between his heartbeats were lengthening. My own heart had difficulty maintaining an even rhythm. This continued for another five, very tense, minutes before if finally happened . . . Tore was gone.

In an instant he was out of our lives forever. Remi threw herself on her son's chest and began wailing. She was hysterical. I turned to look through the window at the cold grey sky as I said goodbye to my angel. I fought back the tears, but felt as though someone had reached into my chest and was squeezing the life out of me. I felt like screaming uncontrollably.

The pain seemed to come from a place inside me that I couldn't locate and, because I couldn't identify its origin, I had difficulty eradicating it. Twenty four short hours ago, Tore was fine and we had our entire lives ahead of us. In a short time all that had been changed forever. I never questioned God's decision to take Tore away from us. He knew best. I asked for strength for all of us to make it through the storm.

I felt a gentle hand 'rubbing' my back as I remained slumped over, crying. I felt that if I stood up, I would snap into two, broken, never to be whole again. Eventually I turned around to look at Remi. We hugged each other and for a moment we understood each other's pain, even though we'd never met before. I told her Tore was now in a better place. I had to believe that.

After his family left I stayed with Tore. The staff allowed me to take as much time as I needed. They removed all the attachments from the equipment, leaving him covered with a plain white sheet. I held his hand and continued talking to him as if he were alive. I didn't quite understand all that had happened—it was a lot to take in. I knew that a part of me died with Tore. Life never stayed stagnant, we had to be prepared for every twist and turn, but this knowledge didn't make me feel better.

The journey home was just a haze. I felt like an alien, arriving on earth for the first time. Everything looked strange to me; everyone seemed to be going about their routine, oblivious to my pain. How could that be?

I promised Franco I'd call him when I arrived home. He asked if I had someone to stay with me and I told him that I'd get a friend to come over. Although Tore's parents had keys to his flat, they preferred to wait until I was present when they visited. They had included me in the decision making process out of respect for Tore's feelings for me. I felt honoured by their compassion and generosity, but saddened by the circumstances that had brought us all together.

The funeral was delayed until early in the New Year, due to the holidays. I had never had to plan a funeral before so I didn't know the first thing about the process. I was relieved when Tore's parents assumed the responsibility for making the necessary funeral arrangements.

When I arrived home I called Dele. On hearing his voice I was barely able to tell him that Tore had passed away before I broke down. To my surprise, he too began crying. I thanked him, but declined his offer to come over and keep me company. I told him that Kunle was on his way. I knew that I'd be fine after a warm bath and a large drink to numb the pain. I asked him to tell the others about Tore's death, and agreed to call him later.

My next call was to Kunle, to let him know what had happened. I felt more composed and was able to talk without crying. He suggested that I shouldn't be alone at a time like this and I told him that Dele was already over at my flat. Another lie-but I needed some time on my own to process all that had happened. He didn't offer any argument. He told me that he'd call me the next day.

I drew a bath before sinking into its warmth. Just as the alcohol began to take effect I heard the doorbell, I wondered who it might be. I was surprised to find Kunle standing before me when I opened the door. I invited him in and we hugged. I sat across from him, still wearing my bath robe, and asked what made him come over. He said he knew that something was up when I didn't put Dele on the phone to reassure him that I wasn't alone.

I suddenly remembered that I needed to call work to arrange some time off. Kunle said there was no rush and I could make that call the next day. He got up from his chair and joined me on the sofa. I began crying again and he massaged my back as I sobbed. He told me that in every life a little rain must fall, but that God would be walking every step of the way with me. I wondered when he'd become so wise.

The next few days were very difficult, but I got through them with the support of my friends, especially Kunle, who took charge of the more mundane chores. He spent the first few days in my flat and insisted he slept on the sofa, although I would have been willing for him to share my bed. He eventually left to give me some space but called every couple of hours to check up on me.

My sleep pattern had been disrupted. Even when I managed to get to sleep, I would dream of Tore and wake up crying. Sometimes my dreams were so vivid, that for a brief moment after waking I would forget my tragedy. The fact that the funeral still hadn't taken place, in my mind, prevented me from experiencing some closure. Tore seemed to occupy my every waking moment and the anxiety I felt about his impending funeral was very real.

Late one evening, Kunle and I talked about how *he* was doing.

"I'm worried about you Kunle, how are you doing?"

"That depends on how you're doing," he replied.

"Cute answer," I said, "but really, how *are* you doing?"

"I'm fine, you're the one who needs support right now," he said.

"I'm doing as well as can be expected under present circumstances," I said.

"I think you're a remarkable person Chris. I know a lot of people who wouldn't have been able to hold it together like you have," he said.

"I couldn't have done it without the help of my friends, especially you Kunle. I don't know how I could ever repay you guys, I said struggling to hold back the tears."

"You know I'll gladly do anything for you Chris, so there's nothing to repay."

"Kunle, I hope you know that I do love you," I said.

"Yes I do know," he said, in almost a whisper.

"Losing Tore has been a very traumatic experience for me, but I have learned a few valuable lessons," I said.

"Like what?" he asked.

"Like taking time to let the people in your life know, how you feel about them. Telling someone that you love them is a powerful gift. We take so much for granted, assuming that others can read our minds. Life is too short, blink and it'll pass you by. We waste so much time holding on to the petty stuff. I read a quote by Maya Angelou once that spoke to my heart. She said she had learned that people will forget what you said, people would forget what you did but they will never forget how you made them feel. There's a lot of truth in that statement."

"You're a lot stronger than you think Chris. And this too shall pass."

"I'm not that strong. I used to think I was, but loving Tore has made me realise that I need someone in my life-I need that special love in my life. I don't know how you do it." Even before finishing the sentence I regretted saying it. I was about to apologised for my insensitivity when Kunle squeezed my hand.

"I believe that each new day brings with it fresh hope, that this day might be better than the last. Sometimes that hope is what keeps us alive," he said.

"I've been replaying the last conversation I had with Tore-wondering whether I'd remembered to tell him that I loved him," I said.

I told Kunle the funeral was due to take place in two days. He asked if I wanted him to accompany me to Crawley. I didn't answer. I couldn't speak, for fear of bawling like a baby. He agreed to pass on the funeral details to my friends.

I asked Kunle whether he believed our fates were predetermined, or if we were in control of our own destinies. He said he believed we had limited control over the things we could change, and that some things were meant to be, regardless of our actions. He felt that we sometimes focussed so much on the destination of our lives that we missed the most important part, the journey.

*　*　*

I knew the funeral would be a very important part of establishing closure for me and moving on with my life. The grieving process and rebuilding my life would not be an easy challenge, but the sooner I started, the sooner I'd get through it.

The sun shone brilliantly on the morning of Tore's funeral. I was reminded of a similar occasion just over a year ago when I attend the funeral of another flower cut down in bloom. Bright sunshine always made things seem better than they were. It was like a fresh coat of paint, covering up what was underneath. The funeral was going to be an intimate affair, involving close friends and family.

The five of us travelled up from London to Crawley for the occasion. Kunle volunteered to drive and picked up Miss Candy and Chez on his way over to mines. Tunde was unable to get time off work so he sent me his apologies. Dele had spent the night at my flat. Dele, Chez and Miss Candy sat in the back. During the long journey my friends tried their best to distract me from thinking about what lay ahead.

We arrived early, and stopped to have some breakfast in a little cafe just on the outskirts of the city centre. It made sense not to face the day on an empty stomach. I didn't have much of an appetite, so I ordered a slice of toast and a cup of black coffee. The others had full English breakfasts.

We arrived at the house with only a few minutes to spare. Remi's home was packed with relatives and friends and I realised it wasn't going to be as intimate a ceremony as I'd first thought. Franco greeted us like we were family.

The room suddenly fell silent and, when I turned around I noticed that the hearse had pulled up outside the house. The huge, black, vehicle held a neat, pine box in full view, with one very large wreath of white lilies on top of it. I thought I had prepared myself for the moment-but I hadn't. I quickly made my way to the bathroom, where I was sick. The sight of the coffin containing my baby had brought back painful memories of the day he died.

A few minutes later I heard a gentle knock on the bathroom door, followed by Dele's voice asking if I was OK. I opened the door to let him in. I told him that I wasn't sure that I could go through with it. He said that I'd come this far by faith and it's the same faith that would sustain me to the end. I needed to be strong for Tore.

By the time Dele and I exited the bathroom, people had begun to leave the house and get into their cars, ready to follow the hearse to the church. I noticed the single red rose amongst the white flowers. Franco had granted my request. There amongst a sea of white, was a solitary red rose to represent my love for Tore.

The entourage made its way to the little church, two miles away. Once we'd arrived, we walked the short distance from the car park to the church. We took our seats and awaited the arrival of Tore's body. The organist started playing a popular hymn as we stood to welcome Tore.

His family had decided on a closed coffin, partly because of the time delay between his death and the funeral, as well as out of respect for Tore's memory. The accident had left scars and they wanted people to remember him the way he was-alive and happy-not broken and lifeless, lying in a box. Franco had asked me if I wanted to say a few words at the service. I thought about singing Psalm 121, 'all of my strength cometh from the Lord', instead I decided to read it.

I rose unsteadily to my feet as my name was called. My nerves almost got the better of me as I walked past the vessel containing my baby. It was a small church, but the walk to the front seemed extraordinarily long.

I avoided making eye contact with the coffin. I took a deep breath and began to speak, pretending that I was at one of my performances. I told the congregation that I'd taken the reading from the book of Psalms, chapter 121. I began to read, "I will lift up mine eyes to the hills, from whence cometh my help, my help comes from the Lord, which made heaven and earth . . ."

Shortly after I began the reading I seemed to lose my way. I had difficulty focussing on the words through tear filled eyes. I looked up desperately searching the congregation for a familiar face on which to focus, a skill I'd learnt as a singer. Everything looked blurred and I began to panic. I didn't want to let Tore down, not today. I tried to continue but it was clear that I had irretrievably lost my way.

I saw a figure approaching me and, as he got closer, I recognised Kunle. With him standing beside me I found the strength I needed to continue. I thanked Kunle for his support and asked the organist to play the hymn, 'it is well with my soul'. As I belted out the first few lines, the congregation joined in, which I found very moving.

Franco squeezed my hand as he walked past to join his ex-wife. Kunle never left my side during the short walk to Tore's final resting place. Dele, Chez and Miss Candy walked a few paces behind Kunle and I. They were sensitive enough to avoid any misplaced humour.

I stopped short of going to the graveside. The thought of them putting Tore into that hole in the ground was not an easy concept for me to grasp, so I looked on from a distance. My mind raced with indecision about moving closer.

The reading at the graveside was taken from the book of Ecclesiates. The priest began reading chapter three, verses one to eight, "to everything there is a season, a time for every purpose under heaven, a time to be born and a time to die, a time to plant and a time to pluck up what is planted . . ."

From where I stood I could hear the soft cries of the mourners as the coffin was lowered into the ground. I closed my eyes in search of courage to stand firm. I had to turn away when I heard a loud wail coming from Tore's mother who was now being supported by several family members. The sound she made was clear and as distinct as a foghorn on a winter's night. A voice in my head screamed, telling me to run as fast as my legs could take me, and as far away as I could get.

I remained motionless as everyone left the graveside. Kunle stood a short distance away while the others went to sit in the car. When Franco approached me, his eyes were still teary. We hugged, and without a single word, he told me what I already knew I had to do. I felt sorry for Franco because Remi still had another child. He told me he'd see me back at the house, before he walked away.

I walked to the graveside where Kunle stood alone. When he turned to hug me I could see that he too had been crying. He left to join the others. I knelt at the side of the fresh mound of dirt and closed my eyes. I sensed Tore's spirit nearby and the feeling of calm was reassuring. I spoke as if he were standing right before me. I told him that I'd been angry with him for leaving so suddenly, but I also understood that heaven was short of angels. I felt at peace with his untimely departure.

I felt privileged that Tore had been a part of my life, even if it had only been for a short time. Now I had my own personal angel in heaven looking after me. I walked out of the cemetery without looking back. I had no regrets. Tore had changed my life at a time when change was necessary. I joined my friends and we drove to Remi's home.

Franco introduced me to a few family members and before long it was time for my friends and I to say goodbye. Franco walked us to the car and we hugged before I promised to call him soon. There was sadness in his eyes as we drove off, like he was losing an important link to his dead son.

On the way back to London I thanked my friends for their unfailing support but told them that the kid gloves were officially off. Kunle took each of our friends to their respective homes, leaving me for last. He offered to spend the night but it was late and I was exhausted, and eager to get some sleep. I kissed him lightly on the lips before getting out of the car. He waited until I was safely inside my flat before driving off.

30. No more tears

I quickly fell back into my routine as the weeks sailed by. Work kept me busy during the daytime but at nights I often cried myself to sleep. I spoke with Franco a few times and he seemed to be coping remarkably well. I was surprised when he invited me to attend the reading of Tore's will. I knew that Tore had been an organized person, but I never expected that he would have a will or that I'd be invited to the reading of this document.

All in all I was getting by. I kept in regular contact with Dele and the others and Kunle had been over to see me every chance he got. I was making progress and although I still missed Tore a great deal, I couldn't sit and watch my life pass me by. I joined a gospel choir and began singing again. This helped me through some of the darker moments.

Returning to Tore's flat with his parents was particularly difficult. I knew it would bring back painful memories, but I was not prepared for how upsetting it would be. Thankfully, the initial dread was replaced by happier memories we shared in his flat. Having his parents present on this visit provided some consolation. We were able to get through it together.

Shortly after sorting out Tore's flat, I accepted Franco's invitation to dinner. I was greeted with kisses on both cheeks when I arrived. I handed him the bottle of wine I'd bought him. He was impressed with my choice. I didn't tell him that Tore had long ago filled me in on some of his favourite drinks. He disappeared into the kitchen briefly, before returning with two wine glasses. I was a little shocked when he asked me if I was seeing anyone.

"No, that's been the last thing on my mind. I've been very busy with work," I said.

"Tore would've wanted you to be happy. You're still young and you have your entire life ahead of you."

"I am happy. I have supportive friends and I've started singing again. That takes up a lot of my free time. I'm sure I'll know when the time is right for me to get back into the water," I said.

"Oh yes, Tore did tell me you were a singer. Maybe you could invite an old man some time to one of your performances. I'd love to hear you sing!"

"I'll do that," I said.

Franco was a most gracious host throughout the evening. He wanted us to remain in touch. Secretly, I felt he thought of me as a link to the memory of Tore. I felt honoured to be thought of in that way. After dinner we retired to the lounge for drinks and to continue chatting.

"You're like a member of this family Christopher. That won't change because Tore is no longer with us. The difference you made in Tore's life during the time you were together was very noticeable and I want to personally thank you for the happiness you brought into my son's life," he said tearing up a little.

I sat quietly as Franco composed himself, before carrying on.

"Are you able to attend the reading of the will next Tuesday?" he asked.

"I have the day off work," I said. "Shall we meet at the solicitor's office?"

"Tore's mum and I are meeting for a coffee before the appointment, why don't you join us? It's a lovely little coffee shop just down the road from the solicitor's office."

"Ok, I will."

"Good, I'll call you with details once I finalise the arrangements."

As I was about to leave Franco reminded me that he was only a phone call away if I ever wanted to talk. I thanked him for a lovely evening and his generous offer. I looked forward to talking with him soon.

* * *

At the reading of Tore's will, we learned that he'd left a share of the proceeds of his substantial life insurance policies, along with other valuable items, for each of his family members. He'd left clear instructions about the proceeds of the sale of his flat. This was to be divided into three parts; thirty percent was left in a trust fund for his sister. Twenty percent was to be divided amongst a few of his favourite charities.

I was blown away when I found out that he'd left the remaining fifty percent to me. Tore's flat was worth an impressive figure and the extent of his generosity, even in death, was overwhelming. I looked over at his parents and they didn't seem the slightest bit surprised by Tore's gift to me. They were pretty well off themselves so they didn't need financial gifts from Tore's estate.

I called Kunle as soon as I arrived home. I told him about the reading of the will and about my plans to hold a memorial service, followed by a party in honour of Tore's memory. He thought it was a good idea and offered to help with the planning. We agreed to speak again soon.

After hanging up, I realised that Kunle seemed a little subdued. I wondered what was troubling him. I decided to investigate further and called him to arrange to meet for a drink. He said he had a headache and intended to have a quiet evening at home. He agreed to call me in a few days. It seemed like he was avoiding me again, so I decided to take matters into my own hands.

I decided not to tell him that I was making my way over to his flat. When I arrived he told me that he still had a headache. I suggested we order a take away and stay in. He must have thought that I was missing the point and told me he didn't feel like having company. I took a seat and asked him what was really troubling him. He looked away and sighed deeply.

He told me that he felt lonely and was tired of coming home to an empty flat. Finding someone new to love was proving difficult. He said he knew he couldn't have me but he couldn't tell his heart whom to love.

My life had changed drastically over the past two years; I hoped that in addition to becoming a little older, I'd become a little wiser. In that instant I realised that Kunle and I wanted the same thing-we both needed to be loved.

I had never stopped loving Kunle. Through all the dramas in my love life, he'd been one of the few constants that kept me grounded. I needed to move on with my life and Kunle was offering me a chance to do that.

I wanted to love Kunle the way he needed me to. If anything, recent events had taught me time was finite and life was for the living. I stood up and walked over to him and with outstretched hands asked him for a dance. He reluctantly accepted my offer, on the condition that he got to choose the CD.

As we held each other close, I listened to the first few words of the song he'd chosen, 'I'm with you, you're with me. This is reality. We're together like never before. And now I want you more. Heaven must have sent you. So perfect your love . . . The Chante' Moore track was a classic and one of my favorite. I'd forgotten all about it. I let her sweet voice blow over me like a cool summer's breeze.

Maybe it had been written in the stars all along that Kunle and I would be together. Maybe the first love is always the strongest. Maybe we were a combination of all our previous experiences, which have lead us to the people we are today. I had no answers to solve the mysteries of life and love.

I felt that I had enough room in my heart to hold on to the memories I shared with Tore, whilst being able to love again. Kunle had been there right by my side all along. I stopped dancing, looked in his eyes and kissed him softly on his lips. He seemed perplexed by my actions, so I kissed him again, this time more passionately, leaving no doubt about my intentions. His body relaxed as he kissed me back.

He turned off the music and looked at me. Without words I told him that I was sure. Maybe this was our final chance for the happiness we both deserved and longed for. I planned to hold on to *love* with both hands this time and to enjoy each moment as if it were the last.

The End

Lightning Source UK Ltd.
Milton Keynes UK
UKOW04n0728261114

242189UK00002B/40/P

9 781477 219546